Nineteen To Go

A Peace O' Farce

By
James Carpenter

www.AMInkPublishing.com

Praise for *Nineteen to Go*

Every bit as good as his last book.
- Wayne Carpenter

It couldn't be any better.
- Chris Carpenter
New York Times bestselling coauthor of
P is for Pterodactyl: The Worst Alphabet Book Ever

Almost as good as his last book.
- Paul Carpenter

…ridiculous[ly]…funny…
- J Carpenter

Grandpa's book has bigger words than Daddy's.
- Mila Carpenter

I'm not surprised.
- Marta Carpenter

- Cleo Carpenter

I'm an excellent reader.
- Don Carpenter

Seriously?
- Rosetta Carpenter

*Caddy went to Winehouse and
wrote o peace a farce.*

James Joyce

*It's good when things in literature are circular.
Gives the impression of profundity.*

Jonathon Ames

Contents

Chapter 1
The Things You Think of When You Shouldn't Be Thinking About Anything at All

---

[Wherein, in the summer of 1953, we meet
Chuck McAllister and Hank Walker by way of
their snap decision to get vasectomies. Which
happens in a bar—of course it does.]

In a single fluid motion and with a kind of disjointed elegance, Chuck set down his Black Label, slid from his stool at the Rusty Bolt Tavern, and declared that he had to take a leak. "Me too," said his friend Hank and slid off his own stool, so mimetically exact to the way Chuck had (both in motion and in rhythm) that a disinterested observer might think he was mocking his friend, but he wasn't. He really just had to relieve himself.

The next thing you know, the two friends were standing next to one another at the galvanized trough urinal in the Rusty Bolt's men's room, not quite shoulder-to-shoulder, but pretty close. When in such proximity to another man before a rusting urinal, there are two things you absolutely *must not do*:

> 1. *Do not look at the other guy's privates*, because if his are bigger than yours, then you will be depressed in a way you would not have thought possible and it will put a damper on the party's mood that might go so far as to ruin the whole rest of the night. On the other hand, if yours are bigger than his, then you will be all smug and full of yourself (so to speak) and the people you're

drinking with will pick up on that (even if the guy urinating beside you is not one of them), and you run the risk of losing friends because of the affect you project, even if nobody can put their finger on exactly why they stopped liking you.

2. *Do not do anything whatsoever to make it appear that you are drunker than he is*—such as weaving your penis around as if you are writing a delightfully naughty ribald limerick on the trough's mottled zinc or mumbling gibberish about why did God make women or throwing up or even swaying more than the other guy—because it is important to be known as somebody *who can hold his liquor*, especially in a place like the Rusty Bolt, where being able to hold your liquor is among the most admired virtues a man can have, and not being able to hold your liquor could earn you a lifetime of disdain.

By the way: Yes, there is that other reason you might not want to look at the other guy's privates: You don't want him to think maybe you are putting a move on him. Before things start drifting off that way (the way that gestures to the space where somebody is sure to get all officious and upset), know that I am fully aware that I say this from the world view of a cisgendered, heterosexual male and that my observation about unwanted sexual advances and sideways glances may not hold across the multidimensional vector diagram of sexual identities and orientations. But trying to capture all of the possible permutations so implied is way beyond the scope of this little book and would make of my simple offering a thing of great complexity and length awkward to its purpose, which is the story of how when it comes to love, even the most seemingly innocent and well-intentioned impulses can lead to decisions you wish you had maybe thought about some more before you made them. (Some of my early readers remarked that they thought it was too long as it is—one of them said she was already thinking it was too long by the time she got to the end of the first paragraph.) Also, as they say back home, "My mama didn't raise no dumb kids." In allegiance to that enduring snippet of homespun wisdom, I'm just not gonna go there. I'm just not.

Anyway, back to Chuck and Hank at the urinal: It was for the second reason above about not doing anything to make you look drunker than your buddy (and the swaying part of that reason) that Chuck, who was feeling pretty woozy, found himself standing in front of the trough with one hand guiding his stream while trying to keep his fingers dry and the other braced against the condom dispenser hanging from the wall above the trough so as to steady himself. As he was finishing, he looked up to see what his hand was resting on and said, "Man oh man, I really hate having to use those things."

"What things?" Hank asked.

"Rubbers."

"You and me both," Hank said.

Back at the bar, Chuck, who was married, said, "Saturday night is complicated enough as it is without having to worry about getting a rubber." There followed from Chuck a rambling meditation on the erotic parry and thrust of marital relations, ending with his wife Mattie telling him to "get it" just as he was about to penetrate her, meaning get out of bed and get a condom from the back of his sock drawer where they kept them hidden from their two girls.

Chuck got way graphic in his meditation about the lead-up to that moment and how his wife could get him pretty worked up, especially when her panties were coming off (the "couple" beers he'd drunk having more than a little to do with what he was saying), so much so that Hank thought about asking him to maybe back off on the description a tad on account of he was getting a little bit stiff by just listening to it, but if showing you were at all drunker than the other guy could get you razzed, just think about what would happen if you told him he was giving you a hard-on. So Hank just crossed his legs and leaned in a little closer to the bar so that any bit of a bulge down there could be explained by the folds in his jeans.

Hank, who was single but did all right for himself on account of he had a rakish smile and real black wavy hair and was just the right combination of polite and bad-boy that the kind of girls that put out were naturally drawn to, responded with his own lament that meandered in a similar way to Chuck's but differed in that he and the girl were going at it pretty heavy in the back seat of his car, not all comfortable at home in bed. When the girl asked him did he have a rubber, he had to pretend he didn't already have a fresh one in his wallet all set to go because it would look like he was expecting her to put out from the second he asked her for the date, which would acknowledge that for him the moment hadn't been all that spontaneous (which he was pretty sure girls didn't like), and he had to put his pants back on and get out of the car barefoot and maybe step on God knows what that could be lying on the ground way back in the woods in the dark and get one out of the box he kept in the glove compartment.

Chuck and Hank stopped talking for a little while and scraped at their beer bottles with their thumbnails some more and silently considered, each in his own way, just how hard life and love can be. Then Hank had a thought.

"You know my cousin over in Youngstown?" he asked.

"Drives a Studebaker?"

"That's him."

"What about him?"

"He went and got himself fixed."

[....]

"He went to the doctor and got an operation and now he can't have kids."

"He got himself castrated?!?!?"

"No, no, no, no, no. Hell no! Like a woman gets her tubes tied. Everything works, just no sperms come out."

"Boy, if we got that, we wouldn't have to worry about the rubbers. We should get it!"

Hank said, "Son-of-a-bitch! Let's go do it!" And Chuck said the '50s equivalent of "Fucking-A!"

Chapter 2
Right the Hell Now!

[Wherein Chuck and Hank make approximate
practical and medical arrangements for their
vasectomies. Also we get an inkling of how
their decision is going to inconveniently affect
other people, especially Mattie. But when you
have had "a couple beers," you don't think
about things like that, which is why there are so
many people in jail and why divorce lawyers
live in really big houses.]

So Chuck and Hank got a six pack to go, said goodbye to the
bartender, and went out to the parking lot where Chuck said
he'd drive and Hank said back that he didn't think it was a
good idea for him to leave his car at the Rusty Bolt because it
was the Rusty Bolt. Hank said they better both drive and
Chuck remembered there wasn't any parking at the hospital
for even one car, let alone two (more about Grove City's
parking eccentricities later). Chuck said why didn't they just
leave the cars at his house on account of he was within walking
distance of the hospital and they both of them figured that
would work and also give them a chance to let Mattie know
what was going on without having to wake her up with a
phone call and scare her half to death when they told her they
were in the emergency room. "Might as well," said Hank. Our
two friends were quite proud of themselves for so brilliantly
figuring things out. A promising future beckoned.

By the way: Forgive me, but I'm going to stop here for
a second and offer up a note on dialect: One of the more
decided of Western PA's peculiarities is its unique accent. It's

a bit lilting in its intonations, most utterances ending on a gentle rise that stops shy of similarity to those Valley Girls' declarative questions. It has a trace of a drawl, especially in the way it elongates short vowels and softens mid-word consonants. Replete with Amish influence, it also still bears remnants of its 18th Century Scotch-Irish ancestry. Upon hearing it, some folks take it as a quaintly innocent pastoral argot, while others bristle at its ignorant parochialism. When Hank affirmed Chuck's idea with "Might as well," it actually came out of his mouth as *my'az-well*. And if he had said Chuck had a good idea when he suggested leaving their cars "up there," he would have pronounced the phrase as the spondee *up-aire*. Though writing such expressions phonetically would be more honest to the linguistic cadences of the region, the effect would not be one of authenticity but of a superciliously motivated dialectical clutter and could quite possibly lead to accusations of white-privileged cultural appropriation and condescension (even though I was born and raised there). Just hear it that way, if you would be so kind, in the same way that you are already hearing my gang drop their *g's*, even though I won't be writin' 'em that way. Because the region shares much of the idiomatic English common to many rural areas of the country (like dropping those g's), you can probably translate most of the standard text to the local dialect without much trouble. However, there are several idioms which I avoid because you just wouldn't be able to. For example, it's highly unlikely that, unless you learned English there, you would nimbly translate "might as well" to "my'az-well" or "isn't it" as "in it." And it would be wrong of me to expect it of you. So out of consideration, and with much resourcefulness, I've worked around the places where such expressions would be natural and appropriate for my speakers. Though some of the resulting substitutions are inexact and so technically dishonest, they are close enough—white lies rather than duplicity. By the way, should you want to hear the real deal, go to YouTube and dial up a Dan Marino commercial.

Anyway: The next thing you know Chuck and Hank are at Chuck's house and figuring out step two. Chuck said Hank should wait outside while he went inside and left a note for Mattie. He went up the porch steps with exaggerated stealth like a silent film actor playing a black-hearted villain bent on stealing some poverty-stricken family's only valuable heirloom, Grandma's silver and turquoise hair combs. Mostly he was just trying to be quiet but part of him was doing it to make Hank laugh. Until Hank laughed real loud. And then Chuck said, "Oh shit!" because he remembered he was trying to sneak into the house without waking Mattie and he shouldn't have tried to make Hank laugh. And he said, "Oh shit!" again because he'd said the first, Oh shit, so loud.

Chuck steeled himself and whispered, "Just walk in the house normal." And he did. (If you are worried about how he got his keys out of his pocket without fumbling so much that he went ahead and made too much noise anyway and how was I going to work my way out of that very real possibility, don't. Hardly anybody back there locked their doors at night. Maybe if they went on vacation for a week, but not just for the night.)

One of the girls' school tablets and a pencil lay on the kitchen table. Chuck tore off a sheet of paper a fraction of an inch at a time and took up the pencil. Bending over the table he wrote:

Dear Mattie,
Me and Hank is going down to the emergency room and get an operation so we don't have to use rubbers anymore.

Chuck stood up and thought for a minute and then wrote some more:

> *Call the shop and tell them me and Hank is taking vacation days. Don't tell them why.*
> *Love,*
> *Chuck*
> *XOXOXOX*

The next thing you know, Chuck and Hank are standing at the reception counter in the emergency room at Bashline Hospital, which was completely empty except for them, it being close to midnight on a Thursday and anybody who got hurt or sick that late usually waited until morning to go in, unless it was something real serious like being in a bad car wreck and they bring you in in an ambulance or you sliced your thumb open from tip to heel while you were skinning a muskrat, the wound so deep and wide that wrapping it with electrician's tape and waiting until morning to see if it closed up enough so you could avoid medical intervention was not a wise option.

Things got a little bit confusing because the nurse quite reasonably wanted to know what they were there for. Hank said, "It's private. Just between us and the doctor." The nurse showed them her clipboard and said she had to put something down. Hank told her to put down that they were sick. The nurse opened up her mouth like she was going to go all prissy on them, but seeing the situation for what it was and not altogether sure if these two would maybe get out of control, just said okay and called back for the doctor. It was actually more than "just" her saying okay. Some of the hospitals around there, in Mercer and Butler County, had put on a workshop about deescalating situations where patient agitation could lead to minor (and maybe not so minor) violence. It was the beginning of a new age that would eventually emphasize patient-centered care, and considering the region's governing zeitgeist, actually pretty remarkable and forward looking. Luckily for the nurse, she picked that night to put her new training into practice, gesturing to the seats and telling the friends it wouldn't be but a minute. (It was probably lucky for Chuck and Hank too.)

Chuck and Hank sat down and whispered back and forth about how great their lives were going to be after this and pretty soon the doctor came out and stood over them the way doctors used to do in those days, all snooty and self-important (he had some work to do on that new patient-centered care thing). He asked what was wrong. Hank looked over to the nurse, who you could tell was listening hard even though she was pretending to be working on her charts, and then he looked at Chuck and back to the doctor and said, "It's private."

The doctor rolled his eyes, thinking what was private was that they both had a venereal disease (the old timey name for STDs) and waved for them to follow him, and they all three went through the emergency room halls smelling of antiseptic, ether, and bleach and into an examination room. Being there was only one examination table and neither friend wanted to give the impression that he was taking charge, they both stood and the doctor sat on the table. He said, "What's wrong?"

Hank and Chuck looked at each other and got a little red-faced, both realizing they didn't know the name of what they were asking for. Chuck got a sad, pleading look in his eyes, which made Hank feel sorry for having got his friend into this. But just for a second. He looked right at the doctor and said, "We want a ball-ectomy." (Had he come of age in some other discourse community, Hank might just have established a reputation as a gifted neologist, the guy who could always be counted on for the precise and apt apercus a tense or poignant moment called for.)

The doctor hadn't been at Bashline's for very long and given that all of his training had been at the Medical School of the University of Pennsylvania, as well as his internship and residency, wasn't really ready for the backwoods world view of many of his patients. He'd also grown up in Scarsdale and gone to a private prep school, good preparation for college maybe, but for Appalachian PA in 1953, not much help at all. Of course, his having all that privileged background and elite training invites the question as to how he ended up in a small-town hospital in the middle of where-the-fuck-am-I? Just suffice it to say that you can be well educated and make bad lifestyle choices just as easily as if you dropped out of high school and fraudulently applied for legacy membership in the Mafia. The doctor's bewilderment was compounded by the fact that Mercer County was (and still is) an odd place, its not being quite sure if it's a patch of Alabama that broke off and drifted tectonically northward until it shoaled on the foothills of the Alleghenies or if it's a sophisticated New England suburb.

Anyway: There was this long back and forth between the friends and the doctor, with Chuck finally saying (because it was how Hank made him understand), "Like when a woman gets her tubes tied."

The doctor rolled his eyes again and said, "How soon do you want it?"

Hank made a little can-do motion with his fist and said, "Right now, Doc. Right the hell now!"

Chuck gave Hank a little sideways glance that said, "Whoa, man, you think maybe we should think about this a little more?"—suddenly becoming a bit tentative now that the getting-tied thing might actually happen. But once you go down one of these rabbit holes being all tough and everything in front of your best friend (and peer pressure being so strong a force even if nobody is actually calling you a pussy for wanting to back out, you know for sure they are thinking it), it is really hard to fly back up, because falling is falling and gravity is gravity. So he gathered up all his resolve and said (with somewhat less enthusiasm than Hank), "Yes sir, right the hell now."

The doctor told them he couldn't do it right now because they had to go at least eight hours without eating or drinking beforehand, and it was pretty obvious it had been far less time than that. But he could admit them and do it in the morning. Hank said, "What about work on Monday?" The doctor said as long as it wasn't real heavy work, they should be good to go. And that was that.

The doctor told the nurse to get them beds and reserve an operating room for nine and ten in the morning. Soon the two friends were ensconced in the hospital, though in different rooms because there were two vacancies in different semi-private rooms, and the staff didn't want to have to deal with preparing a whole other room just for these two weirdos, even though there were several such double vacancies available.

The next morning, the staff prepped the two friends for surgery—just the normal routine, including the shaving part. In those days, they shaved you around what was going to be the surgical site with a straight razor because of the then-current thinking that hair harbors bacteria that might lead to infection and are hard to kill even with antiseptic. To be sure of getting them all, you had to shave real, real close. This was especially true of pubic hair should the surgical site be anywhere near the groin area. Of course the profession eventually discovered that the tiny skin abrasions resulting from blade shaving were even more welcoming harbors for bacteria and the practice has been pretty much abandoned. Now days they just use an electric shaver so they don't get hair in the incision. But not for Hank and Chuck in the '50s. They had to get shaved and of course the youngest, least experienced nurse on the shift drew the short straw—no nurse wanting any part of shaving strangers' pubic areas because, seriously? Being's the youngest nurse that morning was also really cute, both the men had somewhat fuller profiles than they started out with, though neither went to full attention, embarrassment and their hangovers coming to a kind of compromise with what-comes-naturally, leaving them just a touch ashamed but not to the point of humiliation.

I should note here (because it's important to the story) that there was actually one nurse who took a kind of sadistic pleasure in shaving men's groins. She'd been an army nurse and understandably held a lifetime grudge against men born of all the sexual harassment she'd endured during her enlistment, which included four years overseas during WWII. She'd had it. Her revenge consisted in "accidently" brushing the frenulum with her starched sleeve or the safety razor's handle. Sometimes she just acted as if she were moving the man's penis to the side with her thumb and index finger to get to the rest of the hair, handling the member as if it were some icky, slimy thing she was picking up off the floor, but making sure to massage it just so as she did. She was good at what she did and when the inevitable happened, she'd shake her head in disgust and look the man in the eye like every mean school teacher he'd ever had, doing her absolute best to leave him red with embarrassment. She was good at that too.

For a long time now, vasectomies haven't even been inpatient procedures. Urologists do them right in the office. But back then you stayed overnight before and then for a couple more days after in case of complications—a practice consistent with other surgeries. They also don't put you under anymore—they just use a local anesthetic which sounds like progress but not necessarily: I myself am highly resistant to local anesthesia and it didn't fully take when I had my own vasectomy. (#$&##, **#%!) (Also the doctor's nurse was a friend of my wife and made a point of laughing through the whole thing, at one point saying that she sure didn't need two hands for *this*, which made it that much harder to deal with the pain.)

In the recovery room Chuck woke up first and screamed, "Oh God, my nuts hurt!" The nurse laughed and said, "I imagine they do." (These days they routinely inject a local anesthetic around the incision area before awakening you so that your first sensation upon regaining consciousness isn't agonizing pain but a cosmic disorientation that makes you think maybe you didn't survive the surgery. The pain comes on gradually now, which might actually be worse in that it's like tiptoeing into the cold water an inch at a time instead of just diving in all at once and taking your medicine like a grownup. [Also the pain made you know for sure you were not dead {see Hemingway}.].)

Hank woke up about a half-hour later but didn't swear or make any big fuss except to groan some and wonder if maybe this whole thing had been a big mistake. The nurses had finished with Chuck and were wheeling him out the door to take him back to his room, so the two friends couldn't commiserate. In a little while they took Hank to his room. It was just before lunch time, but Hank couldn't eat a bite. All he could do was lie curled up on his side and moan.

It wasn't too long after that when Chuck came into Hank's room. He could barely walk and was all hunched over and breathing in little sputtering spurts. He would have been a whole lot better off if he'd stayed in his room and rested, but he had something to tell Hank and he was determined to tell him. He shuffled and moaned his way over to Hank's bed and said, "You son-of-a-bitch!" Hank squinted through his half-opened eyes and said, "What?"

"I said, 'You son-of-a-bitch!,' you son-of-a-bitch!"

[….]

"I swear if I could get my foot off the floor I'd kick you right in the ass!"

Then Chuck did the equivalent of stomping out of the room in a huff, a jerkily poor approximation given that he couldn't muster up anything more than a straggling limp as if he were dragging both feet behind him at the same time, and any breath he had in reserve had to go for getting air in to deal with the pain and not be huffy about anything.

The two friends stayed out of each other's way all that day and evening, but by the next morning were all chummy again in spite of the fact that they were both in serious discomfort (feeling a little like teammates who've been beat up pretty bad while winning a really physical football game with an archrival) and delighting in talking about how great their lives were going to be now that they weren't going to have to wear rubbers anymore and how they couldn't wait until tomorrow to get out of here and have sex the natural way, Chuck thinking Mattie was really going to love this and Hank going through his mind to think who he could call on short notice for a date.

Chapter 3
Mattie Reads the Note

[Wherein Mattie reads Chuck's note and understandably panics. Also wherein is plunked down a complicating thread of dramatic irony, which some readers will consider just plain pathetic but the smart ones will recognize as a stroke of ironizing genius.]

When Mattie read Chuck's note, she understandably panicked. She didn't think anything of it the afternoon before when Chuck walked in from work and asked her if she minded if he took the car and went out to the Rusty Bolt with Hank. She told him to go on and enjoy himself—he deserved a night out. And she meant it. First off, Chuck hardly ever went out and even if he ended up having a little too much to drink, she wouldn't have to worry about it. He never got mean when he drank. If anything, he would get silly. Also it broke up the routine for her and gave her an evening to herself (except for the girls of course) and she could find something to do just for her.

Mattie's first reaction was, *Oh my God, what happened?*, followed by *Rubbers?* Then she real quick called down to the hospital to see what was what and they told her that Chuck was being prepped for minor surgery and she could call back in a few hours to find out about his condition.

By the way: In those days, anybody could call a hospital and say you wanted to find out the condition of one of their patients. They would transfer you to whoever would know (like the nurses' station on the floor where they were being treated [remember that there were no computers then] and they would tell you). They didn't give a lot of detail. They'd say the patient was in stable condition or good or critical or whatever. You could ask if they were in surgery and they would tell you. No HIPAA Privacy Rules. Anybody at all could call, even robbers who, knowing you wouldn't be home for a while, could safely go to your unlocked house and steal your television set.

Anyway: Mattie thought, Screw calling back, I'm going down there. The next thing you know, she's taken the girls to her mother's and is in the waiting room waiting for Chuck. She was able to see him for a little bit after he got back from the recovery room, even though the nurses told her she would have to wait for evening visiting hours and she told them she didn't have to wait until then and if they didn't tell her where Chuck was, she was going to go door to door until she found him and why don't they try and stop her.

This is when that army nurse showed her other side, which was the side that held true compassion for all those boys who got wounded in the war, including the ones that made like they were trying to grab her ass with their dying breath. Even though Chuck's situation was nowhere near as bad as a soldier getting all shot up, it was enough to worry his wife half to death and it was her solemn obligation to ease pain wherever she found it, even if a moron like Chuck was the one who caused it. She told Mattie she could see Chuck for a little while and took her back.

When Chuck saw her, he got all mawkish and emotional, grateful that Mattie had come. That is until he told her the story about how Hank told him about his cousin and how in the moment, they thought them doing the same thing Hank's cousin did was a great idea. (He didn't tell her how the whole thing got started while he and Hank were taking a leak.

Neither did he tell her that he had been to Hank's room to call him a son-of-a-bitch, because when somebody is shooting bullets at you with their eyes, you don't hand them a fresh box of ammunition.) Chuck got a lot less emotional when Mattie said, "Jesus Christ, Chuck! I could have used a little warning don't you think!"

Chuck almost snapped back at her, because that is just natural. But even with the anesthesia still staggering through his system, he was smart enough to hold back, because given what he was in the hospital for and how sensitive that could be and the fact that Mattie had a point, he just said she was right and he was sorry. To do otherwise, would make moot the entire motivation for getting fixed in the first place, because if he did snap back, one thing he would know for sure: It would be a good long while before he would need a rubber if he hadn't gotten fixed. In that moment, being sorry (even if it was a disingenuous sorry) wasn't just the best option. It was the only option. Anything else wouldn't be like handing over a box of ammunition, it would be like giving up the keys to the whole arsenal.

Given that you can never tell in situations like this what little thing it might be that would lead to grave danger, both Mattie and Chuck wanted the visit to be over but neither one wanted to be the one to say that on account of just saying that could be that little thing. (Oh how the sentences ramble, straddling the fine line between profound sense and ridiculous absurdity, but that's just how relationships, especially marriages, go.) They were saved by the army nurse who came in and said Mattie had to leave. Chuck and Mattie kissed (a quick peck) and Chuck told Mattie not to worry about visiting, it was only going to be until tomorrow and he would walk home.

The next thing you know, Mattie is in her kitchen and thinking that as much of a pain as this was, maybe it was a good sign. Maybe Chuck was getting a little bored and this was his way of shaking off the habit their life together was falling into. Maybe he was looking for *different*. Mattie sure was.

For example: The way mornings worked at Chuck and Mattie's house was that Mattie would get up first, put on a house dress, and go downstairs to get the percolator started and some bacon and chopped onion frying before setting the table for her and Chuck. By the time Chuck came down, she would have his eggs just about cooked (which he always had over real easy, because he liked the yolks soft but runny whites would be a little like eating snot) and the potatoes browning just the tiniest little bit and the bacon draining on a plate covered with a dish towel. He'd sit down and she'd pour his coffee, which he took black with two sugars, and spatula out his eggs and potatoes, with the eggs always on the right side of the plate and the potatoes on the left. Then she'd spread the onions over top of the potatoes and lay the four strips of bacon (always exactly four, and just getting crispy) in a line like skinny soldiers standing at attention all across the whole plate.

She did all this without ever saying anything, because Chuck was decidedly not a morning person and couldn't abide one single word of conversation until he was at least halfway through his coffee and sometimes not even then—sometimes it took a cup and a half.

By the way: I know a "guy" who has been married twice. He traces the genesis of his first marriage's slow lingering death to the morning, just three or four days after the honeymoon, when his bubbly-in-the-morning bride was just chattering and twittering away (like one of those goddamn birds outside!) across their tiny little kitchen table about something he couldn't care less about at 6:30 in the morning, and he looked across his coffee cup (and just beneath his eyebrows because that's about how much he could stand to look at her in that moment) and said, "Why don't you just shut the fuck up!"

Anyway: After Chuck left for work she would clear the table and get the kids up and start their breakfasts, the older daughter always having a single poached egg on buttered toast and a glass of tomato juice, and the younger a bowl of Cheerios and, if they had any, a banana. She'd kiss the girls goodbye and tell them to be good at school and out the door they'd go and Mattie would have herself a nice slow cup of coffee before starting her day. Every weekday, exactly the same.

Every weekday, exactly the same.
Every weekday, exactly the same.
Every weekday, exactly the same.
Every weekday, exactly the same.
Every weekday, exactly the same.
Every weekday, exactly the same.
Every weekday, exactly the same.

It wasn't just weekday mornings that were like that. Sunday mornings had their own routine, even if they were different in the details. Mattie got up early and put something in the oven for Sunday dinner. Ham or a chicken or roast beef or a pork roast or maybe if Chuck was lucky, she'd work on braising some round steak, which is a whole lot more complicated than you would think. And those were the only five things they ever had for Sunday dinner, which Mattie found boring but Chuck thought was surprising enough to make him look forward to Sundays to see what they were having. Then Mattie made French toast or pancakes and the whole family ate together, not in shifts like weekday mornings. The girls would put on their Sunday school clothes and watch some TV until 9:30 when Chuck would load them up in the car and drop them off at the Covenant Presbyterian Church on Main Street. On his way home he would stop at the newsstand on the north end of Broad Street and get a paper. He and Mattie would have another cup of coffee while they read the paper and by then it was time for Chuck to go back and pick up the girls. While he was gone, Mattie set the table and put dinner on.

Every Sunday morning, exactly the same.
Every Sunday morning, exactly the same.
Every Sunday morning, exactly the same.
Every Sunday morning, exactly the same.
Every Sunday morning, exactly the same.
Every Sunday morning, exactly the same.
Every Sunday morning, exactly the same.

And not just mornings. Every weekday afternoon, Chuck would get home from work a little before 4:00, say Hi to Mattie, and go upstairs to take a nap. The girls would come in a little after 4:00, change out of their school clothes, and watch TV while Mattie got supper ready. To be sure, there was some variety to supper, Mattie randomly cycling the meal among the few that Chuck liked, meatloaf, beef stew, spaghetti, pork chops, liver and onions, hamburgers. On Mondays and Tuesdays, maybe leftovers from Sunday. One of a very few others if something was on sale at the A&P. Except for spaghetti nights, Mattie always made potatoes, mashed or scalloped or fried, each matched with a particular meat. Like never, ever did she make scalloped potatoes with beef. They were for leftover ham and that was it.

At 6:00, they'd all sit down to eat and then the girls would go do their homework while Chuck watched the news and then whatever shows were on. Mattie cleaned up the kitchen. When she was done, she would go sit beside Chuck on the couch and the girls would come down when they were finished with their homework. At 9:00 the girls went to bed and Mattie and Chuck would watch another hour of television and then they would go to bed.

Tuesdays and Fridays were a little bit different. Tuesdays, the girls had their Brownies meeting and on Fridays the whole family went down to the A&P and did the week's grocery shopping.

Every week, exactly the same.
Every week, exactly the same.
Every week, exactly the same.
Every week, exactly the same.
Every week, exactly the same.
Every week, exactly the same.
Every week, exactly the same.

And not just weeknights. On Saturday night Chuck and Mattie made love (unless she had her period). They would go upstairs at 10:00 like on weeknights. Mattie would put on her nightgown and get under the covers and wait for Chuck. He would turn out the lights and Mattie would watch him undress ghostlike in whatever light worked its way in from the streetlamps outside. Chuck would slip into bed and slide over and put his hand on her face and kiss her. That part was nice. Then he would slide his hands over her in the same pattern every Saturday. Cheek, neck, shoulder, arm, side, belly, shoulder again, arm. Breast. Down her side again and then gently down her thigh and then inside her thigh and then gently *there*. And then he would do all that again. And then one last time before slipping off her panties real slow (which was also nice) and getting on top at which point she would remind him to get a rubber and he would get out of bed and put one on and come back and get on top exactly where he had left off. Chuck moved his hips in the exact same way every Saturday night and for about the same length of time, which wasn't real quick and done like some of Mattie's friends complained about, but it was always the same. Mattie always thought that it was really kind of nice or would be nice if it was the first time, or maybe the first hundred times, but they were way past a hundred times and it had become like making breakfast, just another part to the day.

Every Saturday night, exactly the same.
Every Saturday night, exactly the same.
Every Saturday night, exactly the same.
Every Saturday night, exactly the same.
Every Saturday night, exactly the same.
Every Saturday night, exactly the same.
Every Saturday night, exactly the same.

Of course there were those weeknights when Chuck wanted to make love and that was different, but only because it wasn't Saturday. The lovemaking itself was exactly the same. Well, not exactly. They would both of them rush it a little because they couldn't sleep in like they could on Saturday night, but that wasn't different enough to make Mattie look forward to it, even if it did add a weird kind of excitement to doing it. In fact, she had started to resist on those nights, even knowing that could lead to trouble because as some of her girlfriends would occasionally concede in a grumbling kind of way, "If you don't take care of your husband, somebody else will." And worse were the ones whose husbands had lost interest in making love just about altogether and didn't touch them for months at a time. Mattie should be grateful that Chuck did want her.

To be fair about it, Chuck was a pretty good husband. For one thing, the girls adored him and he never said no when they asked him if they could go to Isaly's for ice cream. And he always asked Mattie what TV shows she wanted to watch. And he took care of things he was supposed to around the house and never missed work and never wasted money like buying another shotgun he didn't need like other husbands did. And when they had a fight, he never hollered at her (not real bad anyway, never so much that it would scare her). And he spent all of his vacation taking her and the girls on day trips to wherever they wanted to go, as long as it wasn't too far and they could be back in time to sleep at home.

Mattie knew that an awful lot of young women like her would kill to have a husband like Chuck, but still. When you only have one story to hear and you've heard it a few thousand times, you start to wonder about what it would take to locate a different ending. Something new. Something exotic. Something, anything, different. And she found it. She'd taken a lover who had drawn her into *his* story. Someone who wanted her like Chuck used to. And why was it that nobody seemed to be telling Chuck that if he didn't take care of his wife somebody else would? And why on earth did he have to bring rubbers into the whole thing? Rubbers, for crying out loud. Rubbers. Seriously? Rubbers?

Chapter 4
More Than They Bargained For

[Wherein Chuck and Hank find out that they
should have asked more questions before
getting their vasectomies. Which is not to say
they wouldn't have arrived at the same decision
(given that hindsight isn't always 20-20—on
occasion it can be quite myopic), but at least it
would have been an *informed* decision and they
maybe would have done a little more planning
before forging ahead.]

Part way through Chuck and Hank's last morning in the
hospital, the doctor gave them their discharge instructions. He
talked to both of them at the same time in a waiting room for
the families of surgical patients, which was a little bit
embarrassing for Chuck and Hank because they had to share
it with a big Italian family who were waiting for their
grandfather to come out from an emergency appendectomy.

It was hard for both of our friends but in different
ways. Chuck was wary of Italians because at the shop where
he and Hank worked they would sweat their asses off for a
nickel an hour raise and then the boss expected everybody to
work that hard and that just wasn't right. He didn't want any
Italian to have something on him like knowing he'd had this
particular operation, and without any plausible reason why an
Italian would turn him in to the boss for getting himself fixed,
nevertheless was worried that they might.

Hank's discomfort came from a different place. He
really, really liked Italian girls and was nervous that the Italians

in the waiting room (given that they were all one big club and Catholics who all went to the same church because there was only one for miles and miles around) might let out what happened and the girls would make fun of him behind his back and every Italian girl for all those miles and miles around would know what he'd done and that might very well have the opposite effect on what the vasectomy was supposed to do and make it harder to get laid instead of easier. (But on the other hand, he also had a shadow of a thought getting started way back in his brain that it might be a good thing if they spread it around because those self-same Italian girls might think he was actually doing them a favor, what with the Pope being so against rubbers, and that he maybe could persuade them that doing it without a rubber was actually less sinful than doing it with one, the way they had been doing it with their Italian dates.)

But our guys needn't have worried. The Italians stuck to themselves in a corner of the room and didn't pay them any attention—they were busy passing around boxes of pizzelles and cannolis and biscottis, and just going on and on over what a shame it was about the grandfather, he was always so strong, and this is going to kill him. "Ah, what you gonna do?" they said.

So anyway: The doctor told them to take the usual precautions like to keep ice on their scrotums off and on for fifteen minutes at a time for the rest of the day. So okay, thought Chuck and Hank, that makes sense. He said for them to make an appointment to come back in five days to get the stitches out and no sex before then. Both friends had the exact same thought: *What the hell! Five* more *days?!?!*

Then the doctor said that after the stitches were out, they still had to continue using birth control until they'd had at least twenty ejaculations. Chuck got a real strange look on his face and started counting off his fingers with his thumb and working his mouth like a fish deep in thought though he didn't actually say anything.

The two friends made their appointments and strolled awkwardly toward the steps down to the lobby. Chuck said to Hank, "Twenty times?!?! At my rate, that's gonna take months! Did your cousin tell you about that?"

"Not that I remember."

"We should have called him."

The next thing you know, the day came to get the stitches out and Hank picked Chuck up and they drove back to the hospital. Chuck told Hank he was black and blue from damn near his knees all the way up to his navel and what's with that and Hank said him too and he guessed it was just normal. The doctor took them both into the exam room again and each one had to be there while the other one got his stiches out, which meant they had to go through the embarrassment of watching the other one (even if they were resolved to look the other way, because a thing like that?— might as well not look at a pit bull snarling on a short leash trying to get off and have you for breakfast), and when it was their turn, they had to hold still and not move or let out with a little yelp or even wince because the other one was watching, but for crying out loud, somebody's got this sharp little pair of scissors digging into your scrotum and making like it doesn't matter is really, really hard—no matter how tough you think you are.

But they got through that and then the doctor told them the nurse was going to give them a specimen jar and they should use the men's room off the waiting area to collect a semen sample so he could have a baseline for their sperm counts. He told them to come back next week and left. Chuck and Hank just looked at each other. "What's he mean, 'Collect a semen sample'?" Chuck said. Hank got that little twisted look you get when something is way too embarrassing to say right out loud and mumbled, "I think it means…" and made a jacking off motion with his right hand. "Oh shit," Chuck said.

The nurse who'd been in the army came in and gave them each a glass jar with their name on it. Chuck got all red, but Hank manned up and said, "Are we supposed to do what I think we're supposed to do?"

She said, "Do you need somebody to show you how?" The way she held her head when she said it, you would have sworn she'd bitten off a chunk of Redman and was about to spit on their shoes and they better take a step back if they knew what was good for them. The friends could only look down at the floor like schoolboys who just got caught trying to get a peek in the girls' outhouse. She said that when they were done just put the samples on the check-in counter and walked out with about the same air of caring as had the doctor.

So there was this strained couple of minutes when neither friend could think of what to do or say and you can imagine what was going through their heads and what they looked like, their expressions and posture and skin pallor. Finally Hank said (a little testily), "All right! I'll go first, but you got to wait out in the hall. And don't let anybody else in. I won't be able to do it if there's somebody in the next stall."

So they got through that and went out and made their next appointments. Of course it had to be the army nurse making the appointments that day. She held the specimen jars up to the light one at a time and shook her head, then got that back and forth, I-don't-know look. Finally she said, "That should be enough," which got both the guys looking at the other's sample to see how they measured up. (The woman was *good*!)

When she filled out their appointment reminder cards, she made it last way longer than it had to, taking her time writing them out and actually shaking her head at one point before tearing Hank's card up and starting over. And the whole time, there were those two specimen jars sitting right on the counter where anybody who walked by could see. (She had this devious little smirk on her face the whole time too.)

When Hank and Chuck got far enough down the hall, Chuck mumbled, "Screw her." Hank said he was almost desperate enough to, which made Chuck laugh. "Me too," he said. Then the laugh made it to his groin and he said, "Uhhhhhh!"

Hank said, "One down, nineteen to go."

Chuck said, "You mean that counts?"

"Sure it does."

And that's how things started to get complicated. Both friends were thinking (though they couldn't for obvious reasons tell each other) that if jacking off counted, the best way to get to not having to use rubbers was to jack off a lot. That would have been a lot easier for Hank since he lived by himself, but harder for Chuck because his wife didn't have a job and it wasn't like he didn't do it in the house once in a (very) long while, but he had to be *real* careful and sneak around almost like he was having an affair to keep her from finding out. Maybe he could wait until she was asleep, but what if she woke up? He was a little jealous of Hank.

But Hank, even though he thought it for a minute or so, had a better idea. He had this sort-of girlfriend Delores who waited tables at the diner on Main and Broad. Hank and Delores were what these days you would call friends with benefits. She didn't really sleep around, but she liked Hank and put out for him pretty much whenever they got together because he was a real gentleman and discreet about it, which he held as a point of personal pride. After he dropped Chuck off, Hank went down to the diner and sat at the counter and ordered a BLT. He asked Delores if he could talk to her after work. Maybe he could stop by later and they could go down to the Rexall and get a cup of coffee. She said, "That's what you're calling it now? Coffee?"

"No, for real. Well, not exactly."

Delores winked and said, "Okay, so it's 'not exactly'?"

Hank leaned over the counter so he could whisper and she leaned in so she could hear. "It's kind of like that, but complicated."

Delores showed a little bit of chest through her waitress uniform and said, "I can do complicated." (The one time Hank was trying to be serious and she's got to be all teasing and playful. Just goes to show, he thought.)

Hank whispered again, "I can't talk about it now. It's private."

"Always has been."

"You're going to make this hard, aren't you?"

"Make what hard?"

And it went on like that for maybe another minute and then Delores said she was good for getting coffee at the Rexall after work.

The next thing you know, they were in the Rexall sitting in one of those little booths they had for the soda fountain and where they could talk without anybody listening in. Hank told Delores about how he and Chuck got drunk and went down to the hospital and got vasectomies so they wouldn't have to use rubbers anymore.

Delores let him get all the way through the story without giving him a hard time like back at the diner, because there is a time and a place for that kind of thing and this definitely wasn't it. Maybe Hank was one of the good ones, but he was still a guy, and you know how easy it is for even the good ones to get their feelings hurt if you laugh at them at the wrong time, even if they are being riotously funny.

Hank finally finished the story, and she said, "So what do you want from me?"

Hank stammered a little bit before he got up the nerve to tell her about the nineteen ejaculations and was hoping maybe she could help him out with that.

"Sugar," she said in a bad imitation of a southern drawl, "you know I would."

"Wait until you hear what I have in mind."

"Okay."

"Now don't get mad."

"Sugar," she started again and Hank held up his hands and said it was serious and she dropped it.

"I was thinking maybe you could come stay with me for a couple weeks and maybe let me pretty much every day."

[....]

"I could pay you."

Boy oh boy. Delores just about split herself wide open, but before she could get anything out, Hank said, "I know, I know. I wouldn't mean it that way. Just that I'd be putting you out and you ought to get something for all that trouble."

[....]

[....]

"How much?"

"Three hundred?"

"Let's go."

Hank (feeling a lot like some kind of criminal conspirator and that they should be real secretive about what came next) said Delores should walk back to the diner without him and drive home and pack a bag and go on over to his house. She told him it would be pretty late because she couldn't leave before her dad got home from work and she had to make arrangements so he wouldn't starve to death. Hank said just whenever. Just come in and wake him up and he'd fix her something to eat. After she left, he had another cup of coffee, then sauntered out and up to the other end of Broad Street, stopping now and then to pretend he was looking at the window displays. He went into Harshaw's Drugs and bought two boxes of Trojans from the pharmacist. They knew each other from high school so it wasn't real embarrassing, although neither Hank nor the pharmacist said anything other than what was absolutely necessary to complete the transaction. And they called them prophylactics, not condoms.

On his way back to his car, Hank stopped in the Five and Ten and browsed through the greeting cards aisle until he came to the thank you cards but couldn't decide on which one, so he bought a box of assorted cards, figuring he could pick out the right one when he got home. Then he stopped at the bank and filled out a withdrawal slip for his savings account for three hundred dollars. He stared at the slip kind of vacant for a few seconds before tearing it up and changing it to five hundred. Finally he walked the rest of the way to his car, got in, and drove out to Kocher's to pick out some flowers.

Chapter 5
Dolores Says Goodbye to Her Dad

[Wherein Hank and Delores take steps to
implement Hank's plan and we learn the true
worth of a septic system.]

Delores took her time walking back to the diner so she could
have a good long talk with herself. Oh boy, who would have
thought when she got up in the morning thinking this was just
going to be another day of juggling multiple orders and adding
up separate checks for tightwad church ladies and ducking
butt pinches and having to flirt with the old-men-who-ain't-
figured-out-they-don't-got-it-any-more (as if they ever did)
breakfast club that something like this was going to happen?
Just goes to show that the future is pretty much always a
mystery and you just never know, and a girl really should live
her life being prepared for the unexpected and recognizing a
good thing when it pops up and being ready to go for it—like
taking Hank up on his proposition without a second's
hesitation.

Well, there was that little bit of hesitation when he first
brought up the money, but he explained it right away and it
wasn't like that, nothing about it being like she was a whore.
Except there was. Being honest for a second and stripping
away all the excuses, she *was* going to get paid for sleeping with
him. But then again, all he really asked her to do was help him
out with a medical need, so really, when all was said and done,
she was going to be more like a nurse than a whore, and a
nurse deserved to be paid. Once you thought about it some,
she was being a good friend just like if he broke his foot or

something and needed somebody to help with the housework while he healed up and he was just reimbursing her for her expenses. (Notice that Delores neatly sidestepped the question as to whether a *whore* deserved to be paid or reimbursed for expenses.)

So that's what you're going to call it now? Housework?

Yes I am. Nothing more, nothing less.

Really?

She had to admit that the way she went back and forth with Hank at the diner, especially that part about making "what hard," was a little on the raunchy side. But it was also pretty slick on her part and just went to show that when she wanted to, she could hold up her end with anybody.

But maybe she should have thought about the amount a little bit instead of blurting out, "Let's go," the way she did. Maybe being so quick had made Hank think she would have done it for less and maybe he'd thought she *was* a little bit of a whore. But Hank wasn't like that. So far as she could tell, he never bragged to anybody about them getting together now and again just for the fun of it the way those couple of other boys she went with in high school did. Hank was about as much of a gentleman as you could ever hope for, even in your most romantic dreams—not that she had any romantic dreams so far as he was concerned. They were just real good friends.

On the other hand, maybe if she had tilted her head a little and said something like, "You think three hundred might be a little on the light side?" and turned the whole thing into a labor union negotiation and maybe get him worrying just a little bit about how she might go out on strike even before they got started and offer a couple hundred more, which would be an honest and businesslike way to approach the whole thing, she could have done even better.

You hold up right there, girl, and take a minute to admit that you're fooling yourself here. Truth is, you are going to go stay in the man's house and he's going to fuck you (what'd he say?—nineteen times!) and he's going to pay you for doing it!

You better hold up yourself! What about him paying for the stock car races and taking you out for hamburgers afterward and then you sitting right up beside him in that Plymouth of his with your hand on the inside of his thigh, which is pretty much a straight-up invitation? Only difference is the price.

So you're telling me you was being a whore those other times, too, but you'd do it for the price of a fairgrounds ticket and a hamburger and a milkshake? Isn't that what they call a *cheap* whore?

It's not about the money, you moron, and you know it! It's about the inside toilet!

Okay, now that last line needs some clarification. What that was about was the fact that Hank lived in a pretty decent house along a macadam road outside of town, an old farmhouse he bought on an articles of agreement, and even though that was risky, he was a real steady guy with a good job and unlikely to get behind. Hank's house being roomy and just-fixed-up was for sure an attraction, but the real appeal was that the house had a septic tank to go with it. Not having to go outside to do your business for however long this was going to take was the real draw.

Once Delores came to this accommodation with herself, she picked up her step and in no time was back at the diner to get her car. Being more conventional than Hank with his Plymouth, she drove a second-hand Ford with a stick shift, which would've had a kind of symmetry to it if she did drive a Plymouth, but she didn't and you can't change what's real. You just can't.

Delores still had about another half a block to walk once she got to the diner because it didn't have a parking lot. Customers just parked on the street—either Main Street or Broad Street. If they could, they used Main Street on account of Broad Street had parking meters, which is confusing because you'd think folks would have called the busier, more commercial street Main Street, and it would have the parking meters. But folks back then and back there didn't quite think like most people in other parts of the country. The only reason anyone can give for Main Street being called that is because that's where the college is (or was—by the '50s, the college had stretched way up the hill and overland across the fields from there almost to Pine Street). But it was always Broad Street which was the real downtown, except it wasn't called downtown, it was called "down street."

By the way, a typical usage for "down street": "What do you want to do?"

"I don't know. What do you want to do?"

"I don't know. Why don't we just go down street and see who's there."

"Okay."

Such a conversation could only realistically happen on Friday nights, because the stores were open on Friday until 9:00. You'd think that if they picked one night to be open late, it would be Saturday. But not in that town, for which there was actually a good reason. Friday was the day the Bessemer paid its men, making Friday the big shopping day. One thing that made down street especially crowded on Friday nights was that the A&P was right in the center of town (directly across the street from Bashline's where Chuck and Hank got their vasectomies). Combine that with payday and you got yourself a whole mess of people all trying to get at the same thing at the same time, which made things even more complicated, because, like the diner, the A&P didn't have a parking lot, so there would be a constant flow of cars circling the three-block stretch of retail space, with all those drivers trying to find a parking spot. (This all got a lot easier a few years later when Kroger's opened up a big store along the railroad tracks and were smart enough to include a big parking lot.)

To compensate for being open late on Fridays, the stores all closed at noon on Wednesdays. (There wasn't a good reason for that, like there was with payday for Friday—they just closed at noon.)

Anyway, back to Delores after her shift at the diner: So Delores got in her car and drove out toward Number 5 where she lived in a house trailer with her dad. (There were [and still are] lots of places around there that weren't real places but had names like they were, meaning they were just neighborhoods or wide spots in the road. There was Hallville and Blacktown and Pinch and several named for numbers, Number 2 and Number 5 the most prominent. These places got their names from the old coal mines, abbreviations for Mine Number 2 and Mine Number 5. [Presumably there once were Mines 1, 3, and 4 {and maybe 6, 7, and who knows how far up, but if there were, the names didn't stick to any little settlement they'd fostered}.] Number 5 still had a long row of shotgun houses that the company had once rented to miners, according to the company a perk of sorts so the miners could live near the mine and not have to have a car to get to work. They could just walk. But the real reason was to make it hard to quit their jobs, since one of the lease requirements was you had to live in the house for two years and pay the rent via a payroll deduction. You shouldn't need a lot of explanation as to how this would lead to blatant worker exploitation. A cruel consequence to these mining hamlets still being lived in was that they were an enduring monument to the mines, enough so to every couple of years precipitate a rumor that "they" were going to open up the mines again. This was still happening when I left there in the early '70s—it was that entrenched a meme. By the way, in case you don't believe there was a town called Pinch, just Google-Map Pinchalong Road in Grove City—it's still there and probably always will be.)

Probably because of its history as a mining town and the fact that you had to be pretty tough and hard to live as a miner, the residents of Number 5 at the time of this story had reputations for being tough and hard too, not to mention a little light on strict compliance with the law. Some pretty rough customers lived out there. Incongruously, given the neighborhood and the fact that he lived in that old trailer, Delores's dad was actually a pretty decent, hard-working guy (though he didn't do anything to dispel the common notion that he wasn't somebody you wanted on the other side in a bar fight—and in fact had in his younger days done a couple of brief stints in the county jail for such internecine skirmishes).

He worked at Steel Car in Greenville, which depending on whether you were religious or not, was either a real sweatshop or a shit hole. It was hot in the summer and freezing in the winter and building railroad cars being such a cutthroat business, they would work you real hard when they had orders and then all of a sudden lay you off until the next set of orders came in. At the time of this story, there was a steady influx of orders and things were good, but there was always the worry that everything would turn south. That's why Delores's dad kept the trailer instead of moving them to a house. That and he wasn't going to go in for an articles of agreement and, given his reputation, he sure wasn't going to be approved for a mortgage, so just keep things simple. Delores lived there because it was free and she could save her money for a rainy day (or to maybe someday buy her own house with a septic tank).

By the way: Delores and her dad may have lived in a trailer, but it wasn't a *trailer-park-trash* kind of trailer, all rusty and with makeshift tin-can sheet metal hinges on the door. They kept it up. It even had a cute touch here and there like the wizened wooden stoop that pretended to be a porch with three sturdy steps leading down to a dirt path that split at the corner of the trailer, one branch leading to the driveway and the other around back to the outhouse.

Anyway: Nice as he was, Delores's dad had been leaving all the housework for her to do (mostly because she had two X chromosomes of course, but also because her dad was working all kinds of overtime on account of the steady stream of orders and just wasn't home that much), and she would be pretty tired a lot of the time because of working a full shift at the diner, then coming home and doing the wash and fixing some supper for when he got home and packing his dinner for his next afternoon shift at Steel Car. (What most of the whole rest of the country calls *dinner*, around there they called *supper*, and lunch was dinner (à la Flannery O'Connor, [q.v.].) She would be asleep when he got home and she'd be up way before him the next day, which meant she had to lay out his supper on the counter (with maybe a note telling him what needed heating up) and where the side dishes were (if they were the kind that wouldn't spoil if they weren't in the refrigerator) and put his dinner in the breadbox so all he had to do when he got home was plunk it in his dinner bucket and he'd be all set for the next day.

By the way: For the colloquial *dinner* and *supper* to maintain some kind of consistency, men who worked night shifts by rights should have called their food pails *supper* buckets. But that just sounds dumb, so they called them dinner buckets like everybody else. Which for that small subset of the language, aligned them ever so slightly with the greater world where dinner really meant dinner.

When Delores got home after talking to Hank, she did all those chores and packed some clothes in an old leather satchel and took a quick bath (they had electric and a well, a pump, and a gray water drain, so there was running water, just no toilet) and did up her face. She put on a crisp starched sundress that showed off her hips and didn't leave a whole lot to the imagination up top either. She checked that there were enough canned goods and bacon to get her dad through the next few days. Then she lay back in the corner of the couch and dozed while she waited for her dad to get home, hoping there wouldn't be a lot of overtime.

Her dad slipped in right around 11:30, being as quiet as he could be (per usual). When he saw her sleeping on the couch, he stepped real soft around the kitchen table and sat down and started on his supper. Part way through he got up to get a glass a water, scraping his chair on the linoleum as he did.

Delores kind of shook her head at the noise and looked around a little quizzical for a second until she remembered that she was on her way to Hank's.

"Hey there, Dad," she said.

"Hey there, kid. Sorry I woke you up."

"No overtime tonight?"

"There was a breakdown. But that just means lots tomorrow, probably do a double. How come you're all dressed up?"

"I'm going to spend a few days with a friend."

[....]

"I'll be back."

"Who's this friend?"

Delores hesitated about a second and a half, during which time she thought about whether to lie or tell the truth and said to herself, The hell with it. "Hank Walker."

Her dad's head went back and forth about four times like he was devil-possessed before he asked her did he hear what he thought he heard and she told him if he thought he heard her say Hank Walker, yeah, then he heard what he thought he heard.

So about fifty things ran right through her dad's head about what he could say to that, every single one of them being the exact wrong thing to say (because of his actually being a kind, considerate, and loving father who valued his relationship with his daughter). What he eventually landed on was, "Kind of sudden ain't it?"

"Pretty sudden."

"What you gonna be doing over there?"

"I figure that's pretty much my own business."

"What if I told you I ain't gonna allow it?"

"I'd say that it's good that you been working on getting yourself a sense of humor, but you still got a little fine tuning to do."

Delores's dad looked at his daughter and thought about all the wild oats he sowed in his day and how he always treated her as much like a son as he could, which was how she got to be able to drive a stick shift by the time she was eleven. Given that he was proud of her for all that and should be telling her more often that he was, all he said was, "You gonna come back and clean up while you're away?"

Delores just snorted.

"Guess I wouldn't either."

Delores said she had to get going and kissed him on the cheek and told him she'd call every couple of days and let him know how she was. She wrote down Hank's phone number and gave it to him.

As she opened the door, her dad said, "Be careful, Dee. Don't go and get yourself knocked up."

Delores laughed and said, "If you only knew." And then she was gone, the quiet she left behind way bigger than what that dilapidated trailer was going to be able to hold. Her dad sighed and turned to his supper and put a forkful into his mouth, the swallowing of which set off a sympathetic peristaltic reaction in his bowels. Setting down his knife and fork and glancing up to the ceiling with a fuck-me look, he said, "Ahhh, no. How could I have forgot to take a crap before I left work?"

He was about halfway to the door when he pulled up short and thought to himself, What on earth did she mean by, "If you only knew"?

Chapter 6
Shut Your Damn Mouth!

[Wherein via backstory we learn how Delores's
early experiences shaped her personality and
how she got really good at making people mad,
which will help us understand why she is able
to take a lot of what happens from here on out
in stride. Also how she is the perfect person to
play her role in this book.]

That argument Delores had with herself over staying with
Hank to help him out and getting paid for it wasn't an
aberration. She'd been having talks like that with herself since
she was eleven. The first time it happened was because she
was mad—real, real mad. She'd heard that the newsstand was
down a paperboy and walked all the way to town and asked
for the route. They turned her down. They said that people
called them paper *boys* for a reason. Delores had said right
back that maybe the reason they called them that was because
of assholes like you (living with her single dad had enriched
her vocabulary in ways less privileged girls don't have access
to). If her being a girl wasn't enough to blackball her from the
news business, that flash of temper sure was.

She replayed the interaction in her head all the way
home, maintaining a running commentary on what the man
said, what she said, and what she could have said instead of
what she did say. What if she had just taken half a second to
think before she called him an asshole, used that time to think
of something that could maybe make him change his mind?

Damnit, girl, you know good and well that assholes like him don't change. They were born that way.

Yeah, I know that! But maybe I could have said something.

And that something would be?

How the hell should I know?

Exactly.

Which settled that particular soliloquy.

One day that winter, there was a six-inch overnight snowfall. At school she heard some of the seventh- and eighth-grade boys talking about how much money they'd made shoveling sidewalks that morning.

Two things about this: First, back then the townships around Grove City still had one-room schools, which explains the seventh- and eighth-graders (I would have actually attended a one-room school if we had moved to the house where I came of age one year earlier). And two, there had to be a lot more than six inches of snow for school to be cancelled. Kids walked to school and what kid doesn't like walking through snow? Plus there wasn't any way to get the word out what with fewer than half the people having telephones and the school sure wasn't going to pay for all of the toll calls if they did have phones. Any announcement would simply be the teacher writing on the board that school was cancelled and if she (always *she*—just think about that) could make it there to write the announcement, then why not just have school?

Anyway: Delores asked the boys how they went about finding walks to shovel and they told her they just got up early and went in town and knocked on doors. She asked them what you could get for shoveling a walk and they said it depended.

"Oh, Christ," Delores said. "Depends on what?"

The *Oh, Christ* impressed the boys and they took her into their secret little society and gave her everything she needed to know. Don't give the price before sizing up the prospect but never do it for less than a dollar. The best customers were old ladies that lived by themselves. Sometimes you could get up to three dollars from them. One good way when they asked how much was to say back how much they thought would be fair and a lot of the time they would get more than they hoped for, because nobody wanted to think they weren't being fair. Stay away from the Boulevard. That might sound like easy money, but they already have somebody lined up, usually whoever cuts their grass in the summer. Plus they're all cheap bastards. That's how they got to be rich in the first place.

Delores listened to the news on the radio every evening and when they predicted the next big storm, left a note for her dad that she was going into town in the morning to shovel snow and she would just go straight to school when she was done. And don't worry, she would eat something before she left. (Which she had no intention of doing—she'd just pack a little extra in her dinner bucket and have that on the way to school.)

At the first house, a middle-aged woman said she was sorry but she had a boy who did her walk and he should be along soon. At the next house, a man scoffed and said she had to be kidding right? Another woman said her husband had just run out to the store and would be back soon and he'd do it. When Delores looked at the snow-covered car in the driveway and then back to the woman with an expression that said Seriously?, the woman blushed and shut the door.

Delores got some variation of snow-shoveling-is-a-boy's-job about ten times before she started her internal give and take.

Maybe you should just go home.

And maybe you should shut your damn mouth.

And that will help how?

It'll give me a chance to think.

Like thinking ever changed anybody's mind.

How about I just shovel one and then knock on the door?

Don't make me laugh.

So whether to spite her internal antagonist or because she actually thought it was a good idea, she picked a house with several walkways, thinking that getting that done right would make the owner see that not only could a girl do the job, but she could do it better. The woman who came to the door said, "What a dear you are. Thank you so much." She started to close the door.

Delores spoke up. "Don't you think it would be fair for you to pay me?"

"I didn't ask you."

[....]

[....]

The woman closed the door and Delores went back to her argument.

See, I told you.

Shut your damn mouth.

Now what?

I'll show you now what.

Delores shoveled all the snow she'd just removed back onto the walks and a little bit extra so that where there had been bare concrete there were now ridges of white. When she was almost finished, the woman opened her door again and shouted out, "What are you doing?"

"Being a dear."

During the summer when she was fourteen, Delores saw all the money high school boys were making filling in summers for drafted young men who, before the war, had worked the local farms. She knew she was up to the job, but also knew she'd be up against the same resistance she'd gotten with everything else she'd tried. So in spite of her determination to make it on her own, she asked her dad if he could help her out, maybe ask one of his friends if he'd take her on. He told her he could do that and next thing you know she's in Rick Carlson's barn and he's telling her to be back at six the next morning and bring a pair of work gloves because hay bales is heavy and baling wire is sharp and you won't be no good to me if you get your hands all cut up.

In the morning, the harassment started before they even got out to the field, covert at first, the boys nudging one another and gesturing with their chins while they waited for Carlson to bring the tractor. A giggle or two and then they were all in the wagon heading out.

The logic of the work was easy enough. Carlson would pull the wagon partway into the field amid the bales. Two workers stayed on the wagon, one on each side. The others carried the bales over and handed them up to be stacked. Logically easy, but physically rough, which got the first verbal harassment started, the boys joking among themselves about how long Delores was going to last and how much you want to bet she don't make it to dinner. Dinner, hell, I say she won't make it to the end of the second row.

When it came Delores's turn in the wagon, one of the boys held a bale up, but not quite enough for her to reach it without stretching. She saw why when she bent down to grab it and the boy leered.

By mid-morning the boys all had their shirts off and of course, one of them had to say, "Hey Delores, ain't you hot with all them clothes on? You'd be a lot more comfortable if you took your shirt off." They all snickered at how clever that was and one of them said he'd give up his thirty cents an hour to see that. Delores fumed.

She hung in there for three more days, through clenched teeth sometimes, but she hung in. And then...

The third day was pretty hard, the boys bolder and bolder, meaner and meaner. That night Delores waited for her dad to get home from work. He asked her why she wasn't in bed and she said she had something she wanted to tell him.

"So tell me."

"I wanted to let you know that I'm pretty sure I'm going to piss some people off tomorrow."

"Since when have you ever asked my okay to do that?"

"One of them is gonna be Rick Carlson."

Her dad looked her straight in the eye and said, "Dee, Carlson's a pretty good friend, but he ain't family. Do what you have to do."

As she took her turn in the wagon toward the end of the next day, one of the boys said, "Hey Delores, I got something heavy right here. You want to see if you can lift it?" And of course, the laughter—and the last straw.

"That depends," Delores said.

"Depends on what?"

"On whether you stopped fucking chickens. I don't want to catch anything."

While the stunned boys were trying to figure out some kind of smart response, Carlson came over and told her to come down off the wagon. He took her aside and told her he didn't want her using that kind of language and she said how come it was all right for the boys to joke about her tits but turn around wasn't fair play. Carlson said because they was just boys being boys but she was supposed to be ladylike.

Delores took off her work gloves and threw them on the ground and said, "Fuck you, Rick! How's that for ladylike?"

So Carlson threw his gloves on the ground too and told her she was fired.

"Good! You can pay me right now!"

So Carlson goes to the tractor in a great huff and pulls down his dinner bucket and takes his money purse out and does the math in his head, but whispering the numbers, "So four days, ten hours a day at twenty cents an hour is two dollars times four is eight plus two-forty for today is nine dollars and forty cents."

"No," Delores said.

"What'd you mean no?"

"You meant to say thirty cents an hour."

They stared at each other.

"You agreed to twenty."

"I agreed to what you said was the going rate. You a liar on top of being a cheat?"

Carlson did that thing people do when they want to insult you by letting you know how much smarter and better they are than you by rolling their heads and holding up a hand and saying, "All right. All right." And they are so dismissive about it that you just want to kick dirt on their shoes but what good would it do?

Carlson counted out Delores's pay and she stomped off the field. All the way home she gave herself a really good talking to.

Well, I guess you showed him!

What's that supposed to mean?

It means was it worth it, cutting off your nose to spite your face?

Shut your damn mouth.

Chapter 7
You Are What You Do

[Wherein we learn about Chuck's and Hank's
jobs and how their approach to their work
predicts their approach to the nineteen
ejaculations problem. Also wherein the
paratactic literary device is adroitly employed in
the service of character development.]

Chuck and Hank both worked at the Bessemer, a manufacturer of enormous diesel engines (up to big-as-a-house enormous) and natural gas pipeline compressors. Chuck ran a turret lathe in the machine shop. Hank was a millwright, one of the three highest labor grades, which meant that he took home top money. The other two high-paying labor grades were electrician and pattern maker. I thought about making Hank a pattern maker because it's such an interesting job, but then I would have to go into this long explanation about how gray iron foundries work and long intricate descriptions about molds and cores and then a philosophical digression about how engineering and craftsmanship complement and collide with each other at the intersection of the pattern shop and how cost analysis enters into quality control and who needs that? But pattern makers and millwrights both tend to be level headed, calm workers, not easily shaken in a crisis, more or less impervious to supervisory intimidation, and all around nice guys, which is what I'm going for here, so millwright works just as well as pattern maker and requires much less explanation.

To make more than a millwright, you'd just about have to work in the office and not just a work-in-the-office-shuffling papers kind of job, but a real high up job where you made actual decisions. Some of the factory bosses made more, some not, on account of bosses weren't in the union and negotiated their own salaries, which all by itself kept most of the men from ever even wanting to be a boss—that, and if you weren't in the union, they could fire you anytime they wanted for any reason whatsoever. The typical worker's response when asked if they'd consider a foreman position was, No way in hell! Also, all your friends would hate you. Those who said they'd maybe think about it should management ever offer such an opportunity would forever be suspect in the eyes of their fellow union comrades, and no one would ever again bend any work rules when they were around, like taking an extra five minutes for a coffee break. Plus they would be shunned hard (shunned just about as hard as an Amish farmer who went and got himself caught diddling the prize heifer).

Unlike Chuck, who stood by his machine for his entire shift and did pretty much the same thing day after day after day, Hank's job took him all over the plant, wherever the engines of fabrication shut down because of old age or misuse or accident, the core and mold ovens and the blast furnaces in the foundry, the delicate, yet powerful machines in the machine shop, and the finishing tools and conveyors on the erection floor. (Really. A third of the factory was called the erection floor, which is a serendipitous semantic accident for me and my story. Erection floor? Who could have made that up?)

Anyway, a millwright has to be skilled at all kinds of trades: metal working, welding, carpentry, hydraulics, fabrication, boiler operation. On any given day, you might be called on to splint a broken part so it could function well enough to get whatever mechanism of which it was a part to the end of the day when the entire monster could be shut down and the problem properly diagnosed and the machine repaired or replaced, or to fabricate a part from raw stock, or blindly spot weld a fissure in a high-pressure hydraulic line from the inside because to do it right would mean shutting the whole mechanism down to disassemble it, which would take an entire crew off-line for a complete shift, or to rig a makeshift lift to get a stranded crane operator down from his disabled crane. The job required an enormous amount of knowledge and skill, but also experience and significant intuition.

Millwrights were recruited from among the most successful apprentices in the Bessemer's apprenticeship program, begun after the war and lasting into the '50s when they finally figured out that putting a man through a six-month apprenticeship only to have him spend the whole rest of his life as a labor grade four laborer, shoveling sand and working a sledge hammer was an injudicious use of company resources.

Apprentices who got offered millwright jobs ran the risk of becoming arrogant assholes. Those who did indeed become anally pompous tended not to last too long in the job. The other millwrights could pretty much tell if a new guy was going to turn into such a disgusting waste of space if from the start he acted like he thought he knew everything. For example, say they'd gotten called down from the millwright shack to look at an electric motor that had stopped running.

By the way: The millwright shack wasn't a shack at all. It could more accurately be called the millwright lounge. It was a surprisingly clean and orderly room up a flight of broad wooden steps between the foundry and the machine shop.

They had their own set of lockers, a brace of showers, and a couple of picnic tables where they hung out playing cards and shooting the shit while waiting for something somewhere in the plant to break down. (Think of the old image of firefighters lazing around at the firehouse waiting for a fire to break out and taking turns cooking firehouse chili.)

While we're here: The process by which millwrights were summoned was to send the least senior worker in the affected department to walk up there and tell them what was wrong, at which point the millwrights would ask all kinds of technical questions about the crippled equipment that the kid couldn't answer (it wasn't until about their fourth trip that the kid realized they weren't even asking real questions, they were making things up, alluding to equipment components and functions that didn't exist and had in fact never existed and never would. Millwrights just really enjoyed messing with innocents). The name "millwright shack" probably did have a plausible etymological origin—I'm guessing that there was at some time in the past an actual shack out in one of the yards where they waited with their tools and acumen. When they removed into more durable and accessible quarters, the name stuck—as names have wont to do.

Anyway, back to the example of the arrogant apprentice and the electric motor: Before the crew even got to the motor, the smartass guy was saying it was the brushes and then as soon as they got to the floor with the problem, he would start stripping off covers and whatever part of the armature he had to remove to get to the brushes and sure enough, they were burnt, and then replace the brushes and put it all back together again, all the time telling ribald stories of how you had to brush them long copper-wound arms just so if you wanted her to purr for you (which actually was a way of trying to fit in with the other millwrights because the telling and retelling of such slightly off-color, mildly clever double entendres was a big part of how they passed their idle hours in the shack), and then stand up and dust off his hands and say, "Hit it," to whoever's machine it was and the damn motor still didn't work.

What made a good millwright was one who didn't guess what was wrong or assume he knew. A good millwright made sure he knew what was wrong before he tried to fix it and never, never assumed that once he'd found a problem that it was the only one. The dirt and grit and temperature extremes of the Bessemer often induced multiple simultaneous problems into its clockworks. More often than not, one problem was merely the symptom of the real, much more serious problem. For example, that malfunction in the motor that seemed to be the brushes could have been because there was a circuit overheating and the brushes' burning out was just the motor trying to draw too much current and the real problem was a fused solenoid (upon which discovering, a good millwright would call in an electrician, something the mediocre millwrights were loath to do, because they saw electricians as inferior craftsman who only knew how to do one thing, and secretly resented that electricians were the same labor grade they were).

Another thing that characterizes a good millwright is how well they can adapt to production pressures. Sometimes you just need to get a piece of equipment to the point where it can get you through to the end of the shift, just splint it rather than repair it. For example, if the conveyer in one of the small-core baking ovens is out of true and it's only an hour or so until the last of the cores would be fully hardened, you can brace the belt's tracks with some angle iron and keep an eye on it. If it needs more bracing, brace it. If not, you get overtime after the cores are baked for replacing whatever parts have ground themselves into old age. Such pragmatic splinting is what management wants you to do.

But say for example that the cupola fans have shut down and when you look, you see that the bearings are shot. Easy job, right? Just grab a bearing puller, back off the set screws, take off the fan, pull the bearing, tap in a new one, tighten everything back up, and voila! Then just restart the heat and watch things in case there is another problem that caused the bearing to go bad until you get to the end of the heat and check everything out in a deliberate manner. That might get you some points with the bosses (restarting a heat was outrageously expensive), but what if there is indeed another problem and that is that the firebrick inside the cupola has burned out and the cupola has burned through a couple of the massive rivets in the barrel (which was what overheated the bearing in the first place) and a half hour after you restart the heat, the whole front side of the cupola blows out, killing two men and shutting down the entire foundry for a month? Against that possibility, you got to be willing to stand up to management, red tag the whole cupola and tell them if they want to finish the heat, they are going to have to start up the spare and yes, you know how much it's going to cost, but you just ain't going to certify that the main cupola is safe. You just ain't.

By the way: The term *heat* refers to the entire process of smelting the amalgam of iron alloy to be poured on a given production day. It is polysemic in its inferences. It can refer to the violent burning mass of scrap iron, steel rails, limestone, and coke that seethes to nearly a white heat in the cupola, as in: "Let's get the heat started." It is also a number that gives the total tonnage of iron to be poured that day. Typical heats ran right around 100 tons, but they could run to as much as 160, a backbreaking, bone-aching work day. As hard as it was to work a big heat, nothing made a foundry worker more anxious than to see the heat sizes go down over a period of days. Once the heat got below 75, it was only a matter of time before they would see four-day work weeks and if it kept up, layoffs.

Anyway: Guys that weren't judicious in temperament and calm under pressure might or might not get a good talking to from the other millwrights. If they did and didn't change their ways (which wasn't necessarily their fault, given that a man's disposition is his disposition, and you might as well fault a tree for not being able to sing and dance) or didn't get that talking to, they would find themselves assigned to some other job, usually labor grade four laborer, which because of their arrogance, they wouldn't be able to stomach. They'd usually try crying to the union, but that rarely worked, because, hey, union guys may be all for sticking together, but they are not going to take a chance on some know-it-all that's going to get them killed. So all in all, the millwrights tended to evolve away from the mean to the bright part of the standard distribution of skill and resourcefulness. Hank was that kind of millwright.

Chuck's job, although requiring a great deal of skill, was altogether different in terms of what made for a good machinist. Instead of creative solutions, he worked in conformity. His job was to put out part after part of identical proportions, with tolerances often down to under a thousandth of an inch. Turret lathe runs these days are computer actuated and an operator pretty much has to be a computer programmer. But in those days, you set up the machine manually, with micrometers and other precision measuring devices. You had to inspect and measure the bits and taps and dies, the buffers and the grinders, and either replace or sharpen any that were out of tolerance. You had to make sure that the reservoirs for oil and water were full and that the injectors and nozzles were free of clogs. Then you set the operation steps, ran a test piece, and measured the test against the specs. If all was good, you let her rip, the machine alchemizing finished parts from block stock and all you had to do was clamp in new stock after every run, an amazing process to see the first time, but actually pretty boring after not too long a while. Depending on the job, you had to check every n^{th} part for tolerances and if it was outside the range, check the last couple of parts to see if they were okay (and trash any that weren't), then find the offending bit and either sharpen or replace it.

Chuck had gone through the same apprenticeship as Hank, but there was no recruiting effort so far as he was concerned. He knew all along that he wanted to be a machinist, because the machine shop was cleaner than the foundry (though with all the whetting oil getting thrown around, you could still leave your shift plenty dirty, but at least you didn't have to breathe in all that foundry dust) and steadier than the erection floor, whose work load depended heavily on sales orders and delivery deadlines and could go from seven-day weeks to laid off pretty much overnight. He straight up asked to be assigned a job in the machine shop. It suited him. He liked not having to think a lot and he liked that once he got to work, he knew exactly what his day was going to be like (maybe not *exactly* but mostly predictable with a little variation here and there to stave off any tedium [and making that day pretty much perfect]).

Given how they spent their workdays and how what they did was driven by their particular psyches, it shouldn't be all that surprising that Hank and Chuck took quite different philosophical paths to get to nineteen. Where Hank was resourceful, Chuck was methodical. Hank approached the nineteen as an interesting problem to be solved—Chuck saw them as specs to be adhered to. Hank was open to novel solutions. Chuck kept it to the known. Hank tended to the fun side of getting to nineteen (knowing there was going to have to be some work and discipline along the way) and Chuck tended to the fastidious (knowing that there isn't any such thing as bad sex so it wasn't going to be all work), thus placing the two friends' obverse plans in a kind of yin-yang symbiotic yet adversarial positioning to each other, once again suggesting that the transcendent does indeed inform the quotidian (or is it the other way round?).

Chapter 8
If You Want Something Done Right

[Wherein Chuck takes matters into his own
hands and also comes to grips with the
messiness of same, literally and figuratively on
both counts. Also it becomes obvious that
Chuck is altogether clueless about his wife's
rich interior life.]

As with most marriages, over time Chuck and Mattie's had its
seasons of frosts and thaws, times when they weren't speaking
at all and times when Mattie could be downright amorous and
fun to be with. And then there were the lukewarm times when
they got along okay and no fights, but she pretty much made
him work for it. They'd been in one of those for a while now
for some reason elusive to Chuck. So maybe she'd be
receptive during the week and maybe she wouldn't and there
was no rhyme or reason why—at least no rhyme or reason
that Chuck could discern.

Because of this capriciousness and its attendant lack of
reliable routine, Chuck, unlike Hank, didn't have a formal plan
yet for getting through his nineteen ejaculations, for getting
from still-have-to-use-a-rubber to *Praise God Almighty, I'm free
at last!* He was too much of a wreck from the very idea of
getting to the magic number.

He was so nervous about even bringing it up with
Mattie (having more sex so they could get the nineteen behind
them and wouldn't that be *wonderful*), what with the way she'd
been going around with that off-putting look that said, "My
mother warned me about you! But would I listen? No, I

wouldn't, which sets me right up there as a legitimate contender for who is the biggest idiot in this house," and no way was he going to get sucked into that trap. Mattie's mother may have said that, but even she knew full well that neither she nor anybody else was going to hold up Chuck and Mattie's nuptials any longer than it took to get the blood tests back, being that they were of the had-to kind. Before he got married, Chuck was as much of a catch as Hank—although not quite resourceful enough to keep a box of Trojans in the glove compartment. They should have been comparing notes all along.

Chuck wasn't entirely sure what Mattie was moody about or even quite what the mood was. It wasn't like she was pissed off at him and expected him to know what about without telling him. He could deal with that. He'd just unwind the tape in his head until it got to the point where it all started and then look around inside his memory of what he was doing right about then to see what it was he did wrong. He wouldn't apologize or anything, but knowing what it was that he did would give him a clue about how long she'd hold on to her resentment and what he could then do to maybe shorten it up a bit. He was thinking that maybe it had something to do with his going off to the hospital without consulting her and leaving her alone with the kids (which he had to admit would have been pretty hard, but so was being on your feet all day beside a turret lathe—and he didn't get himself all hang dog because he had to work [well sometimes he did, but not often—mostly he was accepting of his place in the world which meant having to do a man's work]).

Oh well, Chuck thought. Whatever it was, his best bet was to hold off and not bring it up until Saturday (he and Hank having got their stiches out on Thursday and even though two more days after a week and a half of celibacy shouldn't make a whole lot of difference, it seemed like a pretty long stretch given that it wasn't just the week and a half, but your scrotum being all weird so that it was telling you every single second that it's there. Also, it's not until you can't have something that you get to realizing just how much it means to you and then you don't just *want* it, you start in *needing* it, that the central fact of your life has transposed itself into an overwhelming *obsession*, and you walk around from morning to night (and most of the times in your dreams) like you got one monster hard-on that starts at your ankles and runs all the way up your spine to the back of your head where it's putting an awful lot of pressure on your brain, like the skull is the hard-on's rightful domain and the thinking part of you has got no right whatsoever to that space (even if it was born there and could claim a right of prior habitation).

As difficult as the two more days were going to be, saying the wrong thing right then, on that Thursday, could turn those two days into an entire month of cold, cold nights. That happened about once a year as it was and holy cow was that hard! Just think how much harder it would be now with him having so much horny already built up and a medical need on top of it. So with significant effort he bided his time until Saturday night when they went to bed, which for some inexplicable reason turned into the typical weekday pursue-and-avoid dance he and Mattie had worked out for themselves the last couple of months and not the normal Saturday where they just did it. He'd push a little and she'd run off, like he was the pathetic adolescent lion who never grew to his full size and never did learn how to hunt on account of the other lions didn't want anything to do with him, didn't even want to be seen with a runt like him and knowing that even offering to lend the poor little guy a helping hand with some stalking-in-dry-brush tips or how to work out at the jungle gym so you could really launch yourself when it came time to pounce, would open them up for serious ball busting from their tough-guy-type lion buddies with their greased-down, swept-back manes. So the little lion was on his own.

Chuck would make whatever lame little advance he thought he could get away with, and then Mattie, the delicate-limbed, disingenuous gazelle, would make like she didn't know what was going on and just prance off a little ways and go back to grazing on the sweet savannah grass, which on weekday nights meant fluffing her pillow and rearranging the covers and settling back down like she hadn't one single thing in the whole world to bother her. But this was Saturday. What the hell?

So Mattie went on with this little ritual for a good ten minutes, which by the end of, Chuck was so hard a cat couldn't have scratched it. But she was just screwing with him (but not really of course), because when the ten minutes was up, she halfway turned to him so she could look him in the eye and said, "My period came on this afternoon."

Oh man. The feeling started way down in the pit of his stomach—a combination of ice cold shards of shrapnel and churning dirty gravel, that feeling you get when you just got caught doing something you are going to be in big trouble for or the sure-thing bet you made on the Steelers just went south and the bookie has got some pretty big guys working for him who don't have a total respect for the law and where are you going to get the money to pay up? Or just got kicked in the balls.

There's a lot of ways Chuck could have gone with this, his first impulse being to go, "Oh, Christ! You couldn't have told me before? Like maybe at supper when I was trying to be all nice and everything (and a lot of good *that* did me), instead of asking when I was gonna get around to cleaning the gutters.

Damn, Mattie!" Or he could have started in sulking (like that ever got him anywhere—except what it *was* good for was getting to a place where he wasn't talking to her and her not talking back, and sometimes he kept on pretending he was sulking when he really was over whatever it was that he'd been sulking about, on account of it was a way to extend the sweet, sweet silence of the absence of her voice).

You may think that the fact that Chuck was so desperate to have sex with somebody he could barely stand to be around right at that particular moment obviously shows what a shit he really was, regardless of how he may think of himself (as a solid family man, a good provider, etc.), but there might be another way of looking at said fact within the current state of Chuck and Mattie's marriage: That they are hopelessly enmeshed in a feedback loop of projection and counter-projection that can only be broken by an epiphanic moment of self-awareness on the part of one or the other of them. (Whoever wants to be first to do that, please raise your hand.)

There were lots of other let's-try-to-get-even tactics like that that he could have gone with (and *had* used to various effect over the years [none of them actually being on the plus side of effective]). What did *not* occur to Chuck was to say, "That's all right, sweetie, we got the whole rest of our lives," give her a peck on the cheek, and then nestle down in his pillow with his face toward her, smiling like she was just the most precious thing in the whole wide beautiful world. For him, this was not even in the realm of the possible, in a way similar to how it would be unimaginable for a color-blind man to tell his date that he couldn't believe how exactly the color of her eyes matched the sky on a crystal clear, perfectly still summer morning.

With considerable effort (manifest as a whole set of autonomic responses such as curling his lips in against his teeth, tightening the cords in his neck so much that they looked like they might rip themselves right out from the bounds of his throat and flail around like the tentacles of some diabolic slimy space alien, and clenching his butt cheeks together so hard his perineum actually went into an intensely painful spasm for a couple of seconds), Chuck managed to act just a little bit petulant instead of righteously pissed off as he rolled over and faced away from her, but being sure to tighten the covers across his shoulders just enough so it would be sure to annoy her, though not enough so she would say anything because it wasn't clear that he did it on purpose. As pissed off as it might make her, she wasn't going to say one single word because it would take her all the way down to his level where he was being just such a child over what was a natural part of life and if he couldn't handle her having her period, then that was his problem, and she wasn't going to dignify his being such a shit by saying anything. In a way Chuck kind of liked it this way, because he could get her all agitated inside without having to listen to her go on and on about it, and all it took was just this little bit of tension on the covers.

But as gratifying as that might be, it still didn't help with his immediate problem, which was his own agitation way down there, where little old Mr. Johnson was acting very much the child himself in the way he was demanding attention and about to throw a tantrum if he didn't get it. So Chuck eased up on the covers and real quiet slipped his hand down to his crotch to see how bad it was, which was a mistake, on account of old Mr. Johnson took that ever so light touch as a promising sign (like a puppy that's just been given a little chuck under the chin, and up he jumps all excited and happy because he's about to get a *biscuit*). But Chuck was just as much the excited little puppy as old Mr. Johnson was and stuck his finger inside his pajama bottoms and found that spot right there (the one the army nurse back at the hospital was so good at finding) and performed a one-finger massage on himself, real, real, quiet and not moving anything except that one finger, not his arm for sure, but not even his wrist, because maybe Mattie was asleep and maybe she wasn't. What's a guy to do, right?

So things were going pretty good and he was to that place where a cat couldn't scratch it and almost to the point of no return, when he realized: Oh shit!, where am I gonna put the mess? He thought if maybe he massaged from the outside of his pajamas, the fabric would sop it all up and it would all be okay (which he knew better than to believe [because way back in his adolescent past it never had]), but then he remembered the smell it was going to make, that distinctive metallic smell that Mattie would for sure know what it was and that wasn't something a patch of thin fabric was going to absorb. So he stopped altogether.

Talk about suffering—it's a sure thing that even the Buddha hadn't taken *that* into consideration when he invented the Noble Truths and the elimination of desire, given that when he was still back in the palace, he'd not had any trouble whatsoever getting any and once he started on his spiritual journey to tame himself, didn't think about jacking off because never having had to do it, he never did and probably didn't even know how. (Jesus doesn't mention it either, the New Testament poignantly silent on the issue. Such silence [along with his little solo sojourns out in the desert] maybe suggests Jesus had his own embarrassing secrets?)

Angry but aroused, Chuck knew he had to get up and find someplace else to finish the job, because lying there trying to ignore the poor guy wasn't going to work, but if he did get up, there would be that jousting lance sticking out and if Mattie was awake, there was a decent enough chance that she'd see it and he didn't want to risk that. Of course, it wasn't as if Mattie had never seen old Mr. Johnson at attention, but there is a time and a place for everything and Chuck knew that if she did see it, given the complexities of the moment, she was sure to come out with something like, "Oh my God," which sounds not all that bad until you figure in all the unspoken, but implied words her intonation would suggest, like *disgusting* and *pathetic* and *sickening*, and she could turn *his* little natural biological response into one of those months of endless drought. So Chuck concentrated on trying to get the damn thing to go down, and of course, the harder he tried, the harder it got (as if there is a stage beyond a-cat-couldn't-scratch-it [up until then Chuck wouldn't have thought there was, but this ball-ectomy thing had emancipated the most private parts of him {not all of them physical} in ways that he would never have imagined possible]).

It was like being back in algebra class and getting called to the board to solve a pair of simultaneous equations just after Becky Mason decided to re-cross her legs (and she knew damn well what she was doing—you'd never convince Chuck otherwise) and you had to go up to the board with one hand kind of casually in front of you with your thumb hooked in your belt like you were just being cool and the other one in your pocket to maybe, if you were lucky, explain the lump in your pants. Then you have the time it takes to solve the problem to talk the guy down, but the problem is too damn easy, with one of the equations having just a $+y$ and the other one a $-y$, which should take about thirty seconds to solve, but you keep making like all of mathematics is an enigmatic cosmic mystery as you try to stretch it out to five minutes or so, writing on the board and then erasing what you did and then you do that over and over until the teacher finally gets exasperated and tells you to sit down and says, "How about you try, Becky?" and there the little scamp goes, just swishing those hips of hers back and forth and gives you a sly little wink as the two of you pass in the aisle.

Since thinking about shrinking the little monster wasn't working, Chuck figured he should think about something else about as far away from the spontaneity of tumescence as he could get and after a while he landed on work. He thought himself onto the hard rubber mat in front of his turret lathe and went through an entire job: Check the machine, make sure the switches and the safety button were working, oil the parts, hand spin the chuck, make sure the midnight-shift man had got all the slivers out of the block, that the drills and cutters didn't have any nicks in them, and all the other things you did without thinking about them but still had to be real careful about just in case. Then get the job from the boss and the blank stock and sign the work order and make sure the scrap box was empty (you don't want to have to account for the last numbskull's screw-ups), set the machining order, and then finally get to work, which consisted of four things, load the stock, push the on button, watch that nothing went wrong, and when the part was cut, drilled, polished, and whatever, take it out. Repeat, repeat, repeat.

Chuck ran through so many iterations in his head that his brain was actually starting to numb up as if he was really at work and he began thinking about what he was going to do when he got home, which included fantasizing about getting it on with Mattie even though it was a workday and not Saturday, which made him remember why he had gone off on this riff in the first place and son-of-a-bitch, if when he checked himself, wasn't old Mr. Johnson, if not flaccid, pretty well drooped over? Damn, thought Chuck, I got to remember that—which really shouldn't have been such a revelation, since Chuck (as do more men than want to admit), extended himself during the actual, real event by imagining his setting a strikeout record while pitching a no hitter against the Yankees. The players in the lineups have changed over the years, but the fantasy endures because it works. Watching himself at work was really just a variation on what he'd been doing for years to slow himself down.

Chuck got up out of bed while it was still safe and headed for the bathroom. No need for stealth in the going, after all it was perfectly common for a person to have to get up and go. But once in, he had to be careful. Now the job was not to hold things back, but to get it over with as quick as possible, since too long in there could by itself raise Mattie's suspicions. But he didn't need to worry. He straddled the bowl and by the time he'd retrieved the guy through the fly in his pajamas, he was just about ready to go and all it took was a couple of feathery, light brushes of his fingers along the full length, from scrotum to glans, to get him to full attention and then it wasn't but about two minutes before blessed relief was on its inevitable way. The hard part then was to not make any noise, no grunts, no deep-throated groans, no atavistic vocalizations of any kind. But boy was that hard. Oh, and to get himself situated over the bowl, so as not to make a mess on the floor. As it was, he was so physically frenetic, what with his hand moving almost in a blur and even thrusting his hips like he was actually doing it (which is kind of the idea for most masturbatory simulations) that he got some on of the lip of the bowl and there was even some dripping down the side. Holy shit!, he thought, didn't think I was backed up *that* much. But boy oh boy, did I ever need that. And yes, it did hurt some. But that's just the price of doing business. So far as the pain of the first few ejaculations is concerned, a vasectomy has nothing on a TURP (Trans-Urethral Resection of the Prostate [don't get one unless it is *absolutely necessary*—trust me]), and nowhere is it recorded that any man so administered to avoided sex simply because the moment of supreme ecstasy would be accompanied by a moment of equally exquisite pain like unto being stabbed through the urethra with a red hot awl. If anything, it may, in fact, enhance the experience. (And men think women don't make sense.)

Which got him to that kind of embarrassing place where the have-to-do-it is over and you're in that kind of why-was-that-even-necessary moment (similar to when the real act has been completed and all you want to do is roll over and sleep and she wants to cuddle), and there are several things that need to be done and in a certain order: Check your hands and clean up as necessary (washing in the sink), clean the old boy off with some toilet paper (which means washing your hands again) and then wiping down the commode with more toilet paper (which includes stooping down to make sure there aren't any creamy, little puddles on the linoleum) and that means more toilet paper and one more hand washing, and finally, flush all the evidence down the commode (which means you have to wash your hands again in case Mattie hears you and being in the bathroom that long had to mean you were doing number two and God forbid you don't wash your hands afterwards). Then a final check of Mr. Johnson and your pajamas and you're good to go.

Chuck got through all that ritual and was back in bed in no time. He slipped under the covers, being sure to leave plenty of slack for Mattie, and when he settled down, he made sure to face her way, where she was facing away from him, so he could see the soft cascade of her hair and the gentle feminine curve of her hip in the glow from the night light and he wasn't mad at her anymore.

Pretty soon, sweetie, he thought. Pretty soon.

He closed his eyes, and as he drifted off into the bliss of dreamless sleep, said to himself, "Eighteen to go.

Chapter 9
Hank and Delores Arrange a Date

[Wherein Hank and Delores work out a way to
get this whole thing about the ejaculations
moving and try to make it really romantic
instead of smutty. Also, some utterly
compelling commentary on the art of
narrative.]

Delores started getting nervous when she was about halfway to Hank's house. Wow, the things that you get yourself into when you're just trying to be funny. It's one thing to have an argument with yourself about whether screwing for money makes you a whore or not, but actually being on your way to said screwing is something altogether different.

It wasn't just that it was the difference between sex-for-money in the abstract and the transactional moments of the concrete act. And it wasn't like it was anything new (after all, her and Hank had gone at it lots of times, well maybe not a lot but enough), except it was something new, something very different about this. She rolled down her windows to let the cool night air sift the smell of fresh cut grass into the car and make it easier to think.

So what's the difference between what her and Hank had before and what it was going to be like now?, Delores wondered. The money, sure, but she already worked that out. She thought some more and decided it was that she was going to be staying in the same house every night and probably all day on weekends other than when she (they?) went grocery shopping or one of them had to work on Saturday or she went to get her hair done or maybe spend some of that three hundred dollars on a new pair of work shoes. Yeah, that was going to make a *big* difference (that being-there-all-the-time thing—not the buying-work-shoes thing).

When you go out on a date, even when you know where you are going to end up (most of the time in the back seat of his car), there is always that thing where he has got to work for it. He's going to be nice (even if that didn't take a lot of work on Hank's part, him being pretty nice by nature, but still). Then he has to take you someplace where lots of people go that shows he's not ashamed to be seen with you, maybe even take a walk down Broad Street holding your hand if it's a Friday night. Plus both of you pay some attention to how you look and smell. And when he shows up, you be just a little bit late even if you've been ready for over an hour.

But when you are in the same house when you wake up and still there when you go to bed, and you all know why, what chance is there for any kind of romance at all? Romance? Hah! Don't make me laugh! Tell me there is one single woman on this whole planet who thinks she looks good first thing in the morning. And there's number two and it's not like number two in the outhouse, it's right there *inside* where you can't blame the smell on the hole in the ground. And what about Kotex? Jeez, she thought, there's a whole lot more to this than I would've ever thought.

What Delores was going through was a lot like what a virgin bride went through way back then, what with there not being any such thing as sex education in school (even the thought of talking about sex in a classroom would likely have got a teacher fired and probably the principal and district superintendent and maybe half the school board) and most parents didn't even acknowledge to their kids there was such a thing. And the poor girl, from about a month before the wedding right up to the "I do's" having all those thoughts of, Is it going to hurt? and What's he going to expect from me? and Will I do it right? and Will we still love each other afterwards? going through their minds all at the same time. If a girl had a smart mother, she'd tell the girl a little bit about it, with advice ranging from "Just keep looking up at the ceiling, it'll be over quick" to "You might have to 'guide him in' and when he gets going real good, move your butt around and make some moaning sounds like a kitten getting petted and when it's over, tell him you never would have imagined how wonderful that was going to be but not to be too enthusiastic because you don't want him to think maybe you are a slut and not a virgin after all and you still are a virgin, aren't you?"

By the time she got to Hank's (where tree frogs chirped in the woods behind his house and the stars were just all over the place like diamonds and diamonds going on forever and the moon hanging way up high so bright it was almost like it was daytime and there were crickets and fireflies and it was just the most beautiful place in the world), she had come to the same accommodation as most of those virgin brides: Well, I got in this boat of my own free will and the boat has left the dock and isn't going back to port anytime soon and that's all there is to it and whatever's going to happen is going to happen, so let's get started.

She half expected Hank to be sitting at the kitchen table with a real expecting look on his face and maybe a little bit of a dirty look too instead of being in bed like he said. But he wasn't. She slipped off her shoes and tiptoed upstairs real quiet and looked in the rooms and could see well enough by the moonlight to find the one where Hank was sleeping. (Yes, I know. People who lived in the country didn't draw their blinds at night. Heck, most of them didn't have blinds at all, just curtains that didn't even close.)

Hank was lying there like a little boy dreaming of long summer afternoons and fishing holes. Of course we all have a pretty good idea what Hank was really dreaming about and how it might lead to his working up one of those nineteen ejaculations in his sleep, but hey, this is Delores's scene.

She didn't have the heart to wake him up. She thought for a second about her obligation but then thought that one more day wasn't going to make hardly any difference at all. She went back downstairs and got her bag and went into the bathroom and peed.

FYI: A lot of country houses back then had the bathroom on the first floor. This was because when originally built, the houses only had outdoor privies. When electric came and therefore the potential for electric pumps to draw water, people put their bathrooms on the first floor right next to the kitchen because you for sure wanted water there and why run two sets of lines if you can run just one and thereby save having to rip out more walls than was absolutely necessary to get the job done.

Anyway: After Delores finished peeing, she was careful to wait for the commode to fill back up before she opened the door so the sound wouldn't awaken Hank, and took a good look at herself and then went upstairs, found an extra room with a bed in it, put on her nightgown, turned out the light, and got under the covers. She was asleep in about a second and slept straight through to morning (well four hours, being that as a millwright, Hank had to be at work at 6:00 am [the same time as the molders in the foundry], which meant getting up at 5:00 to make coffee and all). It was when she woke up to the sounds Hank was making down in the kitchen, that Delores realized this was for-absolutely-freaking real.

By the way: That last paragraph was a little tricky. Having Delores go to bed instead of waking Hank up is obviously an important moment, but it introduces some logistic complexity to the following morning's narrative. Like if Delores had to get up to go to work too because of the breakfast crowd, then she would need an alarm clock since she couldn't be sure if Hank used one, and why would there be an alarm clock in a spare bedroom? Depending on Hank to wake her up would have said something (I don't know what) about Hank and then that would have to be made consistent with other of his actions maybe scores of pages from here and who needs that? I could have had her bring a clock from the trailer, but then I'd have had to say something about that, which would have disrupted the rhythm of her getting out of there and you can't just say she packed an alarm clock without saying what else she packed and one thing I really hate is when a story gets bogged down in all kinds of things the reader really couldn't care less about. Maybe she had a travel alarm clock and kept it in her car just in case? Come on, gimme a break! So maybe she just always naturally woke up without a clock? For crying out loud, she's twenty-four years old and sleeps like a baby because she *is* a baby! So here's the way it is: Delores's boss always scheduled her to work dinner and supper on Fridays (and this is a Friday remember) because there will be a lot of people down street in the evening and a big supper crowd and Delores was the best waitress he had and the only one who could handle a half-dozen tables on her own. So she didn't have to be to work until 11:00 am, plenty of time for her to wake up without an alarm. So it all works and not too much fuss.

Anyway: As soon as Delores woke up and realized Hank was already in the kitchen, her first thought was, How should I handle this? Just stroll down the stairs in her nightgown, looking all sexy (except she wasn't—remember that thing about women not liking the way they look in the morning) or get all the way dressed, in which case she would have to take it all off again if Hank decided he wanted a quickie on the kitchen table (which she sure hoped he didn't on account of that would *really* feel like she was a you-know-what) or about a dozen other ways to go. What she finally ended up with was giving her hair a quick brush and dabbing on a little powder and lipstick and going down in her robe.

Hank was at the counter with his back to her when she walked into the kitchen. She made a little noise so as not to startle him and when he turned around and looked at her, they both went through this long, awkward moment of not knowing what to say and everything just hanging in the air and both of them wondering if it was the polite thing to say something first or wait for the other one and if maybe they should give each other a quick, married-folks kiss. Delores broke the silence. "Hey there, big guy, do you know if the bus for Pittsburgh stops here?"

Hank snorted so hard snot came out his nose, which was even more embarrassing than the financial transaction just hanging there in the air of the kitchen, and he turned around real fast and grabbed a dish towel to wipe it off his lip. "Whoa there," he said. "You always know the exact right thing to say, don't you?"

"I do my best."

Hank asked her how come she didn't wake him up last night and she said because she really wasn't quite sure if it would be all right, what with it being the first night and maybe he wouldn't want her coming on too strong and besides, he looked so peaceful laying there in his bed, that she just didn't have it in her. Hank told her that made sense and did she want some coffee and some breakfast. (You, Hank, and I all know that what Delores said does *not* make sense, because what man cares about being awakened regardless of the hour for *that*, but his saying it does illustrate how nice a guy he is down deep.)

She told him about her shift not starting until eleven and if it was all right with him, she was going to go back to bed and sleep a little bit longer. He told her that was fine and there was a half a pot of coffee left and she could just heat it up and there was all kinds of things she could have for breakfast, just poke around. She turned to go, and Hank asked her to wait up a minute.

"I was thinking that this being our first night, maybe we could go out to Rudy's for spaghetti and then go to the late show at the Guthrie."

About a million things went through Delores's head right then. Like it sure didn't seem like he was in any kind of a big hurry to get on with the nineteen ejaculations, and was he being nice just because this really wasn't all that nice when you thought about it and he was doing his best to at least try and drag it on to the road to nice, or was he trying to make her feel comfortable, or maybe even it was a joke? And a lot more than that, but just those couple gives you an idea. Put yourself in Delores's shoes for a minute: What would you think?

What she came out with (quick enough that Hank wouldn't know she'd been considering alternatives) was: "If I didn't know better, I'd think you was trying to get in my pants," and if you think Hank was nonplussed about the bus to Pittsburgh remark, he came close to crapping himself over this one.

Now it was Hank's turn to go through over a million things in his head that he could say, and him being experienced enough with women to know that every single one of them would be the exact worst thing he could let come out of his mouth, he kept them all to himself. And then he thought of a couple dozen gestures that he could make like shrugging his shoulders and holding his hands open at the same time and all of those gestures would be the exact worst thing to do too.

What he did was go over to her and take her face in his hands real gentle and look her right in the eyes and say, "Well, maybe I am, but ain't nothing wrong with a little romance first now, is there? Besides, if we go out, I won't have to cook." Now it was her turn to laugh. He gave her a quick little kiss and said he had to get going and he'd see her back here when she got off work.

Hank pretended to head for the door and Delores went back upstairs. When he heard the door to her room close, he went out on the porch and got the flower arrangement he'd bought at Kocher's, a bubble of red carnations and daisies, which to an outsider might have looked a little on the gauche side, but it's the thought that counts. It had taken him a considerable amount of time to choose the right thank you card, given the delicacy of the situation, and had finally settled on the simplest one in the pack, just a white card with "Thank You" in a formal-looking script on the outside and nothing on the inside, where he wrote, "Your the best!" He wasn't sure if he should sign it "Love, Hank" or just "Hank," given that she might get scared off if he said "love," but would it be worse if he didn't? For a while he thought he might sign it "Your partner in crime!" But that could lead to all kinds of unintended consequences beyond his ability to imagine (but it sure would be hilarious if it made Delores mad, because the girl sure could do mad when she got herself worked up to it).

Finally he took the card and threw it in the garbage ("garbage" not "trash." Which incongruously aligns this rural region with urban New York and makes no sense whatsoever. But "garbage" is what we said). Hank took out another card just like the one he discarded and on the inside drew nineteen hearts. He didn't write any words, just drew the hearts. Didn't even sign his name (like who else would it be from?). He got four hundred-dollar bills out of his wallet and laid them neatly in the card, put the card in its envelop, wrote "For you" on the outside, and wedged the card among the flower stems where Delores would see it first thing when she got up again.

Driving to work, Hank went over in his head what he'd done (the kiss and the note and the extra hundred dollars [yes, he did withdraw five hundred dollars from the bank, not four—the extra hundred was for the flowers and date money and odds and ends that he was smart enough to know he wouldn't be able to think of ahead of time]) and wondered if that had been the right way to handle it and if Delores would understand about the nineteen hearts or just think he drew a bunch of hearts and if she would take the extra hundred as saying how much he appreciated her or maybe she would think he had thought he was feeling guilty because he had been too cheap and that maybe she should have held out for more from the very beginning.

But then he decided that he was being ridiculous. Delores was as smart as they come and they had never once been the least bit mean to each other, never argued over anything, which maybe wasn't that big of a deal on account of they never really were boyfriend and girlfriend, more like they was just buddies, so maybe it didn't count, but that didn't make it any less true that they got along so well. Hank decided that what he did was at least as good as anything else he might have done or said and smiled to himself. All the rest of the way into work, he marveled at how lucky he was.

When Delores came down and saw the flowers on the table, the first thing she thought was that Hank was trying to make the place look nice for her, which he didn't really have to do, given that she lived in a house trailer and next to that, Hank's place was a mansion even if it could use a doily here and there. But then she saw the card and thought, Well ain't you the romantic little devil! When she opened it and saw the four bills, any doubt that she had had about all this just disappeared. She should have been ashamed of herself, having any doubts at all in the first place. Had Hank ever been anything except a gentleman with her? And why would she think it would be different now?

She turned the burner on under the coffee pot and got some milk out of the refrigerator and stuck a couple pieces of bread in the toaster and opened almost all of the cupboard doors looking for a coffee cup. And then she got a funny little quizzical look on her face and went back to the table and picked up the card and counted the hearts. She thought, That may not be romantic, Hank Walker, but I got to admit it's pretty clever. This was all going to work out.

The next thing you know Hank and Delores are home from work and getting themselves ready for their date, and each of them go the extra mile to look nice for the other and Delores is in the tub getting a little bit turned on imagining Hank out there imagining her naked in all that warm sudsy water.

When about 7:30 or so that evening they left for Rudy's, Hank was real smooth about holding the car door for Delores both when she was getting in at his house and out at Rudy's, not like he was trying hard or anything—he just did it real natural, a little like the way when he was at the shop and confronted with a breakdown. There was a certain way you went about it just because you want to make sure you got it right and after a while, it just comes natural.

By the way, about Rudy's: Rudy's is a restaurant and bar that sits across the Pine Township line. Pine Township and the Borough of Grove City may as well be the same place. Not only does Pine Township completely surround Grove City, but pockets of Pine Township are themselves islets of sovereignty within Grove City, so that both municipalities bind and are bounded by the other (a clever grad student could turn that into a decent enough dissertation provided they used smart-sounding phrases like *interdependent loci* and *emergent assimilation*). Pine Township is more rural and Grove City richer, but the important thing about them in regards to Rudy's is that both of them are dry, except for the Moose and the VFW of course, which as private clubs could do what they wanted. Anyone could join the Moose, and the VFW had an open-guest policy, which simply meant that if you had the price of a beer in your wallet, you could get in even if you'd never served your country, no questions asked. But the Moose and the VFW were pretty dilapidated, especially inside, and if you wanted someplace a little nicer, you could just go over the township line to Rudy's. The Rusty Bolt was across the township line too, but nobody in their right mind would take a girl to the Rusty Bolt (even if it was cheaper because it was in London, which was a "suburb" of Number 5, and looked the part), and Rudy's had way better food, especially the spaghetti and meatballs.

Anyway: Hank and Delores ordered their dinners, just spaghetti and salad, everything the same except Hank had French dressing and Delores thousand islands. Hank had a Rolling Rock and Delores a Coke. They took their time. They told each other about their day, Delores telling how she "accidently" spilled a glass of orange juice on some old coot she never saw before when he tried to pinch her butt. Hank said she should've gone in the kitchen and got a whole pitcher and poured it on his head and did she want him to track the dumb geezer down and beat the snot out of him. She said maybe hold off on that for when she got somebody she couldn't handle on her own but she had it covered for now. Hank told Delores how it had been a pretty slow day up until dinner time when a young kid on the erection floor mixed up the gas and air on a torch and burnt off the release valve and came about that close to blowing himself up. You should've seen him, what with his eyebrows singed half off and everybody ragging on him so hard he was blushing and then they *really* started on him. She asked him was it hard to fix and he said it was real easy, just throw the old valve away and twist on a new one. If it took twenty minutes it was an exaggeration.

And they went on like that for more than an hour, talking and taking turns keeping the booth juke box fed with nickels, Delores favoring Patsy Cline and Hank picking just about any rock and roll song. The way the songs came out was sometimes a little abrupt at the changes, "Crazy" followed by "Oh Boy," which you would think would be a little harsh of a transition to make, but on that night seemed somehow to be just right.

After they ate, Hank waved for the waitress and asked for the bill. She said it was seven dollars and forty-seven cents. Hank took a ten from his wallet and handed it to her and said just keep it and was Delores ready to go. In the car she asked him if he always tipped like that and he said he pretty much did. Delores said it was no wonder the waitress took such good care of them. Most of the tightwads around here didn't even tip the usual ten percent, them thinking that they didn't have to tip on account of the waitress was already getting paid. It was lucky for her that Mike (who owned the diner) paid them enough to make up for it. He just upped the price of everything on the menu ten percent. He said as long as it all came out the same, what did he care if customers thought they was being slick not tipping and that he was thinking about raising the whole menu another ten percent just to screw with them.

It was a little after 9:00 when they got down street, so there were lots of parking spots on the south end of Broad Street right near the Guthrie and you didn't have to worry about putting anything in the meter because you only had to pay for parking up until 9:00. A ton of people were pouring out of the theater because the first show was a Lewis and Martin and a lot of people had brought their kids, so Hank bought their tickets and they both of them had a cigarette while they waited for everybody to leave, even though back then you could actually smoke in the theater.

By the way: There were two movie theaters in Grove City, the Guthrie at the south end of Broad and the Lee at the north end. Both had two bills a week, Monday-Wednesday and Thursday-Saturday (closed Sundays). Both had double features with cartoons and sometimes a newsreel. First show was at 7:00 and second around 9:15 or so, depending on the length of the first feature. Both charged 50¢ (10¢ for kids twelve and under) and a nickel for a red and white box of popcorn. Most people thought the Guthrie was the classier of the two and it was true that it had better cast plaster ceilings, but there really wasn't all that much difference between the showings because they were both competing for the same audience. Sometimes a movie one of them showed one week, the other would show the next. The shows tended to westerns and comedies with a monster movie here and there. A few years after our story, when the Guthrie played *Splendor in the Grass*, holy cow! Was that ever a dustup!

Anyway: After Hank gave their tickets to the usher and went in, Delores asked him if he remembered when they were in high school and used to make out in the balcony and Hank said did he ever! She said how about they see if there are any seats up there, and what's Hank going to do, say no to that? So up they went. There was one couple already there, right down front by the railing that I don't care who you are, if you walked in the space between the first row of seats and that railing, you are going to think about falling down into the main seating, making it a mystery as to why anybody would sit there unless every other seat in the theater was filled, but there they were. Maybe they had some kind of bizarre fear-of-flying sexual fetish?

Delores gave Hank a little nudge and canted her head up to the corner a little ways off from the projection window, which was where they used to sit, and Hank led her up there where they got started on their popcorn and watched the commercials for the concession stand and the previews of coming attractions and then pretty soon a Popeye cartoon where Bluto was holding Olive Oil captive on a desert island and Popeye's boat sank and he had to swim halfway across the ocean to save her. It was actually pretty funny and lightened up any awkwardness that may have been left, although there really wasn't much of that left at all, this having turned into the phatic familiarity of a date. The show was a drama with Gregory Peck and Audrey Hepburn, which had an okay story that both Hank and Delores could get into, but the couple down by the railing not so much, and they left not quite halfway through, which left Hank and Delores all alone in the balcony.

Delores looked around to be sure there wasn't anybody else up there and sort of stretched her neck to see if there was somebody down on the lower level who could see them and she couldn't even see the front seats from where they sat. She did one last check to see if the projectionist had a view, which he couldn't possibly. Secure in knowing that the coast was clear, she pushed herself tight against Hank and laid her hand on the inside of his thigh and sort of worked it back and forth real easy, not dirty or anything, just smooth and delicate like she was petting a cute little puppy. Taking Hank's popcorn and putting it in his other hand, she moved her hand all the way up to the front of his jeans and started working on his zipper, which given how straight up he was sitting gave her some trouble and he had to slide down a little so she could get at it and even then he had to get it started for her, but let her do the most of the work because it seemed like that was what she wanted and who was he to contradict?

Then she had to work her way through his undershorts, which was a bit tricky because of him wearing briefs but he squirmed a little and that helped and out came the master, which she brushed ever so lightly for a while and then stroked with a little more pressure and then a little bit more and what with all that had been going through Hank's mind the last few days and it being a little bit dangerous and that can be pretty exciting all by itself, he came in less than five minutes, at which point Delores stopped stroking and just held him there gently in a way that was actually pretty romantic and nuzzled his neck and murmured in his ear, "That's one. What say we get ourselves home and make it two?"

Delores's suggestion raises an interesting question. Why wasn't there something in that sentence or the one before or an extra one that would come after that says something about the mess they had to clean up? Remember Chuck's masturbation scene where he had to clean around the toilet and even the floor and double check that there wasn't any embarrassing evidence he might have missed? Well there would for sure be some of that embarrassing evidence up in that balcony and don't forget they were going to walk out where there would be that usher still checking tickets and stubs and then they'd walk to the car and if there was a dark spot on Hank's jeans, that could get some funny looks all by itself.

But that's the way it is in most book and movie sex scenes, like a couple comes back from a bar where they just met and can't even wait to get in the door of her apartment before they are tearing off each other's clothes and they do it against the kitchen counter or wherever and there are these barbarous orgasms where he's going all Cro-Magnon and she's just screaming in ecstasy and they fall into each other altogether exhausted and no gestures or mention of cleanup?

Even Salter, in *A Sport and a Pastime*, gives the issue the briefest of mentions. Without a hint of embarrassment, he has Phillip and Anne-Marie dive into encounter after encounter across the spectra of emotion and method. Vaginal, oral, anal—from tender to atavistic. And afterward the couple just lie there exhausted and maybe talking about how great it was, but can you imagine the mess they would have made? In the two or three spots where he mentions the seminal discharge at all, Salter gives such messes the stingiest of nods, a bit of an ooze here, a dabbing finger there, those nods more analogous to a single tear on a virginal cheek than the lapful of vomit that would be closer to the truth. Even the master just goes with the Venn diagram where the circles are primordial sex and romance and the intersection the best parts of each and who cares about the parts that aren't so best?

One counter-example that I can think of is Joyce's having Molly Bloom tell in that last section of *Ulysses* how she "pulled off" her young military man into her handkerchief and then slept with the handkerchief under her pillow for a while because the perfume in that part of Spain was awful. But that's an outlier (the exception that proves the rule?).

Of course, there is that one other broader example where semen is not just acknowledged but esteemed, the porn industry with its money shots, which actually belie intimacy, what with the way the man has to masturbate at the end to generate the visual and how can anybody even stand to look at that (other than to conduct research for an extraordinary little novel and that is just the price you have to pay for being an artist).

Chapter 10
Getting to Nineteen from Here

[Wherein we learn of the different ways Hank, Chuck, and Delores think about the goal of nineteen ejaculations and thereby illustrate some of the processes men and women use to arrive at the same destination by very different conceptual routes. (Mattie is mentioned here, but in passing. Her particular thoughts and machinations regarding the count are postponed to future chapters.)]

Hank, Chuck, Delores, and Mattie each had a different calculus through which they adduced the curve that began at point Here and arrived at Nineteen. But what they had in common was the attempt to estimate how long in calendar time those nineteen discrete moments were going to take (a kind of quantum-to-analog calculation, though that in itself is an inexact analogy because calendars show time in distinct days]). There was one interesting commonality that broke along gender lines: Hank and Chuck both counted down (without having collaborated on which way to go), as in nineteen-to-go, eighteen-to-go, seventeen-to-go, and all the way down to zero-to-go while Delores and Mattie counted up (also without having collaborated), as in that's-one, that's-two, that's-three, and so on. I'm pretty sure that says something about gender roles or identity or conditioning, but for the life of me, I can't hypothesize just what that might be. You'd probably get more clarity about that if you asked a woman.

By the way: I did take my own advice and asked my wife how she would, if given such a situation, keep track.

She said, "How would I know?"

"Know what?" I pressed.

"Whether he was taking care of himself."

!?!?!?!?! Please know that her remark did *not* inspire other passages following from here in this chapter. I asked her during a rewrite, when I realized that if I myself did not ask a woman as I'd suggested, I might get criticized as being either a hypocrite or a sophist. And God knows, nobody wants *that* (but even that assumption is patently suspect to anyone who's ever been to AWP [the nobody wanting to be a hypocrite or sophist assumption]). And though her remark may, to you, seem brilliant (which she truly is), there is the possibility that it was also her disingenuous way of hinting that she harbors suspicions about *me* when I retire to my private place (suspicions altogether unwarranted I assure you).

Anyway: In regards to our characters' various mathematics, Hank's math was the simplest, not even approaching the complexity of basic algebra—he was more at the first-grade-arithmetic level—just erase his nineteen mental tally marks as quick as he could without having to service himself even once. Not that he was above that (as we've already noted—living alone as he did, that was a given), but it seemed somehow un-medical, since the whole idea of the vasectomy in the first place was to get to where he could have sex anytime he wanted without the disruption (and attendant personal responsibility of using a rubber—he couldn't forget that [and wouldn't, him being the real decent guy that he was and also not one bit interested in being married—which was where not using a rubber could land you]). So what was the point of all that discomfort and trouble if all you were going to do was jack off nineteen times (twenty if you included the baseline sample, but that didn't really count because that was doctor's orders). So far as his time estimate was concerned and the fact that Delores had agreed to his proposal to let him every day, that meant nineteen action days pretty close together. But after that first date at the movies and what happened when they got home (Wow!), it was going to be quicker than that. The *most* it was going to take was nineteen days plus however many days was in her period, which would add up to twenty-six days or so, and as it turned out, he didn't even have to factor in her period, given that Delores was working up her own solution, which we will get to pretty soon.

By the way: What this illustrates about Hank (and everybody else) was that they were trying to solve an optimization problem, in his case a discrete optimization problem, but that doesn't really matter. What matters is that there are all kinds of ways to get to a number, but which one is the best? And that can be different for different people depending on what they are trying to achieve, like conserve the most resources or realize the most revenue. Really smart people with lots and lots of advanced degrees have spent their entire careers attacking optimization and are thrilled if they discover (or intuit, deduce, maybe even accidently come across) a way to tweak just one term in an extremely complex equation designed to address optimization in some ungodly esoteric field of endeavor that nobody living in the real world would ever care about even a little bit—and thereby increase the value of the various solutions by even just no more than the shadow price (which is just asking what happens if you relax all of the constraints by 1, and by the way, that little bit of gain opens up all kinds of opportunity for philosophical inquiry because if you can relax a constraint by 1, then it isn't, as a point of fact, a constraint). If they are successful in making that tiny mathematical leap, then they will be ridiculously famous within an infinitesimally small audience of colleagues, who will be furiously jealous, which was probably the goal all along. That and getting a paper published in just the right journal to grab them a prestigious named chair in some math or business or engineering department at a top-tier research university and who can put a price on that? Hank and the others were wrestling with the messiness of the real world, with all of its myriad variables and they are all the time changing and if you can think of half of them, then you are a genius. For them and the rest of us, that "If I do this, then…" but "If I don't to this, then…" and "What if it doesn't matter and how will I know?" can get you pretty close to batshit nuts.

Anyway: Chuck's math was the most complicated, given that his path to nineteen *did* include self-pleasuring (though the sneaking around and the anxiety inherent in finding someplace reasonably likely to be private in a house with three other people always took away a considerable measure of the pleasuring part). Inherent to his particular private complexity was that he had to maintain two counts. First off there was the actual number of solo and conjugal ejaculations combined, which was the number that would get him to the goal of no swimmers and he could go to the doctor's and get checked to be sure (which he was absolutely not looking forward to, what with that witch of a nurse and the general embarrassment of the whole thing because *that* is supposed to be totally private). And then there was the number of conjugalities by itself, which also had to add up to nineteen, because if it didn't and Mattie was keeping track (which he was pretty sure she was), how would he tell her it was okay to not use a rubber anymore? So he would have to keep on going past the real nineteen to get to the ostensible nineteen so far as maintaining his counts was concerned.

At first he thought that keeping track of the "real" sex ejaculations would be the hard part because of how long it would take, but then he came up with what was actually a pretty elegant solution (because of its simplicity)—just adjust the number of condoms in the sock drawer to nineteen. If he remembered right, there were eighteen, a dozen in the unopened box and six in the one they'd been using. (He always made sure to have an extra box on hand because that is one thing you absolutely never want to run out of. He faithfully replenished the supply as soon as he and Mattie finished a box, and he always did a quick count with his fingers of how many were left in the open box every time he grabbed one.) It turned out there were seventeen instead of eighteen, which didn't seem right on account of Chuck was such a nut about routine and would have sworn he'd counted eighteen the last time. But on further reflection he decided it would be easy to make a mistake in the heat of the moment and with the room being dark except for the night light and the only really important number was one (which meant time to buy a new box). The difference between seventeen and eighteen wasn't worth worrying about. He'd just say it was right, whether it was or not.

The next day he stopped off at the drugstore on his way home from work and bought two more and put them with the seventeen. So that half of his formula was all set. Also, he made sure to tell Mattie that he'd bought those extra two so that there were exactly nineteen rubbers in the drawer and he would be absolutely fastidious about using them and would go to the doctor when they were all used up just to be on the safe side and if there were any swimmers left, he'd buy more. (This also relieved the pressure Chuck felt at knowing that Mattie was going to be keeping her own count.) When Chuck did tell Mattie about his plan for keeping track of his ejaculations, a shadow went across her face, not too dark or deep a shadow, but enough that he noticed it. At first he thought it might be because she was thinking how disgusting it was that he could talk about such a private subject so casually, but she right away smiled the shadow away and told him it was a good idea and he didn't think any more about it.

The other half of Chuck's calculation was all about how he could keep track of the number of solos, which of course was complicated by his fundamental paranoia that Mattie might barge in on him when he was doing it (when he envisioned that, what he always saw was him at the moment his climax hadn't actually started but being beyond the point of no return and even if he stopped stroking that very second, the semen would just start appearing in gushing spasms right there in the open, and that would increase the embarrassment by an order of magnitude at least [which he actually knew what that was, Grove City High School always having been real strong in the math part of the curriculum]) or that she would guess what he was doing from some telltale signal he was sending that he had no idea he was sending (like a poker tell). For example, if every time he made a move on her when they went to bed and she wasn't in the mood, he got up for ten minutes or so and came back all relaxed, she might put two and two together.

He thought about maybe some nights when it got to bedtime, he would tell her he wasn't sleepy yet and he was going to watch part of the movie and go up in a little bit, and then wait to give her enough time to get in bed herself and then slip down into the basement. But there were two problems with that. First was the basement, which was just plain base, which to Chuck meant it was all musty smelling and not at all conducive to any kind of fantasizing (a necessity if he was to get off in any kind of reasonable length of time, except at first when it had been awhile and he could come in about a minute no matter where he was), and he'd have to make sure to take a rag or something because you couldn't just wipe it up off that dirty cement floor with some toilet paper and then there would be the sneaking around with the rag and what if he was coming up from the basement with that scummy thing just when Mattie had come down to the kitchen to get a glass of milk because she couldn't sleep? (In case you think I'm being absurd here: Ever notice how truck stops always have lots and lots of packages of tube socks right near the checkout?)

The other problem with telling her he would be up in a bit was that for Chuck, hope sprang eternal. What if it was a night when she would be okay with it? He wouldn't want to pass that up. He had no choice but to be resourceful (as strange as that felt) and find novel places and times. Like 1:00 in the morning in the toolshed and behind the hedge along the back fence and once under the car when he was supposedly changing the oil. But it was hit and miss.

All of this made any kind of prediction as to the total time to get to either of the nineteens almost impossible. He could pretty much count on one act of coitus a week. If he was especially lucky, maybe two or three. So say he would shoot for three ejaculations a week, with anywhere from one to all three being solo. Except figuring out how to get there was always going to be tricky, so for the sake of the count, say two and a half per week. Then there was Mattie's period, which maybe he could get off three on his own that week, but you have to consider what if her period straddles a weekend? What would that mean? He couldn't really abstract out what that would mean—he'd just have to deal with it as it came up.

So say all in all it came to two and a half per week over time. That would mean 7.6 weeks. Holy Christ! Almost two months to get to the combined nineteen! Now say there was on average five "real" sessions a month to get to the nineteen rubbers (being conservative and not counting on a week with three, that would mean two most weeks and an occasional week with only one and the period week which was zero). Four whole, very long months!

Eventually Chuck accepted all this, being as it was what it was and what could he do about it anyway? All that was left was keeping track of the solos, which even this he was paranoid about, nervous that Mattie would come across whatever it was he was using to keep track (like a piece of paper in the bills drawer with pencil tally marks on it) and want to know what it was for and he'd maybe get all flustered (or worse yet pissed off, because sometimes a person will just lash out with the truth if they are cornered when the best thing you could do is to keep your mouth shut and just about every man who has ever been married knows this and every single one of them every once in a while will make the mistake of *not* keeping their mouth shut and just blurt it out [except the I'm-better-than-you-are saints, which we know are just putting on a show to make all the rest of us look bad]). Oh man, would that ever be a mistake!

What he came up with was actually pretty clever. Whenever he'd jack off, he would go out in the garage (not right after, but like the next morning or whatever, close enough in time so he wouldn't forget or get two mixed up and wonder if it was really two or maybe just one) where he had shelves with tin cans of odds and ends of screws and bolts and such and take one of the quarter-inch bolts and twist a nut onto the end and start a new can with just those in it (he always kept the nuts and bolts separate so there wasn't going to be any way to make a mistake and confuse the bolts with already screwed-on nuts from before this whole thing started). Mattie would never in a million years figure out what he was doing because first off, she didn't even care what the difference between a nut and a bolt was—she just called them both screws. And second, she saw the garage as Chuck's turf and didn't care one iota how he arranged stuff out there. In the end his formula was fairly simple too: $e = r - b$, where e is how many ejaculations to go, calculated from r which equals the number of rubbers left in the drawer and b which equals the number of bolts with nuts screwed on (the irony of the term altogether lost on Chuck—also on Mattie, come to think of it).

By the way: To any close readers who may have stumbled upon this little book: the above passage and its referencing of bolts is *not* a unifying device glancing back to my introduction of Chuck and Hank in Chapter 1.

Delores's mathematics was somewhat more mercenary than either Hank's or Chuck's because there was money involved. And when there's money involved, well…. Starting with the $400.00 (which was real nice of Hank to throw in the extra hundred), there were two ways she could look at things. One was how much she was getting per ejaculation, which was straightforward and couldn't change no matter what: $400.00 divided by 19 equals $21.05 per. The other way was to think in terms of how much on average she could make a day. For example on that first day (if you didn't count the night before when she got to Hank's late and didn't wake him up as a day), she got $42.10. $21.05 for the thing in the Guthrie's balcony and $21.05 for doing it back at Hank's (which was pretty amazing and reminded her of why she didn't mind at all doing it with Hank and made her think [for just a second] that maybe it wasn't right to take his money, him making her feel so good and all). Less easily calculated were the intangibles, like the indoor plumbing and how she didn't have to buy groceries for herself and having somebody besides her dad to talk to in the evenings, because as close as she was to her dad, there's some things you need somebody your own age to talk to about. And then there was the going out, like supper that first night at Rudy's, which was real nice, and life isn't just about going to work and paying your bills and keeping house. (All of her qualitative considerations technically makes Delores's optimization problem a continuous multimodal optimization problem, not discrete, but the point of what we're getting to is the same: Life is freaking complicated!)

Getting to how long it was going to take: If she went with once a day and added in her period (which for her was usually just five days, but was due in a week and she was nothing if not regular, you could set your watch), then she was looking at twenty-four days, twenty-three after the first day. She thought for a minute that it would have been good luck if she'd only finished her period right before Hank made his proposition. Then it would have just been a straight nineteen days, eighteen after the first night. But she felt bad right away because that could make somebody think she was just using Hank and she pushed that thought right out of her head because it was Hank who had asked her for a favor in the first place. The vacuum created when she pushed out that first thought made room for a new idea to replace it: That Hank's whole reason for whatever that operation was called was to get himself to where he didn't need to use a rubber anymore and so he could go out with a girl and if she liked him, not have to worry about getting her pregnant. Which surprised her when she had *that* thought, because she had a little twinge of jealousy when she did, even if she did know good and well that who Hank went out with wasn't any of her business, just like it wasn't his who she went out with.

She had another thought too, this one just the least little bit salacious: That it had been so long since she'd had sex without a rubber that she couldn't quite remember how much better it was, only that it was. And maybe after the nineteen, her and Hank could have a couple more, just to remember for sure what it was like. So after all this, Delores decided that it would be best for everybody concerned to go with the per-day calculation (and get creative if that's what it took to cut the number of days down as far as she could). She would be doing Hank a *big* favor, getting him to where he wanted to be that much quicker and doing herself a big favor too by getting out of her indenture as soon as possible. Plus thinking about doing it without a rubber was getting her pretty turned on and making her wanting more and more to get there faster. So she went up in her head and did a few visualizations and thought to herself, I bet I can get there in under two weeks, maybe even just a week and a half.

Which leaves us just Mattie, whose calculation was the most complicated of all, and it was complicated because Mattie herself was complicated. Real, real complicated.

Chapter 11
A Scar Is Forever

[Wherein we learn about Mattie's bittersweet inner life. Also the writing is really, really clever.]

All four of our main characters had been in high school at the same time, Chuck and Hank in the same class, Mattie and Delores a year behind. The school hovered right over Main Street a block down from the diner, its dark-maroon brick façade as imposing and morose as an English teacher. In the not-so-complicated adolescent social strata of the day, Hank dated Delores because he was a halfback and she a cheerleader. Chuck went out with Mattie (from time to time at first and then "steady") because he was a lineman and she a majorette.

This is how that worked: Cheerleaders perched, cute and perky, at the very top of the social order, usually girls from better-off, well-to-do families, only occasionally from the working class (Delores). They had names like Becky and Melissa, and they embodied status. They didn't always date football players—sometimes they dated basketball players or wrestlers. Rarely did they date track and field boys (unless they were also basketball or football players—track was where young men's dreams of romance went to die).

Majorettes, on the other hand, were technically part of the band, which back then was a really nerdy bunch of social outcasts (the word *nerd* just then coming into the American vernacular but hadn't made it to Grove City, a place whose thoughts on child rearing leaned more toward Mother Goose than Dr. Seuss). So to compensate, majorettes tended to date rougher kinds of guys like linemen or one of the jaunty hotrod boys.

By the way: The term *hotrod boys* may suggest mechanical ability rife with both sophistication and aesthetic flair. But not generally true. "Hotrods" in that place and time were usually just old cars brightly painted and maybe with flames on the fenders rendered with house paint or racing numbers on the doors and if the boy was lucky enough to have weekend and summer work, whitewall tires and a glasspack muffler, chopping and fabricating not in the boys' wheelhouses. Eventually these boys would in places (usually in the East) become known as greasers but in the vernacular of Western PA would become known as hoods (as the notions of juvenile delinquency took hold as a war cry for the nascent politics of right-wing evangelical Christianity, which actually had an altruistically motivated genesis regardless of how it ended up). Hoods would in time adopt the name as a mark of distinction and pride, with all the clichés of cigarettes rolled up in tee-shirt sleeves and slicked-back DA hairstyles, which all by itself has got to be one of the dumbest style fads in the history of this country. Who says, "I think I'll make my hair look like a Duck's Ass today"? Seriously?

Anyway: In contradiction to the band gestalt, majorettes were as a group pretty much believed to be sluts (saying he was dating a majorette gave a hood instant gravitas, because, hey, she had to be putting out for him, right?). They had names like Louise and Charlotte.

Cheerleaders had an aura (mystique?) of the innocent, even with their shorter skirts, shapelier legs, and bouncing hair. Majorettes had to wear those band helmets with the white plume up the back, so they tended to shorter hair and what with the helmet and short hair and epaulet-crested jacket (like Robert Preston in *The Music Man*, all chest bands and braided cords), they looked anything but frilly. In fact, they were quite military in appearance. Also they tended toward thicker legs and waists than cheerleaders but not so stocky that they would turn a guy off. (The sad fact of the day was that no chubby girl would ever make it on to either squad, regardless of how well she could cheer and kick or step and twirl.) So cheerleaders had a different kind of reputation, as in maybe you could get them to put out if you got them to fall in love with you and made them believe you were in love with them, but it had to be for real and it had to be the first (really momentous) step on the pathway to marriage.

In the real world, things are not so clear cut. Delores put out for Hank after about two months, and even in high school, the both of them didn't see it as anything all that meaningful. Mostly they did it because it was fun. And nobody ever knew what they were up to, because Delores, being a *cheerleader* for crying out loud, wasn't about to tell anyone. And Hank (bless his heart) was a perfect gentleman, even though he wore his hair a little swept back (but not all the way DA) and smoked Lucky Strikes. Also, he knew which gas stations had condom machines in the men's room.

A cynical reader might read into this that Hank was just being self-serving, thinking that if he kept their couplings a secret, he could keep them going, but the fact of the matter was that with those bad-boy looks of his, that wasn't going to be a problem. He did get jealous from time to time when Delores went out with someone else because he couldn't help but think that if she did it with him, she must be doing it with them. But if he'd taken the time to think about it, he would have recognized that most of those *thems* were the kind of male youth who wouldn't have been able to keep their doing it with a cheerleader a secret and if she was putting out for them, there wasn't anybody anywhere around who wasn't going to know about it.

Mattie, in a (maybe) conscious contravention to the majorette persona, kept her legs tighter together than a nun's. Even after the homecoming dance, where Chuck asked her that night to go steady and she started wearing his class ring (he'd picked the one with the white gold band and the onyx stone with a diagonal white stripe of mother-of-pearl embedded across the stone and a silver pine tree glued on, one of the few times in his life Chuck ever bucked any tide [getting the vasectomy obviously one other time], which was pretty cool and the other majorettes all wished their boyfriends had picked something like that instead of the toned-down frat-ring styles that were more popular), she wouldn't even let him put his hand under her sweater. They made out of course. Who didn't? But no touching either up top or down below.

By the way: You will think I am making this up, but I swear on my mother's grave that I am not. The local lover's lane wasn't a back dirt road way out in the country as you might naturally think, but a street in town now known as Greenwood Drive that winds down Wolf Creek right by the police station. Local parlance had it tagged as "Cow Belly Bend." Kids actually went there to park. Who calls their trysting place Cow Belly Bend? Also, how could we possibly have called it that when we were young and now believe that academic elites have their heads up their ass and calling it Cow Belly Bend would just give them one more reason to look down their noses at us (which would be a real trick, what with their having their heads up their ass and all)?

Anyway, back to Mattie and Chuck: Gradually and with great patience, Chuck got Mattie to allow him to brush his hand over her sweater, but held the line at underneath, all the way through that school year and through the summer after

Chuck graduated and started his apprenticeship at the Bessemer—which abstinence Mattie considered a point of personal pride and gave Chuck a real good excuse to masturbate when he got home, sometimes not even waiting to get home but stopping alongside the road on his way (which should have given him some ideas about how to handle his nineteen ejaculations [but when I became a man I put away childish things]).

Though Chuck had not done it with a real girl, he was not inexperienced. There were a select few men who secretly took their sons to a brothel in Mercer, often on their sixteenth birthdays. The Dog House (yet another perplexing entry in the Western PA lexicon of idioms, as everywhere else in the USA calls such places cathouses) sat way back a dirt lane, backed up against a creek with woods all around. The fathers would take their sons in, tell the girls to show them what to do, and afterward tell the boy to not go getting any girls pregnant. Chuck's father was one such man (and whether one thinks these men enlightened or twisted, when Chuck came out, he knew what went where, what a rubber was, and how to use it [if only he'd been religiously diligent in practicing what he'd learned]). After graduating from high school, Chuck would go up there on his own every now and again on account of he really did want to stay true to Mattie, but hey.

Mattie was more complicated than being a majorette that didn't put out. She was smart and liked school and didn't really care all that much about that thing where smart girls didn't get the best guys. She studied hard, and though not quite salutatorian material, was on track to graduating about sixth in her class.

By the way: Back then and in that place salutatorian didn't mean second best, it meant best *girl*, which is righteously screwed up because it could happen that the top graduate was a girl, but she still didn't get to make the speech—that was for the first boy. At least that's one area where we've made a little progress.

Anyway: Mattie had it in her mind that she was going to go to college and maybe be a nurse or a teacher. She was leaning toward teacher and either English or history because of all the stories, but nursing was tempting because it paid better even if you didn't get summers off. She was going to figure all that out during her senior year. Which turned out to be seriously abbreviated.

Mattie and Chuck continued going steady, although they didn't call it that once Chuck graduated on account of he was a grownup then. Gradually, bit by bit over that first summer, Chuck got himself closer to the inner Mattie. Under the sweater. Under the bra. Bra off. Kissing her breasts. But still nothing down below.

When football season started, he made a point of going to the games in spite of the hassle (Friday nights of course—there was so much traffic surrounding the high school on Friday nights during football season [because of so many people going to the game and adding to the traffic for the A&P] that when the games ended they had cops on every corner for about five blocks all around to direct traffic and untangle the snarls). By then Mattie was one of the top majorettes. All of the girls carried batons, but all except three only carried them in the crooks of their arms and used them like scepters during the dance routines, tracing circles in the air with one end of the baton while holding on to the other. Sometimes they handed their batons off to one another, the three ranks of girls handing off in opposite directions with the last girl on the receiving end tossing hers up in the air in the direction of the girl on the other end, who maybe would catch it but mostly not. The top three baton handlers got to be twirlers and they would have their own little halftime routine in front of the home-side stands while the band was marching out shapes and getting out of step on the field. Mattie was not only one of the three—she was so good that she twirled with a fire baton.

After the first couple of games, middle-aged men sitting in the first row would motion for her to bring the baton over so they could light a cigarette off it. Mattie obliged, thinking it kind of cute. What she didn't see was that they had her set up so she would have to bend over and they'd work themselves a little sideways so their friends could see her butt and even though she wore the gold panties that went with the uniform, it was a pretty cute butt and as far as those perverts were concerned, was as good as naked. Mattie didn't realize what was going on, but her mother did, and she had a good talking to with Mattie about how she shouldn't do it and Mattie said she had no idea and it did make her a little mad but it made her a little prideful as well. After that she stayed away from the stands and put everything she had into her routines, throwing the baton higher and higher so that everybody was just amazed at how good she was.

Important note: Chuck went to every game, even the away games, where the visiting team's band got only a short stint on the field at halftime, and Mattie would really go all out twirling fire because she had that much less time to make an impression.

Mattie had to ride on the band bus for the trip to the away games, but how she got home was her business. Lots of band parents who went to the away games had their kids ride home with them because it was faster and they didn't have to wait around at the school for the bus to arrive. So of course, Mattie rode home with Chuck, and they would stop and park somewhere along the way home and make out, Chuck trying to push things just a little bit further each time.

At the Oil City game that year, Mattie misjudged one of her throws and caught the baton by its end instead of the middle and burnt her hand badly enough that she jumped back and jerked her hand up to her face and gave out a short little scream. Old Chuck never even thought twice. He just reacted, hauling himself down out of the stands and sprinting right out on the field and taking her arm and looking at the burn and telling her he was going to take her to first aid, which was just an ambulance sitting outside the far end zone in case a player had to be taken to the hospital.

Well—after she had her hand tended to, she wanted to go back and sit with the other majorettes so nobody would think she was wimping out and Chuck said he'd rather he just take her home but she insisted and he gave in but told her he was going to keep an eye on her. He pointed to where he was sitting and said if she started feeling faint or anything, just give him the signal and he'd be right there, no matter how little a thing she thought it might be. The real reason Mattie wanted to go back and be with the other majorettes was so she could hear them go on and on about how romantic that had been, Chuck not caring one little bit what anybody thought about him running out on the field like that or even if there were any rules against it, and it proved that he must really, really love her.

On the way home, Chuck found a logging road going up into the woods and pulled in and they started in making out, but this time he went real slow. After kissing her a couple of times he asked her how her hand was and she said it didn't hurt hardly at all and he took it up in his own hand and softly kissed the oversized Band-Aid that the doctor had wrapped around the base of her hand and then he kissed her palm and on to her wrist and all the way up the inside of her arm and then on her neck about an inch at a time, which got Mattie breathing real hard and tingling down around her vulva and even inside.

By the way: A citation is required here to acknowledge my wife's contribution to the predicating research this scene needed (her being a woman and all) and for putting up with another one of my inane questions, like "Rosetta, when you are horny, where do you feel it and what does it feel like?" Also note that sometimes while assisting me with this project, she was successful in hiding from me the fact that she was rolling her eyes, but not always. Through this process we have concluded that silly as it may sound, couples really don't know much about what the other feels, and that the world would be a lot better off if they delved into silly a whole lot more than they do. (Also asking your wife this kind of intimate question about her wants and needs helps her think maybe you weren't such a bad choice after all.)

Please know that I didn't just turn to my wife while writing this book merely to score points with her, but because I really do see her as an expert on topics erotic and sensual. She is Sicilian and not second or third generation either, but the real deal, "off the boat and through Ellis Island" Sicilian. There is a lot I could tell you about that, but this should be enough: You may think you have had stellar sex at one point or another in your life, but unless you've had makeup sex with a Sicilian after a big, big argument (and nobody can argue like a Sicilian [especially when they start swearing in a language you don't know a single word of but understand completely what they are saying]), you haven't.

Rosetta didn't always cooperate. Sometimes she wouldn't say anything in response to one of my questions. She just canted that stunningly lovely Sicilian face of hers haloed in jet black, naturally curly hair laced with the slightest hints of silver threads, arched one eyebrow, which I am sure now is where Sicilians get their reputation for the evil eye, and just stared at me—the exact same look I got when I told her I was considering buying another motorcycle to replace the last one (which I'd crashed in Tennessee, an accident that required multiple surgeries and nearly a year of recovery time before I could walk without a limp).

Anyway: The next thing you know, Chuck's got his hand inside her panties and his jeans are open and she's got hold of his penis (and it's probably a good thing it was too dark for her to see it, because holding it was enough of a shock, it being stiffer than an oak branch) and after not a real long time, they both climaxed, Mattie having two simultaneous thoughts: One, that she never would have imagined how wonderful this was with another person. And two, holy cow! There was a lot of whatever that was that was so warm all over her hand!

Mattie wanted to go on kissing and so did Chuck because that was the moment he really did fall in love with her and wanted her to know it and wanted her to also know how much he really wanted *her*. They stayed there for maybe an hour, winding down until they were just sitting there with Chuck's arm around Mattie and her head nestled into the soft spot under his shoulder, almost asleep. When they finally drove home, Chuck opened the door for her (and not just because she'd given him the handjob—he always did—but this time with deliberate gallantry which was a little bit exaggerated, but not much) and walked her to her door and gave her a lingering kiss, a long thank-you-for-being-you kind of a kiss. The next week they went all the way and kept it up week after week, usually using a rubber, but clearly not often enough, because by January, Mattie had missed her period and they had to get married.

What happened next is a sin. Education was a top priority back then and there, and the schools were tough. Grove City had a rule that if you missed twenty days of school, for whatever reason (sick, farm work, death in the family, it didn't matter) you got Fs in all your classes and would have to repeat the whole year. The penalty for getting married was a twenty-day suspension, which simply meant that if you got knocked up, don't bother coming back.

Nobody who left school that way ever went back to finish. So that was the end of Mattie's dream of a college education and being a teacher or a nurse, the dream replaced with a bittersweet longing that never went completely away, bitter because of the future she had lost and sweet because she lost it for love.

So what does all this have to do with counting up to nineteen? Where Delores, Hank, and Chuck all were motivated to get to nineteen (or zero) as fast as possible, Mattie eventually found herself in a place where she had to plot how to intervene in the count in ways that might look to an outsider erratic and absent purpose but were actually terms in an exquisitely elegant equation that modelled in the abstract how important it was to her that somebody want her. Beneath her skin, she was still a dreamer, the dream a faint trace of what she had been instead of what she had become, just like the scar at the base of her thumb—the indelible souvenir of the night she knew for sure that Chuck loved her and the constant reminder that knowing somebody wanted you was worth as much hurt as you were able to stand and maybe even a whole lot more than that.

Chapter 12
A Long, Slow Weekend

[Wherein Delores and Hank begin to discover
that there is more to their transaction than sex
and we see the incipient sprouts of something
tender that were probably there all along but
they were too blind to see, sprouts working
themselves up through the slimy soil of those
nineteen ejaculations.]

The morning after Hank and Delores's dinner-and-a-movie date, she had the breakfast shift at the diner, so she was the one who got up extra early, the diner opening at 6:00 for breakfast and her having to be there at least fifteen minutes before. Hank had fallen asleep pretty quick after his second ejaculation of the night, but he absolutely was not quick actually getting to that second one—he'd been real slow and gentle and kissed her like she was just the most precious thing he'd ever seen (which she had to admit was probably true) and when he fell asleep, they were both of them naked and he had his arm wrapped around her so her face was on his chest and it was nice.

Once Hank was in a deep sleep, she'd slipped out from under his arm and around to his side of the bed (pretending like she didn't see the shriveled rubber oozing semen in the ash tray) and got his alarm clock and took it into the next room and set the alarm for 5:00 and left it on the dresser in there because she was pretty sure she'd hear it but maybe Hank wouldn't and he could sleep in. Before she slipped back under the covers in Hank's bed she reached for her nightgown, but thought about what if he woke up in the middle of the night and they could do it a third time (which would have been a record for her [except she wondered if the handjob in the balcony would count for one of the three—if it didn't, it wouldn't be a record, just tied for it]). So she just left the nightgown on the floor and got in bed and was asleep herself in about two and a half seconds.

Hank did sleep in until a little after 9:00, which was pretty late for him, but last night had been one heck of a night and he'd been about as relaxed afterwards as he could ever remember being. Down in the kitchen he found a note on the table that said Delores was going to go out to check on her dad after work and see if she needed to run to the store for him. She'd be back right around supper time. The card he'd filled out with the nineteen hearts on it lay right next to the note. He laughed out loud when he saw that two of the hearts had arrows drawn through them. That girl!

Hank took his time over coffee and watched a couple of Saturday morning cowboy shows and then went out and tinkered in the barn and had some leftovers for dinner and took a nap and went out and cut the grass with his new power mower, finishing up about 3:30 in the afternoon. After taking a bath and putting on clean jeans and a good shirt, he went out on the porch and sat in one of the rockers to wait for Delores. She drove up just before 5:00. Halfway up the porch steps, she said, "Hey there, big boy, what're you waiting on?" As soon as she said it, she wished she hadn't because he maybe would have thought she was making fun of him on account of the nineteen ejaculations and that was the last thing she wanted to happen. But he just shot back, "They said there was a bus to Pittsburgh comes by here, but I been waiting all day and there ain't been a bus heading anywhere, let alone Pittsburgh." And she knew everything was all right.

Sitting down in the other rocker, she asked did he cut the grass and he told her he did. Laying her hand on the arm of his chair and just so very lightly brushing her fingers along his, she said the yard looked real nice and how much she liked the smell of cut grass and that she wished her and her dad had a big yard. He told her if she wanted a yard, it would happen someday. He asked her how her dad was and she told him he was about as mean as he ever was, which was somewhere between mean as piss and mean as a rattlesnake and even so, she had to admit the old guy was cute in his own way. They went on like that for a while and then Hank asked her if she wanted to go out again tonight and she told him that she would surely love to, but she was really tired from getting up so early and being on her feet eight hours and running errands for her dad and would it be all right if they just opened up a couple cans of something and watched television. Hank told her that sounded a little bit better than perfect and did she want chili or Dinty Moore. She said did he have any Spam— she could go for some Spam and eggs. "Coming right up," he said.

While Hank was getting their supper ready, Delores gave herself a quick wash in the bathroom, put a little makeup on, and then went upstairs and got into her nightgown (a creamy white, shiny, and clingy little bit of a thing) and robe (pink and a touch see-through, so it set the nightgown off just so and reached to just beneath the knee because the girl knew how good her calves looked). When Hank saw her, he almost dropped the spatula, which gave her a little bit of a twinge herself.

They ate, not saying much, just more of what they'd been talking about on the porch. When they finished, Delores started clearing the table and Hank told her to just go in the living room. He'd put the dishes in the sink to soak and they'd worry about them in the morning.

They sat close together on the couch and watched a couple of shows until it got dark, Hank thinking about getting to sixteen-to-go and feeling himself stiffen up some because of it. Just a little bit after it got all the way dark, with the only light in the room coming from the television, he felt Delores's hand slip off her lap and brush his leg. He turned to look at her and was just about to say, "Ain't you in a big hurry," when he saw she was knocked-out, dead-tired asleep. As delicate as was humanly possible, he reached his arm around her and held her by the shoulder and watched another show, Delores sleeping right through the whole thing, even when the commercials got a little on the loud side.

Now what should he do? If he woke her up, it would look like it was for just one thing and her being so tired, he just couldn't get himself to want it that way, her spreading her legs just to get it over with. Last night had been too nice to just start humping away at her. Finally, he kind of slid away from her in a way so gentle it was nearly motherly, letting her slide with him, so that when he was to a point where he could stand up, he held the back of her head like she was a week-old baby and lowered her down on the couch.

He went upstairs and got a blanket and a pillow and came back and eased the pillow under her head and covered her up. In spite of Delores's being out cold and unlikely to wake up to any noise softer than a gunshot, he turned the television down real slow until you couldn't hear it at all before turning it all the way off, even dilatory doing that and covering the knob up with both hands to mute the click.

In the morning Delores awoke to the soft scruff of the front door closing and Hank's boot soles going out across the gray-painted porch boards and a minute later his car starting and the tires crunching on the gravel driveway. Rising on her elbow and looking around, sleepily bewildered, she remembered. She thought, How sweet. She lay back and stretched and rolled her head and saw the sun on the damp grass and the prismatic light it raised.

Lighting a cigarette, she got up and went out on the porch herself, into the birds' choir and the morning's yellow glow and wondered would she ever live in such a place and how come nobody ever trapped Hank and then thought about that and realized she already knew why. No way. Marrying was not for Hank and not her either, for sure. She'd seen too many romances smolder out on account of marriage (like the way Mattie's seemed to be going) and what if you want to run around a little bit? Then you are royally screwed (which she realized was a pretty funny way to think about it).

Flicking the last of her cigarette out onto the grass, she turned to the porch and turned back again and looked at the wisp of blue smoke out of place there and stepped down to the lawn and bent and picked it up. A car went by, a man in a suit driving and a woman in a high-necked dress and white hat beside him, the woman eyeing Delores in her nightgown and robe with a puritan's glare. Screw you, Delores thought and then laughed. Not likely. She imagined the man and woman in bed, the man clumsily inept and his wife with her fists clenched and teeth gritted down tight and her legs in a vee stiff as boards. She shook her head hard to bounce that image from her thoughts. Some people!

Back inside, she thought a minute about getting dressed because maybe Hank would want to go someplace but then thought, Hell it's Sunday morning—just laze around time.

Besides she needed some coffee and figured Hank already made it, but he hadn't. Bless his heart, he didn't even want to make that little bit of noise. And besides that, she looked pretty good in her nightgown and robe, even if she said so herself, and why not give old Hank a treat on a Sunday morning?

She emptied out yesterday's grounds and started the coffee going and moved on to the dishes in the sink, the egg leavings on the plates soft from sitting in water all night, and the skillets easy to scrape clean on account of how Hank always kept them seasoned just right. After rinsing away the dirty water, she ran clean and squirted dish soap in and washed everything and put the skillet on the stove and set the burner to low so the pan would dry but not get too hot to handle. She rooted around for bacon drippings and found the can in the refrigerator, which was itself yet another wonder, because most people kept their grease in a coffee can under the kitchen sink so it would stay soft and just start over with a new can went it went rancid. (One thing there was never a shortage of was bacon grease. Another was heart attacks.) Lifting the dry pan from the stove, she scooped a little of the grease up with her fingers and wiped it around the pan and set it back on the burner for a couple minutes to season—which, unbeknownst to her, was almost exactly the way Hank did it.

The next thing you know Delores hears Hank's car again and his boots on the porch and in he comes. It turns out he went out to get a *Post-Gazette*, a loaf of bread, and a pint bottle of cream. He set everything on the table and Delores came around and kissed him lightly on the cheek and asked him how come he didn't wake her up last night (which really meant, How come you decided not to screw me last night? And they both knew it, but weren't about to say it because it would make this whole thing sound dirty and in that moment at least, it didn't feel all that dirty—it felt nice).

For the same reason she didn't wake him up on Thursday, he told her. She just looked so peaceful that he didn't have the heart and she told him he really was a softy, wasn't he, and he said not to spread that around too much, he had a reputation to keep up, didn't she know.

"Your reputation's safe with me. What's the cream for?"

"You'll see."

Hank disappeared down the cellar steps and came back up with a quart jar of canned peaches and a jar of homemade apple butter.

"No way, Hank, don't tell me you know how to can too!"

Hank made that little tissing sound that men make, not really a tsk-tsk, but a kind of dismissing sound that always has a wiggle of the head and squinting of the eyes to go with it, which is just a polite way of saying, Hell no!

"There's an Amish Dutch family across the way comes round every month or so with whatever they been making and overcharges me for it."

Pulling down bowls and dessert plates from the cupboard, Hank said for Delores to have a seat. He got the butter out of the cupboard and some spoons and table knives. (Just trying to keep it real: Most people kept a half-pound or so of butter in the cupboard to keep it soft, just like the bacon grease under the sink.)

Hank put bread in the toaster and while it was getting ready, pried off the jar lids with a beer bottle opener and spooned peaches into the bowls and opened up the pint of cream. He asked her how much she wanted on her peaches and poured the cream over her peaches until she said,

"When." Toast done, they buttered it and spread on apple butter.

"So you went and made me peaches and cream?" Delores said.

"You know what they say about life not always being peaches and cream?"

"I heard it. Never had it, though."

"Me neither. Life might not be all peaches and cream, but this being such a pretty morning, it came to me that if it ever was, this would be the kind of day it would pick."

He told her to taste her toast.

"Wow, that's good," Delores said.

"You ever see them make it?"

"Never did."

"All the women come around and they build a big fire in the yard and mash up apples and cook them down in a giant copper kettle—got to be thirty gallons at least. They take turns working a big wood paddle that's hooked up to a crank to keep the apples from burning. And they got a secret recipe for the spices. You can't buy it in a store that would be anywhere close to this good."

And the morning went on that way, their finishing their breakfast and having extra cups of coffee and reading the paper, Hank going for the sports and funny pages, and Delores for the style and editorials, neither of them saying much at all. Except for Delores looking like the contestant that beat out Marilyn Monroe for first place in a national beauty pageant, they could have been a couple of long-time buddies having beers at the Rusty Bolt.

When they'd had enough of the paper, Hank asked Delores if she wanted to get dressed and go for a walk and she told him she had a better idea and took him by the hand and led him upstairs where they made love with a silvery indolence, so slow and sweet it took the better part of an hour for them to finish just once and by then it was close to dinner time and Hank said why didn't they go out to eat. Delores said it sounded good and give her a little privacy so she could make herself decent. He told her she was already about as decent as anybody ever been. Too much more and he might have to fight for her honor, depending on where they went to eat.

Delores took her time cleaning herself up and getting dressed and doing her face. She put stockings on and high heels and looked at herself in the mirror and thought, This is getting pretty close to a fairy tale, while Hank downstairs was thinking that maybe it wouldn't be so bad a thing if it took more that the three weeks he figured it would to count down to zero. Delores came down and drew an arrow through the next heart on Hank's card.

Chapter 13
Of Petty Bureaucrats and
Cream-Colored Convertibles

[Wherein Mattie is rescued by a handsome
stranger on a day that was *different*. Was it ever!]

On a warm spring morning a few months before Hank and Chuck's fateful decision, Mattie had to run up to the courthouse in Mercer to straighten out a clerical problem with her and Chuck's property taxes. They'd received a notice from the county telling Chuck (not Chuck and *her*) that he owed several thousand dollars in back taxes and threatening a sheriff's sale if he didn't address the matter forthwith. Obviously the form was addressed to Chuck because as the man, he was the one in charge and also the main owner on the deed, making him the go-to guy, smart enough to pay the bills and manage bureaucratic investigations without messing the whole thing up like his wife would. But at their house it was actually Mattie who paid the bills, her being a woman who could handle the complexities of writing out a check and getting all the zeros perfectly ordered when she was doing it—not too many and not too few. Also, she *always* filled in the memo line.

This whole tax thing was ridiculous. First off, Mattie didn't have to pay the taxes because the bank did that, taking them out of the monthly mortgage payment, just like now. And second, the amount declared in the notice to be due was so high that it was obvious the county had got their house's records mixed up with some other piece of property. The whole thing could probably be worked out in a few minutes, but still meant taking up the better part of a day what with waiting until the girls were off for school and going to the courthouse and rushing supper preparations. What a pain!

Mattie drove over to Mercer with the windows down and had to admit to herself that it was almost like having the day off and using it to go for a drive in the country, Route 58 from Grove City to Mercer actually being pretty pleasant in the landscape department, gently rolling farm country and acres and acres of woods. She found an empty spot right on the courthouse square and went in, leaving the windows down and the keys in the ignition (because that's what people did back then, that's why—not for some esoteric literary purpose [but feel free to read in a literary purpose if you are so inclined]). So far Mattie's day was going pretty well. But then....

Mattie went in and asked the deputy at the door how to find the clerk's office and climbed those ornate marble stairs with the polished brass balustrades and the domed ceiling just letting the light shine in and it was like going back in time to when people were civil. Just as she was thinking that this day wasn't going so bad after all, she walked in the clerk's office and there was a line (all women). And of course the woman handling the counter just had to go on and on with every single person that came up, rambling about the weather and her grandchildren and the price of groceries. By the time it was Mattie's turn, she was almost to a place where she could forget how important it was to be polite with people like that. Almost forgot but didn't on account of there was the easy way and the hard way and it was the woman on the other side of the counter who decided which.

Mattie dug down for some composure, finding a little bit, but not quite enough. After her turn with hearing about the woman's grandchildren while trying hard not to look impatient, she showed her the notice and said she was pretty sure there was a mix-up and what did she need to do to straighten things out, but in a voice that had just a touch of an edge to it. The woman raised her eyebrows and took the document and made a big deal of putting on her glasses, which were hanging from her neck on a string of purple beads, and took her good old time reading every word, as if she never before in her whole life saw such a mysterious missive. And then she said, "Hmmm" and read the whole thing a second time! Finally, she took off her glasses and canted her head just a little too far west of genuine concern and said with a velvet voice, "Oh yes, definitely a mistake, no property in that neighborhood is worth anywhere close to that." She smiled a sweet venomous smile that just dared Mattie to get pissed off and then she would see how mixed up things could really get. The woman was about as secure in her beadledom as any such petty bureaucratic could be.

Mattie didn't take the bait. She just said that she had thought the same thing and was there a form or something she had to fill out. The clerk just twiddled her hand in the air (the gestural equivalent of *Pshaw, I got this*) and said, "This shouldn't take but a minute." She sashayed back and disappeared behind a row of big wide shelves holding leather-bound volumes of very important papers. Mattie heard a door close. And then she waited. And waited. And waited some more. She waited so long that a new line formed, with her at the head, which is where you think you want to be when there's a line in a government office, but is so not where you want to be when there is no one at the desk helping you, which makes everybody else, whose business is obviously way more urgent than yours, think you are some kind of miscreant with a problem so non-routine that the county solicitor has to be summoned just to understand it, and you came here today with no other purpose than to make things hard for the rest of us, you goddamn loser you!

Finally, after twenty-some minutes of Mattie drumming her fingers on the counter and tapping her foot and looking back at the growing line with what she hoped was a look of abject apology, the woman came back out, dabbing with a paper napkin at the corner of her mouth where there were plastered crumbs of what sure looked like the last bits of an apple dumpling. Mattie took a deep breath, pursed her lips, and smiled.

The clerk said it had taken longer than she thought, but she'd figured out what happened. They had a new girl who had typed up all the delinquent notices this month and it looked like she had mixed up the two addresses, Mattie's card being right behind the one for a business that was delinquent, which was odd, since business property taxes were supposed to be handled by a different girl altogether.

By the way: It's always "the new girl" or often just "the girl" who was responsible for any error. Never "the young woman" or better yet, "the woman" or even better yet, "the clerk." Or even better than that, "Me."

Anyway: Mattie again asked if there was anything she needed to do and the girl said no, it was all straightened out now. Mattie said, "What about the notice?"

"Just ignore it."

Mattie didn't say what she had more than half a mind to say (which you can figure out for yourself). Instead she said, "Thank you so much," and turned to leave, to which the clerk said in an exaggerated syrupy tone, "Oh don't mention it. Happy to help." And now you can figure out for yourself what flashed through Mattie's mind and what she was thinking about saying and thinking about doing, which would have gotten her a short trip to jail, given that the county lockup was right in the same building and there was a deputy sheriff stationed on every floor, but she didn't. She just went out and headed to her car, thinking that she was sure glad that was over and at least she could enjoy the drive home.

And then she saw the flat tire.

Imagine yourself for a second spewing out your very best string of profanity-riddled obscenities. Whatever your concatenation of naughty words might be, and regardless of how creatively you might mix them, and no matter how shocking you think you would sound should you shout them out in public, your vision of yourself is but a pathetic and feeble approximation of what was going through Mattie's mind in the moment after she saw that flat tire. But she held it in—almost held it in. She did mutter *shit*, pretty much beneath her breath and with resignation. She said it a couple more times as she got the keys out of the ignition and unlocked the trunk.

By the way: Flat tires were common occurrences in 1953, so much so that people routinely went out to check the tires about fifteen minutes before they left for wherever they were going so they'd have time to change any flats. If they had kids, they'd send one of them out. Nobody liked changing tires. Except for young boys. They thought it was cool. So fathers taught their boys to change tires when they were around twelve, give or take, the length of the give or take roughly corresponding to how far out in the country they lived, with farm boys often being able to perform the chore about the time they went into first grade.

So a Sunday morning might go like this: The family's almost ready to leave for church and the father tells his teenage son to check the tires and the boy goes out and comes in and tells his father the right rear is flat and the father asks if he changed it and if he did that was pretty fast wasn't it. And the boy says no, he didn't. "Jesus Christ!" says the father. "Go change the damn thing!" Which considering the whole reason for going out was to go to church, is damned ironic.

Girls typically didn't receive such instruction. If a family had only daughters, there was a better chance that they would, but not one hundred percent. In Mattie's case, her father hadn't taught her, but Chuck had, a couple months after their first child arrived, a gesture more pragmatic than egalitarian, that gesture a natural reflection of Chuck's propensity for order and structure. If Mattie had a flat tire when she was out running errands or something, she wouldn't have to worry about finding a pay phone to call him and his finding a way to get to wherever she might be to change the tire.

Anyway: So Mattie got the jack and lug wrench out of the trunk and set the jack and pumped the handle a few times to get the car's weight off the flat tire a little but not all the way up so that the wheel wouldn't spin when she wrenched the lug nuts off. She had the tire almost to where she could start working it off when she heard a resonant male voice say in a Hollywood drawl reminiscent of bayou sunsets and magnolia-scented mornings, "Excuse me ma'am. Would you let me lend you a hand with that?"

Mattie turned to the street and there he was—a tanned, red-headed man in a denim work shirt and a brand-new cream-colored Pontiac convertible.

Mattie's first impulse (before she actually saw the man) was to say thank you, she got it and how kind of you to offer. But oh my. Her next immediate impulse was what she actually did say, the same thing but without the *got it* part, "Thank you. That's so nice." The man pulled his Pontiac to the curb and unfolded all six foot two of himself out of the car and strolled across the street as if his shoulders and hips were gliding on ball bearings greased with baby oil. (He was also wearing pointed-toed cowboy boots which certainly didn't hurt things one little bit.) When he got the right amount of close, he touched his fingers to his forehead like he was tipping his hat, except he wasn't wearing a hat, and said, "Good morning, ma'am. I'm Hunter." Mattie's right hand rose involuntarily. (Back then, proper etiquette had it that a man did not thrust his hand out to a lady—he waited for an invitation, the decision on whether to so engage resting entirely with the woman [alas, if only the custom had extended to *any* interaction between genders that involved physical touch].) Hunter took Mattie's hand as gently as if he were cradling up a fledgling songbird fallen from its nest and it was all just as natural as the sunlight cascading down all around, and his smile was right about ninety-five percent sunshine itself and the other five percent Mattie pushed out of her mind, her being married and all, although she did let that five percent linger for maybe a second and a half before she did.

"Mattie," she said.

"A pleasure to meet you, Mattie. Now let's see about that tire."

So Hunter took the lug wrench out of the jack handle and stooped down next to the crippled wheel, and oh boy, did that ever show off his broad shoulders and narrow waist. He pried off the hubcap and laid it near the tire, showing that he really did know what he was doing, because you always lay the hubcap close by so you can put the lug nuts in it like a bowl and that way you won't lose them. When he twisted at the first lug nut, it resisted and he had to give it a really hard yank, so much so that it squealed as it suddenly broke free.

"Wow" said Mattie. "I'd of had a hard time with that. It's a good thing you came along. I don't know what I would have done." (And yes, this moment of semi-flirtation is also a foreshadowing.)

Now Hunter's turn: "Ma'am, there is not the least bit of doubt in my mind that you would have done just fine without me." (Oh yes. Out of the mouths of handsome strangers.) Mattie blushed.

Once he had the nuts off but before slipping the tire from the wheel, Hunter went back around to the trunk to get the spare.

By the way: You always got the spare out before taking the flat tire off because it was really dangerous to leave a car up in the air with nothing holding it there but a bumper jack, because a car could slide off that jack with no warning whatsoever. A shove from a stout seven-year-old would do it. For sure wrestling a heavy spare out of the trunk could. But knowing that and practicing it were two different things. Once a year or so, you'd hear about some moron who'd lost a hand because he was fooling around under the car when the jack picked that particular second to slip sideways and the wheel came down and crushed his wrist. On the bright side, hardly anyone died that way. Once in a while, but not often enough to waste time writing about it.

Anyway, back to Hunter and the spare tire: He lifted the tire out of the trunk and set it upright on the pavement and said, "That doesn't feel right."

"What do you mean?" asked Mattie.

Hunter put his weight on the tire. "The spare's flat too."

Mattie came close to crying. She was in that spot where you have felt too many disparate intense emotions in too short a time and are just plain out of ways to react. She'd used up about what mad she had in her in the clerk's office and expended a lot of joy-in-the-moment when Hunter pulled up and now she had to deal with this?

Hunter saw. Hunter acted. He ever so lightly laid his fingers on Mattie's forearm and said, "Ma'am, we'll take care of this little bit of trouble, you and me. Let's just take a breath and figure this out."

Mattie breathed. Hunter breathed.

Hunter said there was a gas station just north of town and why didn't he drive them up there with the spare and see if they could get them to fix it while they waited.

Mattie said she didn't want to put him to all that trouble. (Ha! Don't make me laugh!) Hunter said it wasn't any trouble at all. He'd just been out enjoying the day and he couldn't see anything more enjoyable than driving Mattie to the station and back. And he smiled again. Oh, if only he didn't have that smile!

Mattie said okay and Hunter put the spare in his Pontiac's trunk and off they went.

At the station, Hunter rolled the tire inside (Mattie at his side) where the mechanic said he guessed they needed that fixed. Hunter said they sure did and was there a chance he could do it while they waited and explained about the two flats.

The mechanic said he couldn't get to it right this second on account of he had a tune-up to finish and he'd promised the owner he'd have it ready before noon, but if they didn't mind a little extra wait, he could take care of them in a half hour or so. Hunter looked at Mattie who was bucking up as best she could and said, "Hey, I don't have anything planned. How about we leave the tire here and find us a place to have some early lunch and wait there?" And she said yes.

By the way: I have off and on played with the idea of making *And She Said Yes* this book's title. But in the end I decided against it, because though that might be a catchy title, it would be a better fit for a much more serious book than this one is (probably in the subgenre of chick lit [also I would have to write it under a female pseudonym, maybe something exotic like Angela Vecoli]). Plus a title like that would take the focus off Chuck and Hank, without whom none of the really icky parts would resonate.

Anyway: The next thing you know Mattie and Hunter are sitting across from one another in the booth of a diner and their food is arriving, chili and a burger for Hunter and a turkey club for Mattie.

Mattie and Hunter made small talk, Mattie asking Hunter if he lived here in Mercer.

"No, I'm up in Greenville."

"Do you work at Steel Car?"

"No, I teach."

"Oh," Mattie said. "At the high school?"

Hunter got that look people get when they know they have to answer an innocent and altogether polite question, but wish they didn't because their answer will change the whole tenor of the conversation and things were going so well—was it really necessary to ruin it? In Hunter's case, it meant he was going to have to tell her he taught college, and trust me, when people hear that, it changes everything. Once in a while the change is good but mostly not.

Hunter almost winced when he said, "No. At Theil."

Mattie made that little stutter step kind of double take people do and then smiled that genuine kind of smile that shows true delight.

"No kidding," she said. "That's great. What do you teach?"

Hunter thought things were really going to go south now, that Mattie's enthusiasm was simply the fates taunting him because, English. If you think people have an insensitive reaction when you tell them you teach college, just try telling them you teach *English* at college.

Mattie's jaw actually dropped. "That must be amazing!" she said.

And things soared from there. Mattie learned that Hunter had written his dissertation on Faulkner, that he taught mostly American literature, but also had to take his turn in the barrel with freshman comp.

Mattie told him about the books she'd read, all of Willa Cather, a lot of Austen, some Steinbeck, and was working her way through *Middlemarch*. She was sorry, but the only Faulkner she'd read was *As I Lay Dying*. Something deep inside of Hunter stirred. And something deeper yet awakened. Oh, ye fates! And in this backwater of the world!

(Hunter had been graduated from Ole Miss, where he discovered his beloved Faulkner and went on to earn a masters and a PhD, his dissertation a brilliant analysis of *As I Lay Dying*, in which he argued that all of Faulkner's complexities and polysemies could be reduced to an understanding of his interrogation of the word *bevel*. Polysemy, Hunter argued, was considerably more complex than its most common uses would indicate. Conceptualizing it as the same morphological unit occupying multiple semiotic spaces was restrictively simplistic [though that way of thinking could occasionally be applied to developing useful heuristics that could lead to minor insights not readily accessible to casual readers]. A richer understanding of polysemy could be reached by including in a word's spectrum of meaning all of the possible contextualizations within which it could be employed—from the starkly quotidian to the hazily abstract. The man was way ahead of his time.)

When the check came, Mattie reached for her pocketbook and said, "Let me."

Hunter said that he couldn't and Mattie said back couldn't they at least go Dutch and Hunter said back to that that he hadn't enjoyed a lunch this much in a long time and it was the least he could do to show his appreciation and that was that. (I know there are a lot of *that's* in that last sentence, but if you reread it, you will see that every single one of them is absolutely necessary.)

The tire was ready when they got back to the gas station. "How much?" Mattie asked.

"Two dollars."

Mattie reached into her pocketbook, then looked puzzled and rifled around in there and finally gave up and said to Hunter, "I'm so embarrassed. I forgot my change purse."

Hunter took out his wallet and handed over the two dollars and put the tire in his trunk and they drove back to Mattie's car. If you think the day was abundant with sunshine *before* Hunter showed up, you should have seen how glorious the day was now that he and Mattie had spent a little time together.

Hunter took the flat tire off, slapped on the newly mended spare, spun down the nuts, banged the hubcap on with his fist, laid the bad tire in the trunk, closed the lid, and turned to tip his missing hat a final time.

Mattie said, "You have to let me pay you back for the tire."

"No, no. I'm happy to help."

"I just wouldn't feel right taking advantage like that. Please give me your address and I'll mail it to you."

What could Hunter say? Not let Mattie do the civilized thing after all of his display of chivalry? (Don't make me laugh—even college teachers can fool themselves.)

"Okay," he said, and took a notebook from a worn leather attaché case on the back seat and wrote out his full name (Hunter Calhoun), address, and phone number. He tore the page from the notebook and handed it over, his fingers brushing Mattie's wrist for just the tiniest fraction of a second, a brief enough touch to indicate *accident* but firm enough to say *on purpose*.

Mattie said she'd put the money in tomorrow's mail and she couldn't thank him enough and Hunter tipped his imaginary hat and said the pleasure was all his and until next time and got in his Pontiac and drove off.

Until next time?, Mattie thought.

On the way home, it occurred to her that today was something she didn't want to share. That is, she didn't want to tell Chuck about it. But she didn't want to lie about it either. Except how would she explain about the tires, the spare on the car and the flat in the trunk without lying? She wondered if maybe the mechanic at the station would trust her for the money to fix the flat and put the tires back where they were supposed to go. But then she would maybe have to explain taking a second trip to Mercer. What she came up with was pretty complicated. She stopped at the first gas station she passed on the way home and dropped off the flat and went home for her change purse. Then back to the station where they put the repaired tire in the trunk for her. When she got home, she changed the tires again so the spare was in the trunk where it belonged and the good tire back on the wheel where it belonged.

Now she could tell Chuck that she'd gotten the flat outside the courthouse and a nice man had seen her plight and changed the tire. Also that she had taken care of getting the flat fixed and swapped that out herself so he didn't have to worry about it. So her story would be mostly true and not really a lie, or maybe just a little bit of a harmless fib and whichever way it was, nobody was hurt. Plus changing the tire right in their own driveway where the neighbors could see and confirm her story just in case it needed confirmation would head off any suspicion.

Mattie almost wondered if the tires' being where they belonged said anything about where it was that *she* belonged but she didn't. Neither did she stop to consider that even *thinking* for a split second about Chuck being suspicious should have set off a whole lot of air raid sirens in her head.

Oh boy.

Chapter 14
A Big Surprise for Hank

[Wherein Delores figures out a third way to
tally off another ejaculation (other than
intercourse and handjobs). Also, she and Hank
learn that just because something is hard to talk
about, doesn't mean you shouldn't talk about
it, and when you do, you will feel a lot better
afterwards (in all kinds of ways).]

When you and your spouse are old and you think back to what
you had when you were young but didn't know it and ask each
other what it would be that you would do differently if you
could be young again, it almost always works itself into the
conversation that you would have a *lot* more sex, because the
farther down the firing range that carnal target takes itself, the
more you miss when it was right close up and almost in your
face and you couldn't miss it with a slingshot. And if you are
a man, you remember to yourself (but not to your wife—
because what would be the gain in telling her?) how you would
(like Chuck) strike out the top of the Yankees batting order
over and over in your head to last longer and you wish you
had that problem now. But when you remember those
younger days, what you leave out is going to work and getting
the car fixed and paying bills and cutting the grass and cooking
and then the kids: Changing diapers and making sure they eat
right and toilet training them, and just when you think it gets
easier when they can do all that on their own, it gets *really* hard
because they have figured out how to get on your nerves on
purpose. No, you don't remember all that. You just remember

Saturday night, what it's like now compared to what it was like on a good night back then.

When Hank approached Delores about letting him every day, he hadn't taken into consideration that even though they were in their mid-twenties, the sweet spot for sex (past all that adolescent ignorance and quick-on-the draw response, but still real virile and real responsive), they also had jobs and chores and responsibilities that took up precious hours that could have been spent naked. It was mostly their jobs that got in the way, Delores never knowing from one week to the next what shifts Mike was going to give her, and Hank not being able to turn down overtime, because if a machine goes down, it's got to get fixed right now and that's what millwrights do—great job but sometimes your time isn't yours. Plus, there was a lot of Saturday work right then and it was in the union contract that millwrights and electricians couldn't say no. All-in-all, they did pretty well the first week, getting in five, but after that it started in being hit and miss, settling in at about two or three, and a couple of times not even one. Just like they were married.

And then there was Delores's period (which, all things considered, they were both of them grateful for her getting, still was an obstacle to getting to nineteen [or zero]). The first time it came after she started staying at Hank's was only on Friday of the first full week, when they were still real gung ho about getting the job done. Delores got home about 7:00 that night and right away saw that Hank was all ready to go with supper warming on the stove and the plates laid out and candles burning on the table. She almost didn't have the heart to tell him on account of they'd just missed a couple of days in a row and it was pretty obvious that he was about as ready as a man can get, but it would have been disgusting, what with blood all over the both of them and on the sheets in the morning, and so as soon as he put the food on the table, she told him and said she was sorry.

For a second he got that "little boy who can't go fishing because Dad has to work Saturday" look, but just for a second. Instead he gallantly said, "What d'you got to be sorry about? Married people have that all the time." Then he was sorry he said it because maybe it would make her think he was taking her for granted (because it was in the movies all the time about the romance dying and you just expect things to get more and more boring once you get married), which was the last thing he wanted. (But he didn't say he was sorry, because why draw attention to it?) Instead, he grinned his almost-bad-boy grin and said it would be just that much better when they could get back to it.

So they went through their routine like usual and went upstairs to bed. Hank kissed Delores real light on the lips and said goodnight and turned out the light and drew her to him so her cheek lay on his chest in the familiar way they had fallen into (which is not the same thing as taking someone for granted—it just isn't). As he was settling himself down for sleep, her hand went down there and she started in kissing him on the cheek and Hank thought it was going to be like the first night at the Guthrie. But Delores kept on going with the kissing, down his belly (not that he had much of one) with her fingers wriggling away in his shorts, kissing him in that special way of hers: Going back and forth across his skin, alternating between kissing and breathing on him and sometimes using her tongue, and the next thing Hank knew she had his shorts off and him in her mouth.

The next thing you know it's morning and they are sitting at the table having coffee, one of the times when they both had to be at work at 6:00.

Hank took another sip of his coffee and said, "Uh."

And Delores said, "Uh, what?"

"Last night."

[....]

"Nobody never did that to me before."

"Which makes us even, on account of I never did it to anybody before."

Hank went Uh again and she looked at him with that look in her eyes that said that in her head she was somewhere between saying something bust-out funny and going-to-give-you-a-hard-time-that-you-will-never-be-able-to-forget. But she just sat there not saying a word. Hank thought what he was seeing was her making him work for it, because she could tell he was embarrassed and it was just like her to bust his balls, which as soon as he thought it, Hank knew was not a good thought for him to have, what with her always being so nice to his balls. Delores finally helped him out.

"Well?"

"Okay. If you never did it before, how did you get so good at it?"

"How do you know I'm good at it if you never had anybody else take a shot? Maybe every other woman in the world is way better at it than me and you don't know what you're missing because when it comes to that, I am dead last." (And then it was Delores's turn to think she shouldn't have said that, because what if it gave him the idea that maybe he should do a little comparison shopping?)

"If that was the worst there is, I'm pretty sure I wouldn't live though whoever is next-to-last."

[....]

[....]

Finally Delores said that she'd practiced because she knew her period was coming and didn't want to let him down, and Hank said now he was really confused because if she never did it before, how could she have practiced?

Delores pressed her three middle fingers together and put them in her mouth and moved them back and forth. "Like that," she said.

[….????]

"You mean that thing I did with my tongue?"

Hank reddened and nodded.

"I know where you like to be touched and I figured if fingers is real good, tongue has got to be holy-mackerel! good."

(The two of them heard different things when Delores riffed out that last line. What Hank heard was that she knew what he himself liked which meant she cared enough to pay close attention to him [you being singular in his mind], while Delores meant that she had been around enough to know what "you men" liked [you being plural]. You might think that this could lead to some serious complications later on in the plot, but it won't, because in that moment, the ambiguity gave them both what they needed, Hank feeling special and Delores feeling like a woman of the world who knew how to please her lover *because* she was a woman of the world, and neither of them had any reason to think the other heard something different. So no potential harm, no foul. No foul, no complication. Besides, what happened next having to do with this form of sexual expression turned out to be kind of sweet, which is not a complication at all but a gradual unfolding of our characters' tender inner selves.)

CHAPTER CODA

Or

What's Good for the Goose….

One night about a week or so after Delores's period, she and Hank had a faltering kind of stop-and-go conversation:

Delores: You know that thing we did when I got my period?

Hank: [....]

Delores: [....]

Delores: That thing?

Hank: Yeah.

Delores: [....]

Hank: [....]

Hank: I remember.

Delores: Well....

Hank: What?

Delores: Um.

Hank: ????

Delores: I was wondering....

Hank: [....]

Delores: Maybe you would want to do that?

Hank: !!!! Yeah, I would!

Delores: [....]

Hank: [....]

Hank (finally starting to understand what she's getting at [and also getting a little bit red in the face]): You mean...?

Delores: Yeah.

Hank (after taking a big breath and blowing it out so his cheeks bulged): I never done it.

Delores: Me neither.

Not out loud, but in his head, Hank was musing about a hundred and twenty miles an hour. Fair was fair, but wasn't it kind of disgusting. Plus even though her smell down their was actually kind of pulse raising, he wasn't sure he'd want his nose right there in it. And what if she farted? But she took an even bigger chance that he might fart (him being a man), and besides that, there was that thing where he came in her mouth and that can't be all that pleasant but she did it for him to be nice, so how could he say No? Oh boy.

An unfortunate linguistic characterization of the act was no doubt motivating Hank's hesitancy. "Eating her out," (as the act was generally known then [still is, if Google is anything close to an authority on the subject]) just naturally brought to mind intimations of Southern Gothic at its worst. "Good boys" didn't do that. Maybe Italian boys, but not good Christian boys.

A case in point: In my late teens I worked summers and then one very long year when I was "between jobs," in a factory much like the one where Chuck and Hank worked. For a while there was another young man on my crew who was very comfortable in his own skin and said what he felt, whether or not it was a blue collar tenet. Once when the breaktime conversation turned to cunnilingus, he told us he did it with his wife. After all the expressions of general repugnance directed his way, he said, "Show me a man who doesn't eat out his wife and I'll take her away from him." A lot of the guys took that as a threat.

Anyway: The only thing Hank's racing mind could get down into his throat was: ?????

Delores (holding up two fingers in a slim V and touching them to her lips like she was going to throw Hank a kiss): You could practice like this.

(Then Delores held her fingers up to Hank's lips and told him to give it a try and he gave her fingers a little brush of a kiss like you would give your great aunt when she was dying in the old folks home but with just the tiniest little flicker of his tongue.)

Delores: Jesus, Hank, show some enthusiasm!

Hank: Tsslpp-ts-ts. Tuh, tuh, tuh, da tuh.

Delores: Or I could bake a split-top banana bread and spread some of that Amish Dutch apple butter in the crack and you could practice with that?

Hank: Ha, ha, ha.

Delores: Does that mean yes?

Hank (nodding with shy temerity): Yes.

Delores: You better be sure because I'm going to drag you right upstairs right the hell now.

Hank: [....]

Delores: But I should still make the banana bread later on. That way you can have your cake and eat it too.

Hank: [....]

The next morning Delores came down the stairs like a movie star, one step at a time, sighing all the way to the bottom (like she did back in her bedroom after the first time a football player kissed her) and her legs snaky under her nightgown and showing everything she had, her face rapturous like she just found Jesus. After a bit Hank followed, his grin so wide it looked like it hurt. The man was sure enough proud of himself. Boy, was he ever!

Chapter 15
Hunter Makes a Breakthrough

[Wherein Hunter finds himself in thrall to his
muse and in a frenzy both spiritual and carnal,
conceives the Great American Novel.]

After making sure Mattie was all set with her car, Hunter raced his cream-colored Pontiac convertible up Route 58 to get home before the inspiration passed. He had not felt such urges since leaving Ole Miss, from sometime before leaving in fact. It was the dissertation that had done him in. Really, he had never been meant for the staid language of academic conformity. He had been born for the art of high prose, to inflame not instruct. That his spirit could be reignited here of all places and by an uneducated woman come across by happenstance almost made him believe in God again.

Once in his own driveway, he didn't even put the top up, just ran inside and rushed to his study where he fed a sheet of paper into his portable and began typing without thinking. You could not will the words this moment called for—you just let them come. The words would tell you what they wanted to say. Be their channel not their fount:

> Our orator seems to appear from nowhere. We will be about our business, on our way to work, or to visit a friend, or to keep an appointment; and there he will just be, coming around a corner or walking out of a store or crossing the street.

He ripped the sheet from the plenum, crumpled it, and threw it on the floor. He spun in another:

> They had been married for over sixty years. Their children had children almost of an age to go out on their own. They had lived in the same comfortable house their entire life together. They loved each other as deeply as when they were first married. That was beyond question. But they had become frail, their days awkwardly tentative, and routine tasks inordinately difficult.

Again he tossed the page aside and took up a fresh, unsullied one:

> Neither of his parents had ever wanted him. They slapped their infant son when he cried and when he cried from the sting of that, they slapped him harder until he learned not to cry at all or to even whimper. As he grew, they took to correcting him with hickory switches and leather straps until the timorous slant of his head and the suspicion in his eyes lent him the constant aspect of an animal that is often beaten.

And again:

> Every morning during that long summer, the pale young woman came down from the abandoned house rotting on the hill and sat on a whitewashed bench in the town square.

Getting closer, he thought. He went on, opening after opening after opening, deep into the night. Paragraphs and pages.

Sometimes a sentence, sometimes just a phrase, once a single word—incipient fables whispered in ever more mysterious tones, in signs ever more alien and undecipherable. The pages littering the floor joined chorus in sublime cacophony, urging him to keep going in spite of his fatigue. He typed until his fingers nearly bled. And finally:

> You are always walking away, the wind blowing your hair and your dress billowing like a white flag of surrender but never to me, and you are always barefoot in the damp grass in late spring, the Missouri primroses staining your ankles yellow as you brush against them and you don't notice them either, or you are walking along a dirt road, your feet powdered beige with the road's dust, and the sides of the road embroidered in chicory and tiger lilies, their blue and orange intertwined like the cross-stitched border of a debutante's sampler and the dust settles on the green leaves of sumac that in another month or so will bleed red into the crevices that lie along the fault line between equinox and solstice and it is near twilight, when the droning insect sounds of the daytime are fading and the music of crickets and tree frogs are replacing them, or you are standing in a gentle autumn rain that dimples the road and rinses the sumac leaves clean and there is no wind this time, just silver-gray droplets splashing on stone fences and gathering in the fields in rills and rivulets that you dance in, your face turned up to the sky, and the rain streams down your face like tears but you are laughing and you are farther and farther away and soon you will walk off where I cannot see you at all, even from a distance and you will walk off into the night, but not into the sunset, not to the west, where

you would eclipse the sun, its corona surrounding you and blazing around you like the wings of a great and perfect flaming bird and there would at least be heat, no not into the west, but into the north, into the cold black sky with stars like ice, and you will still be barefoot even in the snow, as you slip into the cold embrace of the aurora, never knowing how my breath could warm you, my embrace illumine you, and if the wind can reach beneath your skirt and ever so lightly touch your white satin legs, why can't I?

He took the page from the typewriter and placed in on his desk and read it slowly. Yes, he could work with this. There was a novel in this bit of a seed, one that could go in any of almost endless directions. Maybe lyrical. Maybe stark. Loss certainly. Hope? Backwoods incest? Violence? Maybe vague adumbrations of some dark, spectral revenant? He took up a pencil and read his snippet again, noting spots that could be tightened or more sadly rendered. He retyped the passage with his emendations and read it once more, this time aloud, his tongue lightly moistening his lips, his breath deepening, his heart quickening.

He laid the page face down on the desk and turned off the light. Leaning back in his chair, he masturbated to two alternating but blended fantasies: Mattie bent over the bumper jack, the curves of her hip and thigh altogether voluptuous and perfect, her supple body flexing as she pumped the handle. And Hunter himself at his debut book signing, earnestly engaging with readers and gracefully accepting their accolades. The images dissolved in and out of each other, each the palimpsest of its companion, each relinquishing itself to the other, each lifting the other up, each informing and informed by the other, elaborations within elaborations—

twin Russian dolls of endlessly nested complications. Sobbing and heaving, he came in massive rolling spasms and then fell asleep amid the several messes he had that day inaugurated.

Chapter 16
Yours Truly

[Wherein Mattie mails Hunter his two dollars and sets the stage for a serious narrative complication. Also, she connives just the least little bit (but mighty oaks). Also, she gets a tingle.]

If Mattie were going to slip off for another lunch with Hunter, she would have a lot to take into consideration. First off was the car. Fortunately they lived just a few blocks from work so that Chuck walked and she wouldn't have to worry about how to have the use of the car to get up to Greenville (or wherever) like wives who lived in the country had to, because she for sure couldn't suggest Hunter meet her anywhere in Grove City because how could they keep that a secret, what with all the gossips just waiting in the bushes for something to go all self-righteous about, and probably a hundred other things you couldn't even begin to imagine until they were right in front of you and you had to deal with them on the fly.

Mattie was also thinking somewhere in one of her mind's back rooms about how it would be kind of deliciously bad to find a place over in Sharon or maybe down in Butler, which would make it a rendezvous and not like she was sneaking around, but practically speaking, she knew it would be Greenville. There was also the chance that it might not happen at all, because, Who knows?, maybe Hunter wasn't interested, but then again, she saw the way he looked at her, and pretty soon the voice from that back room took over the whole house and was all she could hear to the point that she finally said to herself that she should shut the hell up and pay attention to what she had to do right now. She thought about the car some more.

The thing about the car wasn't having it, but how to explain the miles she would put on it driving up to Greenville and back which was a good twenty-five miles each way. Chuck would notice for sure. He kept track of everything, not like he was checking up on her, but he knew to the tenth of a mile the last time he got the oil changed and checked the odometer every single time he got in the car to make sure he wasn't going over the 2,000-mile limit. It was like a religion with him. If he started seeing big chunks of miles on the car, he'd for sure get suspicious, maybe not that she was running around on him, but was wasting gas and wear and tear going to card parties or something. Except he wouldn't be against card parties—he was pretty good about things like that.

Then there would be the phone calls. She couldn't risk Chuck seeing the toll calls on the phone bill, which meant she'd have to keep a supply of change so she could walk down street to a phone booth, but the change wasn't a problem because they both of them tossed their end-of-day change in a Mason jar on the kitchen counter and pretty much only used it to give to the girls for candy and ice cream. But what if Hunter tried to call her here and Chuck answered the phone? And, oh sweet Jesus, what wasn't she thinking of that could trip her up?

Finally Mattie put all of those potential complications aside for the time being, because regardless of what other steps there might be down the road, the very first step was to mail Hunter the two dollars he'd paid for getting the flat fixed, which she did the very next day like she promised. She'd go back to worrying about all those other things later. So as soon as the girls left for school, she got out her good stationery, writing pen, and ink bottle.

Okay, before I go any further: What Mattie was about to do was write a "letter." A letter was a primitive method of communication which was commonplace for centuries until cheap phone service and the internet came along and made it obsolete. People would sit down and write their thoughts out on paper in "longhand." (An adequate discussion of longhand is way beyond the scope of this book [it's a little like cursive, but way more complicated]. But briefly: You can think of it as a fast way of writing, where all of the letters have these swooping, curvy lines to link them together and all the letters are on a slant unique to each individual rather than the utilitarian, perfectly vertical alignment that they are supposed to have so that normal people can read them. [I know, WTF? Right?] Don't worry if you can't read longhand. Anything anybody wrote that way was a long time ago, so why even worry about it.) People of means often had small desks just for writing letters, called writing desks (though called writing desks, people used them for other things as well, like setting down their pocket books when they came in from running errands), but Mattie, a member of the blue collar working class, just sat at the kitchen table.

People could have conversations by letter, but they would take a long time to develop since you had to mail your letter and then wait for it to arrive at the home of the person you wrote to and then for them to carve out a space of time to write their "return" letter and then for it to get back to you. (This process was called "correspondence"—think of it as slow motion texting.)

If you were a considerate letter writer, you didn't just sit down and knock something out and tap send. You would write a "draft" on scratch paper and then read that over a couple times and make any changes that you thought would make it easier for your reader to understand your letter (you could use a pencil for this part). Then you would copy the letter over on good "stationery" (you can look *stationery* up on dictionary.com). There were entire stores devoted only to the sale of stationery and sundry writing accouterments. Often they were called *Stationery Shoppes*. You would write on your stationery with a pen, which in those days would not be a ballpoint, but a stem-like handle (called a pen holder) into which you would insert a curved metal point (called a nib). You would then dip the nib in a bottle of ink and then use that little bit of ink to write a few words and then go back into the bottle for more ink and write a few more words until everything that you'd written in your draft was on your stationery.

Once you were satisfied with your letter, you would blot it to make sure the ink was dry, fold it according to the strict rules that they used to teach in school (and that they don't anymore is one more step on the slippery slope that will plunge our civilized world all the way back to another Dark Ages), place it an envelope which you had addressed to the person you were sending it to, stick a stamp on the envelope, then put it a mailbox and wait for a reply. (For those interested in learning more, just go to my Web site and use the contact form to express your interest. I will be happy to explain everything to you in more detail—maybe even in a "letter.")

Anyway, back to Mattie and her letter: She started with a draft on yellow tablet paper, "Dear Hunter," she wrote. Then erased that and wrote, "Dear. Mr. Calhoun." Then changed that to, "Dear Professor Calhoun." Then put it back to, "Dear Hunter." Oh, boy, this was going to be a lot harder than she thought it was going to be. She went all frantic inside because she had to get the letter in the mail today so the postmark would be a signal to Hunter that she really was interested in him and hadn't just taken advantage of his good manners to get out of a sticky situation and the mailman (note that the gender-neutral *mail carrier* had yet to be thought of) would be here in a couple of hours. Oh boy.

Mattie set her pencil down and took a deep breath and said to herself that she should just compose herself and then write whatever came into her mind and she could change the whole thing later if what she put down wasn't any good. So that's what she did, and once she got started, things really started to roll, so much so that she felt herself starting to get a little bit excited and not in a wow-this-is-going-to-be-a-great-letter kind of way but in a little bit of a sexual way, which on a different day might have embarrassed her but today she was able to accept it by telling herself that it was just a natural reaction because who wouldn't get a rise from a handsome chivalrous stranger on a day that had been on its way to complete shit. As long as she didn't act on it, what was the harm? (Yeah, right! Like all those complications that she'd been projecting wasn't also projecting her acting on it.)

She started out telling Hunter again that she just couldn't thank him enough and enclosed was the two dollars she promised to send and she still felt so embarrassed for forgetting her change purse. She went on to say how much she had enjoyed their conversation over lunch and that she planned to go to the library and take out a couple of Faulkner's books and could he recommend one or two to get her started. (That part was pretty disingenuous because it meant Hunter would have to write her back, which was the polite thing to do if somebody asked you a question in a letter. Just thinking about seeing a letter from Hunter in the mail gave the sexual feelings she was having writing *this* letter a real boost, not quite to the point of desire but down the road a pretty decent stretch.) She put in the letter that maybe Hunter would let her repay him for their lunch by going again, this time her treat, maybe someplace in Greenville.

The first draft was pretty good. Mattie made a couple of minor changes before turning to her pen and stationery. She got the first sentence or two down and then set the pen aside and thought a second. Picking up her pencil, she crossed out the part in her draft about maybe having lunch again and went back to the pen version. When she'd finished, she added the thought about lunch as a P.S.

P.S.: Mattie will successfully deal with all those complications she was worrying over, the mileage on the car and the phone bill and arranging her assignations around the girls' schedules, etc., etc., etc. It will be hard and always tense, but she'll get it done. However, I am not going to explain what she has to do for every single little episode, because then we would end up with page after page of really boring details such as how she arranged for the girls' supper on a particular day (which is freaking hard to make interesting, let alone funny—plus there are only so many times you can use that "the next thing you know" trick before it gets annoying). And most likely I would have to write a chapter about how Mattie used Vacation Bible School as camouflage for not one but three lunches, but I would have to explain what Vacation Bible School was and how it is different from Vacation Bible School now and because I took a step down that road, I would feel obligated to throw in a slant nod to an enigmatic Bible verse (which would lead to complications of my own, like whether to pick something from the Old or New Testament and agonizing over whether I should connect the verse to the army nurse that had it in for Chuck and Hank and should I make her an angel of mercy or retribution). I will, however, in the pages to follow try to make one concession to realism by infusing Mattie and Hunter's interactions with tension-inducing semantics and anxiety-laced syntax.

P.P.S: Or, putting it another way: Who is this that cometh up from the wilderness?

Chapter 17
Three Books and a Letter

[Wherein Mattie and Hunter flirt long distance,
which people always think is safe because who
does it hurt? And which is almost always a little
less safe than soaking your fingers in molasses,
sticking them through the opening of a
beehive, and wriggling them around like a
Carolina debutante waving too-da-loo.]

Mattie waited for a return letter from Hunter with not quite bated breath, but with a lot of anticipation, the kind of anticipation where you are hoping for something but not real sure it's going to happen and also where you are afraid you maybe have embarrassed yourself by setting the wheels in motion in the first place and have set yourself up for a huge disappointment. But Mattie needn't have worried. About a week and a half later, there was a slip in the mailbox that said there was a package for her down at the post office with a Greenville postmark.

Mattie ran out to the car without even taking her apron off and three minutes later was in one of the parking spots in front of the post office with twelve-minute parking meters (it cost a penny for those twelve minutes). The package wasn't real big, but it was real heavy for its size. She raced home, went in, took off her apron, and tore open the package. Books! Three of them. And a letter taped to the front of the first one. It began with *Dear Mattie, I too enjoyed our conversation over lunch.* Mattie's heart fluttered. He went on to say that he'd enclosed three of Faulkner's novels and please consider them gifts. He had multiple copies of each of them and space on his bookshelves was getting quite sparse. She'd be doing him a favor. (In point of fact, Hunter only had a second copy of one of them.) He could indeed recommend some more of Faulkner's books and maybe they could talk about that over lunch (he would take her up on that kindness, though she was not indebted to him in any way, that if one of them were beholden to the other it was he, for her lively company and her charm). He closed with the suggestion that she phone him so they could arrange for their lunch and even included his phone number again just in case she had misplaced it. Oh my.

Chapter 18
Sanctuary

[Wherein Mattie and Hunter find refuge in
discussing books over lunch, each perceiving
the exotic in the other. And honest to God,
both of them really only meant for it to be
lunch.]

Mattie was ready for her lunch with Hunter way early. Ever since they'd talked on the phone and arranged a time (noon Friday) and place (Paxton's), she could hardly think of anything else. By Tuesday she had decided on her black pleated skirt and pink sleeveless blouse. Most of Wednesday went to waffling on whether or not to wear stockings. Going out bare-legged in the summer was perfectly acceptable but what with Hunter being a professor and all, shouldn't she try to lean toward the formal just a little bit? If he showed up in a suit, bare legs would look really Tobacco Road. But Hunter had been wearing a work shirt when they met. He couldn't possibly wear that to class. Or could he? What if being a Faulknerite, he was a little on the Tobacco Road side himself and didn't care if people knew it?

She planned to leave a little after 11:00, so at 9:30 she put on her face and got dressed, checked herself out in the mirror this way and that, and went downstairs to read. At 11:00 she gathered up her pocketbook and headed for the car but stopped halfway down the walk and thought for a good long while (which was maybe three seconds altogether—but a lot can go through your mind in three seconds, especially when you are on your way out on a Friday morning to meet a college professor and talk about books). She went back inside and upstairs where she put on a garter belt (not the sexy black one, but the going-to-church white one) and stockings, checking the seams half a dozen times before starting back out.

The next thing you know Mattie and Hunter (in denim shirt and black-satin string tie) are sitting at a booth in Paxton's and there was a little bit of tentative small talk, with Mattie being the more nervous but Hunter pretty nervous too. Fortunately he salved that over with his elegant Southern manners and natural charm and pretty soon they were just talking like they had been having lunch every Friday for years and years and they stopped being at all nervous and turned back into themselves.

Mattie thanked Hunter again for the books and he told her it was his pleasure and asked her if she'd had a chance to look at any of them. When she told him that she was most of the way through the second one, Hunter had to hold himself back from looking surprised (shocked really) because that would have come off as patronizing and it was the last thing he wanted, on account of his Southern manners reminding him that though the main reason for such manners was to reflect well on your parents, the second most important reason was to try to make everybody who was part of the immediate social situation comfortable. Also, he was really starting to like Mattie and he didn't want to screw that up (so to speak).

By the way: A good "question for discussion" might be, *Which of Faulkner's books do you think Hunter gave Mattie?* I have my own thoughts about that, but won't waste your time by laying them out. Also, if I did that, then I would have to have all kinds of references to said books peppered throughout my story and also drop in here and there obscure suggestions about what those particular books have to say about the culture of the times and how that affects people's values and the corresponding relevance to both 1953 and today and how men and women interact (then and now) and so on and so on. And this just isn't that kind of book.

Anyway, back to Hunter's question to Mattie about whether she'd had a chance to look at the books he sent her: He asked her what she thought about them and she told him that she was really enjoying them and though she had expected that she would like the stories, she found herself just as involved with the rhythm of the writing. It was as if Faulkner had used the sounds words make to set his stories to music. Hunter got an erection.

Mattie's remark was the spark that really lit their conversation. They went off on a long mutual meditation about the stories and the characters, the places and times. How experience informed their reading. (Neither of them used the word *informed* of course. They said things like such and such an action by a character reminded them of something that happened when they were kids or that the setting of some particular scene was reminiscent of a place they'd passed through once or twice and never before assigned any significance to [neither of them using the words *reminiscent* or *assigned* either].) And how much insight into the human condition Faulkner had. Both of them wished they could write like that.

They revealed details about their lives, Mattie confessing that she'd never been much farther from Grove City than Pittsburgh and the only other state she'd ever been in was Ohio. When Hunter talked about how he had first been drawn to Faulkner because he was raised in Mississippi, Mattie asked him if he missed it and if he ever wanted to go back. Hunter told her yes to both, that Mississippi had always been a place of sanctuary for him, a place to be just himself, and that talking with her here and now about the then and there made it almost seem as if he were already back in Mississippi.

And then:

Mattie said he must have a lot of books and he told her quite a few. She said she would love to see them sometime. They looked at each other across the table and got real, real quiet. Mattie because she realized what that must have sounded like and she didn't mean it like that. And Hunter because he was wondering if Mattie's remark had been innocent or was she suggesting something more and yes, he was physically attracted to her but what had really intrigued him was how she understood so much about books with virtually no education and what did she mean by "sometime." The silence across the table got real close to too long.

The waitress saved them by swimming by and asking if they'd like some dessert. Again they looked at each other, neither one wanting (and not wanting) to say, "What say we get just the heck out of here?" which would really mean something else completely different than it was time to leave, and they were at that point where both of them were wondering if they'd tripped over a stone right next to a cliff and were about to fall way down into something they couldn't take back but not sure if the other one is thinking the same thing and which if they aren't, could lead to a seriously awkward exchange that would end with one or the other indignant as hell and the other one humiliatingly embarrassed and ashamed.

[....]
[....]
[....]
[....]

Hunter said, "Do you?"

"I don't think so."

"Coffee?"

"Yes, coffee." (Thank God.)

The waitress asked how they took it. Mattie said, "Black." Hunter said, "Black." Oh boy.

The next thing you know Mattie and Hunter are standing in his study after driving up to his big Victorian house in his cream-colored Pontiac convertible with the top up. The study was huge, the room having been intended by its builders as the living room. (Hunter used the sitting room as the living room.)

Mattie had expected there to be a lot of books, but not for this. And she'd also expected the house in need of redding up, given that Hunter was a man living alone, but it was neatly arranged and kept, not to the point of fanatic where you would have to be terrified you might drop a cigarette ash on the hardwood floor but to the point of comfortable. Her first impulse was to ask him if he had a cleaning lady, but that didn't seem to fit the mood of the day (which is quite an understatement). Instead she said, "There must be a couple thousand books here."

"Just about," Hunter said. "Give or take."

"Have you read them all?"

"Not all. Most."

Mattie walked around and ran her fingers lightly over the books' spines. In spite of Hunter's being a gentleman, he wished he were one of his books. He couldn't help it.

Hunter said, "You can borrow some if you want."

Mattie said she just might take him up on that and then she noticed his desk with the portable typewriter and a stack of pages sitting next to it. "Are you writing a book?"

"Yes."

She asked him if he had written many books and he had to tell her that this was his first. He didn't add, "Except for my dissertation."

"When did you start?"

"The day you had the flat tire."

[....]

[....]

[....]

[....]

Mattie said, "Could I read a little?"

Hunter paused for just a fraction of a second before saying, "Sure. But don't expect too much. It needs a lot of work."

Here's what went through Hunter's mind in that fraction of a second: If I say yes, she could think I'm showing off. If I say no, she could think I'm insecure. Or that I think she's stupid. Will she think I set this all up to seduce her? But I didn't. She doesn't know that. But here we are.

Here's what went through Mattie's mind in that fraction of a second: Why's he hesitating? Does he think I'm too stupid? But we just had that great lunch. Maybe he's ashamed of it? Maybe it's about *me*? What am I doing here? Oh Jesus.

Hunter turned the stack of pages over so the opening page was on top. He handed it to her:

In layered quiet the woman went slowly upslope through young hardwoods budding green. She followed along a small stream in tentative shuffling steps, the hem of her long-skirted dress damp where it had dragged through the woods' winter detritus. From time to time she rested, wiping her face with her sleeve and looking upward. Her hair was working itself free of the black ribbon with which it had been tied back and hung in moist tendrils across her neck. She clutched to her breast a clear Mason jar half filled with a delicate gray-white dust that shifted and stirred as she stepped, as if it were keeping pace with the tides of some ancient and long lost ocean whose caliginous heart's interminably long beats still thrummed nearly mute beneath the earth's farthest horizons.

She came to a place where small moss-covered boulders and rounded rocks littered the ground and through which the stream dripped like the tap of a blind man's cane as he felt his way through a land of uncaring strangers. In spots the stream ran tight between rocks where there was insufficient space for her to pass and she detoured wide around them, sometimes retracing her steps where the stones made of themselves a barrier too dense for her to breach and found yet another way, always working back to the stream until the course from which it descended became too steep for her to straightway climb. From there she quartered like a dog seeking scent and found less demanding ground and switched her way up across the hill in a slow, milling march that took her by early afternoon through twists and turns too numerous to account for to the stream's springhead. (How Hunter got here from those nascent bits of opening he wrote the day he and Mattie met might be another good question for discussion.)

"It's beautiful," Mattie said.

"Thank you."

"Whose ashes are in the jar?"

Nonplussed, Hunter froze. He hadn't thought a working-class woman from here would even recognize the image, here where only earth ever embraced the dead, never fire. That if she questioned anything, it would be to ask what was in the jar, not who. Why did he keep underestimating her?

"Her son's."

"A baby?"

"No, full grown boy. Not quite a man."

"What happened?"

"He killed somebody and tried to run away. They tracked him down and shot him."

"Why?"

"Because he wouldn't surrender."

"Not that, why'd he kill somebody?"

"For love."

[....]

[....]

They fell right off that cliff and into their first hungry, lingering kiss.

It was the little things that Mattie would remember. How Hunter was gentle but manly. The way he cupped her face in his hands, how warm and soft they were. How, as they climbed the wide staircase side by side, he held his hand firmly in the small of her back as if they were dancing. How slowly he undressed her, how she breathed with the release of the first button as if she had never before tasted air. How they were both trembling as Hunter slid his body over hers and it was time.

Hunter would remember how Mattie was yielding but eager. The way she kissed his chest through his shirt, how that whipped up his heart. How she lifted her face to give him her neck. How she ran her fingers down his back. How her naked shadow gave life to the sheets. Thinking that she was poetry incarnate. How when he caressed her hand and saw the scar below her thumb and told her how much that must have hurt, she said, "Not anymore."

There was that one moment that briefly broke the mood—when Hunter rolled halfway over and got a condom from his bedside table. And of course that meant carefully tearing the wrapper open so as not to damage its contents and getting rid of the wrapper and rolling the thing down on himself and where's the romance in that? And when he did all that, Mattie felt a jolt like what you feel when you realized that today was the very last day you had to pay this month's articles of agreement bill and you left the check on the table and you are too far from home to get back before the bank closes and you are going to lose your house. Why? Because it just that second dawned on her how big a chance she was taking and how much bigger it would have been if Hunter didn't have one and they'd just fallen into one another without protection.

But of course he had one, she thought. With manners like his and looks too (not to mention him being a college teacher), you can for sure bet he didn't live without women (though she secretly hoped it wasn't a lot of women but she put that thought aside right away because it wasn't any of her business really). And what with him being so considerate, he wouldn't take a chance on getting somebody pregnant. Then she couldn't think at all, because the mood-breaking moment was over and he was inside. Skin to skin from cheek to foot, they almost stopped being two separate people.

The next thing you know, Hunter is dropping Mattie off in front of Paxton's and there was that awkward moment when Mattie was about to get out of the car and both of them were wondering if they should kiss, but there could be people watching and maybe they could get away with just a quick peck, but that would belie what had happened between them. Hunter saved the day by taking Mattie's hand in his so that their fingers interlaced, kissing the back of her hand, looking right in her eyes, and saying, "You are so very beautiful." Then he got out and walked around and opened her door. As she turned to go, he tipped that imaginary hat of his.

Mattie stopped at the first gas station she came to and while the man was filling the gas tank (not filling actually— just two dollars' worth so there would be about as much gas left when she got home as when she left), she went in the women's room and washed her face and reapplied her lipstick, but not as heavy as when she was getting ready for lunch—about the same as she would if she was going out for a loaf of bread. Looking at herself in the mirror, she wondered to herself if she had made what happened today happen. Or if it was out of her hands. And if redoing her makeup was a way of acting out a lie. Oh God, she thought. Did I mean for this to happen? She washed her hands and started out—but then stopped and took off her stockings and garter belt. She stuffed them deep down in her pocket book and went home.

Chuck had left a note on the table saying that he and the girls had gone to Isaly's for ice cream. Mattie went upstairs and set her pocket book on Chuck's dresser. She put her stockings and garter belt away before changing into a house dress. Being in her and Chuck's bedroom reminded her that tomorrow was Saturday and what Chuck would be expecting and how big a thing it would be after today, and how small. Oh God, she thought again. Something that felt very much like a little notched wheel clicking against a spring jerked inside her. She went into Chuck's sock drawer, got out a just-in-case condom, and put it in her change purse before going downstairs to get supper started.

Chapter 19
A Nasty Message

[Wherein Hank and Delores are reminded that
what they have been doing is outside the
norms of polite society by someone who is too
much of a coward to tell them to their face,
and they decide that they are not going to just
take it without doing anything or turn the other
cheek or return hate with love. They are going
to get even by going to church.]

As Delores's stay at Hank's stretched out from weeks to
months, the snubbing from prudish neighbors grew into
shunning and that in turn metastasized into just plain mean
and hostile nastiness. Hank even got flak at work, although it
was more on the why-him-and-not-us end of the spectrum of
possible plaints. Sometimes as he climbed the stairs to the
millwrights' shack, the raucous laughter of the other
millwrights rolling down the steps would stop all at once as he
came into their line of sight, one of them giving a quick nod
in his direction and raising a finger not much more than a
couple of millimeters to the other millwrights. Other times it
was a quick guilty look.

Delores got it at work too, middle-aged ladies from the
Boulevard in modest Sunday school dresses slumming at the
diner for lunch and glaring at her through the veils of their pill
box hats and flapping their gloved hands like drag queens and
tsk-tsk-tsk-ing in judgment as she waited the table across from
theirs.

By the way: If an author were so inclined, he could go off on a subtext here about one of the ladies. You know, like say something about how when she looked at Delores, she wondered if it was true what people said about her and Hank and if she had had an abortion in some rogue doctor's office in Youngstown and ended up in the emergency room down at Bashline's and almost bled to death and would have if they hadn't given her an emergency hysterectomy and even then, she had a tube in her side to drain the infection for over a month. And you could say something about how more than one Boulevard lady had those old-style hand massagers that were really vibrators that you strapped to your hand with cloth-covered springs so that your fingers vibrated and that's what you touched yourself with (or touched your partner with), not the vibrator, which if you think about it, is way more intimate that today's Magic Wand (but it would numb your hand after a while—so in that regard the Magic Wand is better) and how after she saw Delores, went home and was very kind to herself, fantasizing as she did that she might get real wild with her husband one of these days and be the one on top. Or maybe she would fantasize about Delores, what it would be like to have that body of hers naked against her own skin. Oh my God!, she'd exclaim to herself, how could I think that? But oh my, if my heart beats any faster it's going to fly right out of my chest. Once wouldn't hurt, would it—just to see what it was like? (That last part was verbatim what Eve thought when the serpent held the apple under her nose [except she thought it in Hebrew {which she should have known just from the Biblical sound that that thought made, that she was making a big, big mistake!}].)

Anyway, back to Delores and Hank being on the receiving end of intolerance: Once when Delores and Hank went to a square dance at one of the Grange halls and stepped onto the floor to join a square that was down one couple, the other six dancers decided that that was the exact right moment to take a punch break and left them out there on the floor all by themselves.

Fortunately (or sadly depending on your world view) they could always just go to the dances at the VFW where you could drink, and by the second set everyone was just drunk enough that nobody cared what anybody else did in their own damn houses. (Plus a lot of the people who went to the VFW were doing the same kind of thing [though nowhere near as brazenly] and would secretly give Hank a lot of credit and wish they knew what it was that Hank Walker had and how could they get it for themselves. Plus the married ones were maybe a little jealous. Plus plus, when they talked about Hank and Delores, someone was sooner or later going to say something on the order of, "He must tuck it in his sock.")

Until it got real nasty, Hank mostly said Screw 'em, and Delores, being that she lived out in Number 5, and had had to put up with such self-righteousness pretty much all of her life, just let it roll right off her back.

But just because Hank had a slow fuse, didn't mean he didn't have one, and one Saturday night when they'd had supper at Rudy's and were on their way out, it smoldered all the way down to *bang*. As they walked past a table of more-drunk-than-was-smart-to-be-saying-something-snide-about-Delores-in-range-of-Hank shit stompers, one of them let out of the side of his mouth, "Goddamn whore," as if Hank wouldn't be able to hear. And like he wouldn't do something about it if he did.

It took about a second and a half for Hank to have that boy up out of his chair and down on his back squirming on the floor and grabbing at his face where the skin around his eye was already changing color and mewling like a little baby.

The other two started to get up, but when Hank looked at them, they just slid back down and looked at something over against the far wall that wasn't there.

You know what?: Someday I'm going to write a whole book made up of nothing but B-movie clichés. Like: "That's not much of a plan." "It's the only plan we got." And: "Whoa, fellas—we're all on the same side here." And: "I hope you're right about this, but if you're not, I'm gonna do what I gotta do." Plot would be tricky, but the dialogue would write itself.

Anyway: The next morning the shit stomper showed up at Hank's with his black eye and the Justice of the Peace (who knew Hank's family, not what you would call family friends, but enough so that they could spend comfortable time together at a community picnic). The JP said, "This boy's swore out a complaint on you. You give him that eye?"

"You already know I did, cause you wouldn't have come out here without you already talked to witnesses. So you know why too."

The JP let out a little snort of a chuckle and gave Hank a quick wink. He said he had to write out a summons on account of Hank had confessed. He took out his book and wrote a ticket for disorderly conduct and winked at Hank again and said it was a fifteen-dollar fine plus a dollar and seventy-five cents court costs, but if he wanted to pay it right now, he'd drop the costs. Hank paid.

Walking back to the JP's official township car, the shit stomper got real agitated and wanted to know how come the JP let Hank off so easy. The JP told him to count his lucky stars Hank didn't give him way more than a black eye and if it had been him, the shit stomper would be in the hospital right now and how would he like a disorderly conduct ticket himself? The shit stomper shut up, but he did glare, not at the JP—he just glared at nothing in particular.

What really tore the scab off was on a Saturday morning when Hank and Delores were inside having their third cup of coffee and trying to decide whether to spend the evening at the stock car races over at the Mercer fairgrounds or go to the Tri-City track up by Franklin. Hank kind of wanted to go to Mercer because it was closer and they'd get back in time for you-know-what (except he didn't say it), but Delores held out for Tri-City because the season was almost over and it was a real raceway with an asphalt track and real race cars, not like Mercer with its dirt track, where anybody with twenty-five dollars to buy a '30s junkyard Buick and a set of socket wrenches and a timing light to get it running could go out and say he was a race car driver, and besides, they wouldn't have a chance again until spring. Hank had just about let her have her way (which he had started doing about ninety-five percent of the time, only holding out if it would affect work or something serious like him going hunting if he didn't) when there was a knock on the door. There stood the mailman, holding Hank's mail.

"Hey there, Bob," Hank said.

"Hey yourself."

"Something I need to sign for?"

"No," said Bob, handing Hank his mail. "But you might want to go out and check your mailbox." Bob went back to his car and, with a wave, went on about his route.

Hank set his mail on the table and Delores said, "That was weird." Hank went out to the mailbox, opened it up, and looked in.

"Son-of-a-bitch!" Hank yelled. "Can you fucking believe it?"

Delores, thinking Hank had hurt himself or got bad news in the mail, not remembering in that split second that the mail was already inside, came running out in her bare feet.

Hank pointed to the mailbox and said again, "Can you fucking believe it?" but softer this time and shaking his head.

By the way: The fact that Hank used the word *fuck* is by itself noteworthy, since in those days foul language was simply not used in what was known as mixed company. It just wasn't. Besides showing how mad he was, his using the word also shows just how much ahead of their time Hank and Delores were. Their cohabiting, not so much. It happened— not a lot, but it happened. But people didn't call it "living together." They called it common law marriage, which is quite an interesting thing to learn about, but such discussion is beyond the scope of this book. For those interested, consult Google. For those whom the Google search makes trepidatious, consult an attorney—now!

Anyway: The mailbox was stuffed with dog shit. I mean *stuffed*. Somebody had put a lot of work into it, no doubt saving their dog shit up over at least a month (unless they had more than one dog—then it wouldn't have taken that long) and probably wearing rubber electrician gloves to keep it off their hands, it was stuffed in so tight. They would have had to throw the gloves away when they were done. Hank hoped the gloves cost a lot.

With one hand on his hip and the other scratching his head, Hank finally said he wasn't even going to try and clean it out—he'd just get another mailbox. He walked over to the barn and came back out with a claw hammer and a cold chisel. What nails he couldn't pry from the mailbox post, he chiseled off, the nail heads making little pinging sounds as they broke, until the mailbox proper fell down on the ground. Picking it up by the flag, he carried it around to the back of his big yard and across the narrow strip of weeds to the woods and pitched it into the brush. He started back and stopped and mumbled, "Oh, the hell with it—it'll just stink forever," and went back to the barn, this time returning with a garden spade. Ambling around a bit while he located the mailbox, he started thinking maybe he should do something about this, but it wasn't going to be easy on account of they were too much of a coward to say it to his face, except that guy at Rudy's and that really wasn't to his face. By the time he'd dug the hole and kicked the mailbox into it, Hank had a plan.

By the way: Through all this he said *fuck* and *shit* and *goddammit* a lot, but though narrating it as it actually happened with all the curses and obscenities would be truer to the facts, it would make for a kind of stuttering prose, so I've Bowdlerized a bit. Just be aware that in the real world, Hank was getting himself pretty worked up and the particular vocabulary he used with himself reflected that. Also, don't read too much into Hank's burying the mailbox. This fragment of a scene is just to give Hank time to come up with a plan for responding to the affront of somebody stuffing his mailbox with dog feces. It's got nothing to do with how Hank buried his emotional shit or assumed somebody else's emotional shit or anything else artsy like that. Also again, his dragging the mailbox by its flag across the yard is so not trying to convey some insight into messages across time and distance—unless its so doing would make you think this piece of writing is an extraordinary, theoretically inspired narrative and therefore truly beyond the restraints of a specific place and time and one of only a handful of such examples of narrative that can be called truly great—in which case, it is.

Anyway, back to Hank's plan: By the time he got the hole filled and the tools put away and went back in the house, he was smiling in a way that told Delores he had something devilish on his mind. "What do you got on your mind?" she asked, not altogether sure she was going to like what she heard.

"Get dressed," Hank said. "We're going down street."

"What for?"

"I'm going to buy you a red dress."

"What for?"

"You and me's going to church in the morning."

The next thing you know, Hank is parking right in front of Flowers' Hardware on Broad Street, just across from the dress shop. He put a quarter in the meter, which gave them three full hours. "Big spender," Delores said.

"Just you wait," Hank said back and took her arm in his and led her across the street, his head high and taking big steps. Inside the dress shop, he said for her to pick out anything she wanted, so long as it was red and by red, he meant, knock-your-eyes-out, it's-Saturday-night-and-I-mean-*business* red. They had chairs for husbands and he took one, except unlike husbands, he didn't have that look on his face of, "Holy crap, how'd I ever let myself get roped into this?" He had a, "This is really going to be good," kind of look.

At first, the sales ladies (after looking her up and down and especially at her hair) took Delores to the modestly priced rack and said these were pretty nice and they were sure there would be something she liked and walked stiffly back to the cash register, flipping their hair.

Seeing what they were doing, Hank strolled his bad self over across the oiled wood floor and stood right in front of the register and flipped his own hair (which sort of worked, because he hadn't greased it down yet) and asked them if they took checks and they said they did. He asked them, "In that case, why are you showing this beautiful lady the cheap stuff?" He was paying and had more than enough in his checking account to cover anything they had in this backwater shop. He said he'd told his lady friend here not to look at the price tags, so show her the good stuff—just make sure it's red. The whole tenor of the transaction changed and they stopped being so supercilious and uppity and got all fawning and syrupy. (Parasites! thought Hank, which though it made Hank a little sick to his stomach, also made him feel more than a little gratified, them having to lower themselves to wait on Delores and feign respect for her while they were doing it.)

They brought out every red dress they had that was anywhere close to Delores's size and no matter which one she put on, they all went on and on about how that dress was *you* and asking each other, "Doesn't she look just *amazing*?" She and Hank eventually narrowed it down to three and she tried each one of them on again and they picked the mid-calf number with a deep V-neck and three-quarter sleeves that covered her shoulders. The thing was tight across her hips and thighs so they showed off what she had and she had *plenty*. It was a little loose in the waist and the owner said they'd have to take it in and it would be ready by Monday afternoon. Hank told her as he took out his checkbook that if she wanted to sell it, she'd have it ready in an hour and she said okay. He made out the check and handed it to her.

Leading Delores across the street to Burdick's, Hank told her that as good as she looked in that dress, he wasn't sure he was going to make it home without jumping her bones and she said it wasn't her bones wanted jumped and gave him a little squeeze on the arm that said this was going to be a real good night. She asked him if he really had that much in his checking account and he told her he almost did. He'd just stop off at the bank after work on Monday and transfer the difference out of his savings account.

Inside the men's store, Burdick asked if he could help them. Hank said he was looking for a suit and what did he have that was a little on the flashy side? Gesturing to the suit racks, Burdick said they were mixed in with the others and eyed Hank and said, "Forty regular?" Hank nodded and Burdick took him to the forty section and said for him to take his time and feel free to try anything on.

By the way: I miss men's stores like Burdick's. I really do. It's still there, but it's just not the same (like everything else around there these days, it's just gotten weary). You used to be able to go into a men's store not knowing what it was you were talking about and they'd put you at ease and ask tactful questions until they had an idea of what you needed and then have you try things on and ask more questions, getting closer and closer to what was right for you. They'd even steer you away from what wouldn't drape just so on your particular frame and explain why, even if it cost them a sale. (Sigh.)

Anyway: Hank finally decided on a three-piece suit cut from a shiny sort of fabric that was mostly dark purple, but depending on which way the light hit the cloth, had hints of red and green shimmering in and out of focus. It fit right off the rack. He picked out a solid yellow silk tie. "You sure about this?" Burdick asked and Hank said sure as hypocrites fight for the front pew. Burdick told him he did know he was going to stand out, didn't he and Hank said he was counting on it. The only dress shirts Burdick had were white so Hank asked could Burdick press the suit and they'd be back in a little bit to pick it up, and Hank and Delores went next door to the Five and Ten to get Hank a shirt to wear with the suit, a long-sleeved dark green sports shirt. "Almost there," said Hank and they crossed back past Burdick's to King's shoe store, where Hank got a pair of patent leather lace ups with Cuban heels and the leather carved to look like alligator scales. They bought a pair of red spiked heels for Delores. The shoes made Hank remember he didn't get socks, so back to the Five and

Ten and three pairs of brightly colored socks: orange, yellow (to match the tie), and neon green.

Once Hank got started, he was like a train picking up speed and down they went to College Avenue where an Italian guy from the old country ran a shoe-repair shop. Hank had him tack double cleats onto the soles of the shoes and to leave the nails a little loose so the cleats would clank when he walked. The old man did as he asked, his bruised, blackened fingers flying and his hammer flailing, all the while asking would Hank want a pair of second-hand shoes, he had dozens to pick from, castoffs people had left off and never picked up. "Gooda, like-a new," he said and lots of other small talk mixed in and within the small talk, the occasional, between-the-teeth *sei una fava* and *puttana*, all with a simian, subservient grin. Hank passed on the shoes. "Maybe next time," he said.

What with all the packages they were carrying, by the time they picked up Hank's suit and Delores's dress, they were pretty bogged down and kind of juggling everything. Hank carefully laid his suit down on the back seat and Delores's dress on top of it and everything else in the trunk. They slid into their seats and Hank started the car. Snapping his fingers, he said, "Almost forgot," and turned off the motor and told Delores to just wait a minute. He went into Flowers' and bought a mailbox and some glue-on letters to spell out his name.

On the way home, Delores kept looking in the back seat until Hank asked her was there something wrong. She said no way. It was just that seeing the way the clothes were arranged on top of each other back there and remembering how Hank dragged the mailbox across the yard by the flag was giving her some ideas about what they could try tonight on the way back from Tri-City—but it would only work if Hank wouldn't mind finding a place along the way home where they could pull into the woods where nobody could see them. Hank grinned and grinned and grinned.

The next morning, Hank and Delores stepped from the porch in their new clothes, their outfits as bright and hopeful as the day, both they and the morning feeling like sure and certain harbingers of the resurrection and the life. In spite of the beauty in all that sunshine, Hank still looked like a guy in a too-flashy suit, but Delores! Crimson red lipstick, new nylons, rings on six fingers, and a ruby-red brooch right where her cleavage ended. (They'd had to go to more stores to get all this stuff of course, but there's enough of that kind of thing up above—just fill in the details for yourself so they show how Hank spared no expense.)

They drove to a small Presbyterian Church just off the Leesburg Road (which actually was the way they would go if they were going out to see Delores's dad). When Hank pulled into the crushed-stone lot and turned off the motor, Delores reached for the door handle. Hank told her to hang on a second, they should have a cigarette first.

"Why? We just had one."

"So everybody sees and so we smell like it when we go in."

Delores was starting to understand and smoked her cigarette with an exaggerated style as if she were using a cigarette holder and Hank just let his dangle from the side of his mouth, sucking on it every few seconds (given that he had those bad-boy looks to start out with, Hank could go all out James Dean pretty easily when it suited him). When they were done, they stepped out of the car and threw the butts on the gravel and made a big deal out of grinding them out with their shoes. The church folks looked upon them aghast and every time they met someone or saw someone looking at them,

Hank would smile like he'd just been reunited with an old war buddy he hadn't seen for years and say (real avuncular and like the person he was talking to was just the most wonderful person in the world), "Morning, brother (or sister)! Beautiful day to be in the House of the Lord, ain't it!" And they'd brightly say "Morning" back, because what else could they do?

Hank led Delores inside and down the aisle to a couple of seats near the front, Hank shaking hands all the way and his cleats clinking and clanking like Bojangles himself about to fly into a tap dancing frenzy and saying what a blessing it was to be here among God's chosen and how much he was looking forward to the singing, but as much as he loved the singing, it was the teaching he really came for and thanking everybody for welcoming him and his lady friend into the sanctuary of the blessed and he'd be sure to visit with them for a while after the service.

The next thing you know, the pastor is settling in to his place behind the pulpit and reciting the opening prayer and the choir is filing in.

The first hymn (the warm-them-up hymn) was "Bringing in the Sheaves," which would fit with the pastor's text for the day. Sharing a hymnal, Hank and Delores sang along, Delores on the respectful side because being in church just did that to her, but Hank just booming out the words, louder and louder and almost on key, until he was all by himself just about as loud as the rest of the congregation put together, even on the closing "Amen."

Then came "There is Power in the Blood," and Hank just about had a stroke over his good luck and sang even louder, because when you can repeat a word like *power* over and over and with *feeling*, you can make a whole room rock (and boy, did Hank ever), and the pastor was thinking maybe he should shift up the hymns to some that were more sedate and reverent, but he couldn't, on account of the numbers were already posted up front, along with the total of the Sunday school offering, the children's combined offering adding up to three dollars and sixty-seven cents. By the time they got to the end of the hymn, Delores couldn't contain herself, her inhibitions because of being in church having evaporated into the ether, and knew that if she didn't do something quick, she was going to bust out laughing and no way was she going to be able to stop once she got started, so she just let out "Praise Jesus!" and that took care of two things: Holding back the laugh and embarrassing every single adult in the sanctuary, but the kids absolutely loved it and a couple of them yelled, "Praise Jesus," too, which had their parents glaring at them, because Presbyterians? Seriously? Even a Baptist had to be a Baptist for a good long time to get away with something like that.

Then came the offering. Hank made a big deal of fishing around in his pocket and after bringing out a roll of mints and then a pocket knife, finally found the quarter he was looking for and made another big deal of plopping it in the plate.

By then the pastor didn't want anything more than to get out of there, so he cut the offering hymn and went straight to his sermon, not even praying before he started because all he was going to ask was for God to open their hearts to His Word and he wasn't sure that was a good idea on this particular Sunday morning. He cut the sermon itself short, culling it down from the forty-five minutes he'd allotted to fifteen. To himself he was thinking, I got to get us the fuck out of here. Which wasn't particularly pastoral but it was the truth and isn't church, if it's anything at all, a place for truth?

After the sermon, he thumbed through his hymnal and said, "With your kind indulgence, I'd like to change this morning's closing hymn to 'Softly and Tenderly Jesus Is Calling,' hymn number 86." He figured the man down front couldn't possibly have the nerve to mess with that, but Hank couldn't believe this second dose of good fortune and just about shouted out the closing line, "Pardon for you and for me." And then the pastor rushed through the benediction like a man in bed with another man's wife leaping for his pants because the husband just started up the stairs: "The Lord bless you and keep you; the Lord make his face to shine on you and be gracious to you; may the Lord turn his face toward you and give you peace." And then he beat it the hell down the aisle to stand by the door and receive the parishioners, who after shaking his hand, went outside and stood around to see what was going to happen next, all of them hurrying too.

And then there was Hank.

He pumped the pastor's hand, squeezing so hard the pastor was afraid Hank was going to break a couple of his fingers but couldn't say anything or even grimace because you got to be brave in the face of evil and be strong for your flock.

"Dandy sermon, pastor!" Hank bellowed. "Just dandy! I got to confess I was hoping for one on casting the first stone or love one another, but what you said about what the Lord requires, I found that to be real enlightening." (Micah 6:8. Interestingly, the same text Reverend Al Sharpton used for his sermon at Michael Brown's funeral, which has to be incontestable proof of the truth of the doctrine of plagiarism by anticipation.)

Hank went on. "Powerful stuff, pastor! Powerful stuff! I got to thank you for giving me a lot to meditate on as I take up my earthly burdens this week. I will try to spend every single second asking myself what God wants of me in that second. Me and my friend just can't thank you enough." Then stepping outside and lighting a cigarette and offering one to

Delores, he led her to the car and they went home. Every couple of minutes, Delores would yell out her window, "Praise Jesus!" And Hank would yell out his, "Amen!" Then Hank said that what she came up with for last night was pretty amazing and she yelled out, "Praise Jesus," all the louder and Hank right back, "Amen." (This became a thing with them for the whole rest of their time together. Whenever the sex was especially explosive, one or the other would let out, "Praise Jesus," and the other would retort, "Amen.")

Over the next couple of months of Sundays, Hank and Delores wore their Saturday-night outfits to as many churches as they could, including the Baptist Church in town just off the intersection of Center and Main, the Church of the Nazarene where Hank actually spoke in tongues in a way that he managed to make sound dirty, but nobody said anything about because if you are sanctified like that, then whatever comes out of your mouth has got to be holy (which is why Nazarenes swallow rather than spit), the Assembly of God, and the First Church of God. They even hit a couple of revival meetings. When Delores asked Hank if they should try the big Presbyterian churches in town, he said they weren't religious enough.

Eventually they quit going to church because they got to the place where they'd gotten all the fun they were going to get out of their unconventional but fervent set of spiritual practices and they also missed lazing around on Sunday mornings and how nice that was, which you couldn't do and also get all dressed up to make church on time. Even though neither one of them seemed to get any closer to God from all that church going, they did get to that place of peace that comes from standing up for yourself when people think they are better than you (also because nobody ever again stuffed their mailbox full of dog shit either).

Chapter 20
Down by the Riverside

[Wherein are briefly described the variations in
Mattie and Hunter's assignations, not all of
which include sex. Also they fuck up. Big time.]

Mattie and Hunter didn't see each other all that often. (By the way: Think about the verb *to see* in this context, the euphemism so often employed that it sounds innocuous, a way to make an affair seem not an affair even though everybody knows what it means. As in a movie where a man admits to his wife, "I'm seeing someone," and then she either starts to cry in wrenching sobs, gets so angry she starts throwing things, or throws up on the sidewalk [if the man was dumb enough to tell her on a public street]. But the construction is hard to avoid. Opening a chapter with the reductive, "Mattie and Hunter didn't fuck each other all that often," would come off as gauche to a lot of readers and downright offensive to others. And given the context, "Mattie and Hunter didn't sleep together all that often," is just ridiculous.)

Anyway: Mattie and Hunter "got together" every other week or so. At the extremes they once went a month between trysts and "met" three times in one week when the girls spent their annual two weeks at Mattie's mother's house. Sometimes they'd have lunch. Sometimes Mattie would just drive to his house (talk about reductive). Sometimes they'd meet on campus—on those days they didn't "see" each other, they just talked. Sometimes they'd go for a drive in Hunter's convertible, maybe over toward New Wilmington to look at the hex signs painted on the barns and think of ways Hunter could incorporate them in his novel or over toward Franklin just to be out in the fresh air of the woods and hills.

One morning when they'd driven up to Tionesta, Mattie saw a pull-off and a path that must wind down to the Allegheny River. "Let's take a walk," she said. Hunter pulled over. When Mattie saw how steep the path was, she took her pocket book back and left it in the car. Then down they went—way, way down that steep and slippery slope to the river. Fortunately, someone had put in some railroad tie steps on the worst parts. But they did slip and slide a few times, Hunter firmly grasping Mattie's arm when that happened to keep her from falling or her holding on to him. They laughed at their clumsiness and the laughter, along with the grabbing and the physical effort of the descent, had them pretty worked up by the time they made it to the water's edge and you know what happened then.

When they got to the point where they were both breathing pretty heavy but still dressed, Hunter gasped out, "I don't have a," and Mattie gasped back that it was okay, it wasn't the right time of month, thinking to herself that climbing back up to get the one in her pocket book would destroy the mood, and being so full of life and wilderness and sun and reflections on the water didn't come along every day, so she didn't even mention that she had one up in the car.

Two facts about what she said:

Fact 1: Mattie had no idea when the right time of month was.

Fact 2: It was.

Chapter 21
Oh Shit!

[Wherein Mattie finally figures out what is important to her, but comes really close to her whole affair with Hunter blowing up right in her face.]

Delores sat at the kitchen table leafing through the *Allied News*. Pretty soon she'd get up and get something started for supper. (She and Hank had worked out a thing, without actually talking about it, that if one of them was home from work before the other or had a day off and the other didn't, that the one who was home first would make supper and the other one would clean up after they ate. Delores was a little bit surprised that Hank went along with this, but if she had taken a step back, she wouldn't have been, because for Hank, her and him in his house was pretty much like deer hunting and staying at a camp where the guys took those kind of turns without thinking about it and when it came right down to it, Delores was a lot like that, at least in the beginning, though she was becoming more and more than that as time went on.) Before she had a chance to start supper though, the phone rang. It was her dad. His car wouldn't start and could she give him a ride to work? He wouldn't need a ride home—he'd get somebody from work to run him down. And he was sorry—he'd tried a couple of the guys but they'd left already.

By the way: There was a reason why he couldn't get ahold of anyone he worked with. One thing about working in factories and mills in those days was that a lot of the guys would show up for their shifts ridiculously early and hang around the time clock shooting the shit. I thought this was really dumb, because why would you want to spend even one extra second at a place you spent most of every coffee and dinner break bitching about how screwed up it was and what you would give to be rich enough to not have to work at all and then this place could go fuck itself. When I told one of the guys that I just didn't understand why they came so early simply to hang around, he told me I would when I got married.

Anyway, back to Delores's dad's car's not starting (note how you can have three possessives in a row and not be nonstandard): Delores said sure, she'd be glad to help him out and would be over right away. Just give her a minute to leave Hank a note. She wrote the note and started for the door and stopped and came back to the table and drew a heart at the bottom with a question mark. Hank would like that.

The next thing you know, Delores is dropping her dad off at Steel Car.

Delores asked her dad if he was sure he wouldn't need her to pick him up and he told her he was good. She said what about in the morning, would he need help getting the car fixed? She could try to get her shift changed if he did and he told her he was pretty sure it was just the starter and he'd get a neighbor to run him over to the junkyard to get a "new" one and he'd be good to go. Delores told him if he changed his mind to call early before she left for work and started off.

When she got to 58, instead of turning left she said what the heck, as long as she was here, she might as well drive up down street. (Which expression may seem jarringly incorrect but it actually is correct. Greenville's shopping district was north of Steel Car and therefore "up" from where she was and because of the colloquial *down street*, also "down" from the same place. In that context to "drive up down street" is perfectly logical—this entire story in microcosm.) She could do some window shopping and maybe pick up something a little slinky to go with that heart she'd left for Hank. He'd like that too.

So she parked on Main Street and just started walking, looking in the shop windows and going inside a couple times when something caught her eye. One of the dress shops was having a sale on light lingerie, probably because they wanted to clear all that out of the stock room so they could lay in a supply of flannel for winter. Delores wondered if maybe there was a way to make flannel sexy and had an abbreviated conversation with herself, taking both sides until one of her drowned out the other of her, and by the end of which she'd come up with the idea of buying a flannel nightgown and embroidering a heart with an arrow through it over the left breast. She had to hand it to herself—she could make the most everyday thing sexy if she put her mind to it. The nightgown would have to be pink though, and the embroidery thread real bright red. So she got those things and went back to walking, looking in store windows and enjoying the day.

A notice taped to the inside of a restaurant's window caught her eye. It was for a local sportsman's club family day. There would be games of chance and games of skill and a fishing contest for kids. A square dance. And a turkey shoot. Delores checked that the turkey shoot would use targets and not live birds. The whole thing sounded like a fun day for Hank and her. She was so busy getting a pencil and notepad out of her pocketbook to write down the details that she didn't notice the tall red-headed man going in, though if she had, she would have thought, Poor guy thinks he's something—he should meet Hank. That would take him down a peg.

For the entire drive up to Greenville, Mattie kept trying to work through in her head just exactly how she was going to tell Hunter that she was pregnant, not just the exact phrase to use, but when. Before they ordered? While they were eating? Right after? Maybe during coffee (which had become part of their routine)? By the way: The fact that Mattie and Hunter had fallen into a "routine" should have been a giant red flag heralded with a claxon loud enough to be heard all the way up in Presque Isle. As Mattie knew good and well, routine is where passion goes to die.

Anyway: For sure, she couldn't just wait for him at the table and the first thing when he sat down, say, "I'm pregnant." Can you imagine? Maybe say she was late and hope he could put two and two together and she wouldn't have to use that word (pregnant)?

But if she waited, Hunter would be thinking that this was just another normal day of illicit romance and this so wasn't going to be normal and would he be disappointed that they probably wouldn't be "sleeping together" on account of that wasn't really appropriate given what she was going to tell him or maybe it would be the most romantic ending to this day there could possibly be? Or would he be disgusted? Or get that look men get when they are caught with their hand in the cookie jar and no one knows what's going to happen next, except they are probably going to run away into the woods and pretend to be scouting for deer? As she was walking into Paxton's, she decided to just wait and see, hoping that the right time would jump up and assert itself exactly when it was supposed to. Hunter hadn't arrived yet so she took a table facing the window where he would be sure to see her when he did. (In those days small restaurants and diners didn't employ hostesses, you just took whatever seat you wanted.)

Hunter let his class out a few minutes early so he'd have time to zip back to his house and retrieve the book of poetry he'd bought for Mattie and like an idiot left on his desk instead of taking it with him to work. But that's the kind of thing that happens when you are in love. You just get so absent minded.

He planned to give her the book over coffee and later on when they were languorously entwined in his bed tell Mattie that he loved her, loved her with his whole heart and there must be a way that they could be together permanently and he knew it would be hard on a lot of people and he was sorry for that but she was all he ever thought about. (He wouldn't tell her that he also thought about his book a lot—just in case she might get jealous of his writing.)

She was waiting for him when he walked into Paxton's, sitting at a table with a smile that was not quite a smile, more like the kind of smile you see when somebody gets a pretty nice present for Christmas but not the one they were hoping for even if the one they did get was way more expensive. And she didn't light up like she usually did when they met. Something was definitely wrong. He went to say something about it when Mattie went ash white and she wasn't even pretending to look at him—she was looking over his shoulder at something else and for a second it came into his mind that that bit of fantasy prose he'd written about the narrator's lover always walking away was coming true. And he was right.

Oh Jesus, Mattie thought. That's Delores Young. Oh God oh God oh God oh God. She looked at Hunter. Hunter looked at her. Hunter went to say something. She shook her head no. Hunter reached for her hand. She pulled it back.

Oh God, what could she do? She couldn't just walk out because she couldn't avoid Delores and she'd have to have a reason why she was here and what could she say—I've been screwing a college teacher from Theil?

And she couldn't get up to go to the restroom or something because maybe Delores hadn't seen her yet and her just standing up would catch Delores's eye. And oh God, what if Delores came in and actually saw that she was sitting with an ungodly handsome man who was not her husband and that could only mean one thing?

Mattie didn't dare look out the window any longer and she couldn't look Hunter in the face, so she just looked down at her water glass. For the longest time she was silent and she could feel Hunter getting more and more uncomfortable and it came into her mind that this was something his Southern manners weren't going to be able to make feel right. And then she thought of Chuck and that night he came out of the stands because she burned her hand and didn't care what anybody thought. The chance that Chuck was going to find out about Hunter was what had her so worked up. On scale, as wonderful as Hunter was, he wasn't Chuck. He probably didn't even know what a majorette was.

When she looked up, Delores was gone. She stared Hunter straight in the eye, told him she couldn't do this anymore, got up, and walked right out of Paxton's without even saying goodbye. Hunter got a look on his face a lot like the one that Jesus must have had when God told him in the Garden of Gethsemane that he was sorry but he'd considered his petition and decided it was best for everybody all the way around if they just went ahead with the crucifixion in the morning like they'd planned.

Mattie's mind raced all the way home, permutations within permutations of desperate plans, mostly really, really bad ideas, like converting to Catholicism and becoming a nun so she could escape to a convent in Brazil. When she passed the gas station where she and Hunter had taken the tire, she said, "Oh shit!" And when she passed the restaurant where they'd had lunch while they waited for the tire, she said, "Oh shit. Oh Shit." And when she drove around the courthouse square to get to the Grove City Road and saw where she'd actually had the flat, she said, "Oh shit, shit, shit, shit, shit, *shit, shit, shit, shit, shit!!!!*" And saying the word so many times in a row like a set of tally marks prompted the thought that she and Chuck hadn't gotten to the goal of nineteen ejaculations and that maybe she could worm her way out of this yet. When she got home, she went straight upstairs and counted the number of condoms in Chuck's sock drawer. Seven. Yes, she could make this work.

"Question for discussion": *What book of poetry had Hunter bought to give Mattie?*

Advanced "Question for discussion": *How had Hunter inscribed his gift?*

Chapter 22
Chuck Passes with Flying Colors

[Wherein Chuck suffers through producing his
semen specimen, soldiering bravely on in spite
of that mean army nurse's best efforts to stifle
said production, and wherein Mattie very
sweetly deceives Chuck, thereby precipitating a
series of events which in due course result in
the couple's much more real crisis and climax.]

On a warm evening toward the end of September and with a
not unimpressive application of resourcefulness, Chuck had
attained the combined ejaculation count of zero-to-go. The
next afternoon he called the doctor's office to make an
appointment for his test, which they set for the afternoon after
that. And of course when he went in, that army nurse was on
duty and she had to roll her eyes in disgust when she handed
him the jar and pointed to the men's room and told him to be
sure and take his time so there was enough to get a good
sperm count and she said that in a rising volume so that
"sperm count" came out loud enough that everybody in the
whole waiting room could hear it. Chuck reddened a little bit,
but wouldn't give her the satisfaction of turning around and
letting her know she got to him. He muttered, "Witch" under
his breath but not really. He actually just said it in his head
because he was just as afraid of her as any of the rest of us
would be and who knows what she could come up with when
she was actually pissed off? (As in: "Witch, huh!?!? I'll show
you witch!" And then look out!)

This time was a little trickier than when he and Hank gave their first samples on account of Chuck didn't have Hank there to stand guard outside in the hall. He'd just have to go into a stall and close the door and hope for the best. But he'd thought the mechanics of the chore all the way through ahead of time. Unscrewing the lid from the specimen jar, he set it on the back of the toilet, then turned around and dropped his pants clear down to his ankles so that if anybody looked under the door they would think he was just sitting there doing his business.

Normally you would face the toilet so that any semen waywardly flung would be more likely to land in the water, though of course not a guarantee. (For you women who are wondering about the authenticity of all this: Imagine that you have been stroking your member and of course that gets it moving in space in various and erratic ways because it's not actually *inside* anything which would govern it and then it gets worse because the closer you get to liftoff the faster go the strokes and then you are supposed to get all that *stuff* into a tiny little specimen jar. Male masturbation is nowhere as easy as you might think it would be. It takes years and years of dedicated practice to get really good at.)

He began by tickling his scrotum to get things started and then lightly brushing Old Mr. Johnson as he got hard enough (and fantasizing about Mattie naked on the bed to move things along because his desire for her was true and had been ever since that first handjob in the car after the Oil City game and in spite of the day-to-day boredom that had set in and their little skirmishes, which really weren't that many, thinking about her naked was the most arousing thing for him, even more than imagining every majorette who ever lived out on a football field twirling their batons and bouncing while wearing only their plumed hats and white boots).

But wouldn't you know it, just as he was finding his rhythm some guy came in and took the stall next to him. And of course the guy was wheezing like a leaky bagpipe (it was a hospital for crying out loud and the man was no doubt sick, but it was still distracting as all get out, even if Chuck could have mustered at least a little sympathy for the poor old guy) and it took the man forever to unbuckle his pants and work his way down onto the seat.

Now it is a fact of life that when you got two men each trying to take a dump next to each other in a public toilet, both are wishing to high heaven the other one would just *get done* so they could relax because they don't want the other one to hear them fart and grunt and the water going splash. (One of the most melodious sounds in the world is another man beside you in a public toilet spinning the toilet paper roll.)

By the way: This does not obtain in a truck stop men's room. Those places are like the ape cage in a zoo—nobody cares about anything. One of these days I'm going to take an audio recording of all that groaning and cursing and flatulence and work it into some piece of conceptual art. Maybe make recordings in truck stop men's rooms all across the country and turn it into a series, *Truck Stop Shitters*. (I wonder if that would necessitate consent forms. Or is there no reasonable expectation of privacy in a public toilet, thus rendering all such sounds open source? Maybe if the restroom is gender neutral? [But it's very unlikely that would ever happen in a good old American truck stop.] Plus claiming open-source prerogatives probably wouldn't be an effective defense if some sleep-deprived driver figured out what you were doing and busted out of his stall with his pants down around his knees, grabbed you by the front of your shirt, and knocked the smart aleck right off your face. You could scream all you want that this being America, the land of free expression, you had every right to record the moving of his no doubt mammoth and utterly manly bowels, but you would still end up slapped into a week from Tuesday.)

Anyway, back to Chuck trying to elicit his semen sample when there is an ailing old man in the next stall: Alas, Chuck lost his erection. There weren't a lot of choices here. One of the things you can do in a situation like this (meaning you can't do your business because there's somebody next to you and that's what Chuck was pretending to be doing) is roll off some paper, make like you're wiping yourself, throw the paper in the toilet, flush, pull up your pants, and go out and wash your hands, and then after all that, exit the toilet altogether and wait for the other guy to come out so you can go back in and finish in peace. But not an option for Chuck, because of old nurse Battle Axe out there, not to mention all of the people in the waiting room who *knew*. Another ploy is that you flush the toilet like you are just doing a courtesy flush with the hopes that the other guy will subconsciously hear it as covering sound and relax enough to let go (or your own body's own autonomic nervous system will itself be tricked into blessed relief—which wouldn't help Chuck at all because relaxing your sphincter all of a sudden and guiding yourself through the stages of sexual arousal and response are completely different animals). Which left Chuck with the only other option left—wait the guy out.

Finally the old geezer gave up and left and Chuck started all over again. He was doing pretty well, getting himself to the place where you know you are going to make it and you're starting to get a little hurried and are smack dab in the deep-in-the-breathing department, but not quite yet to the point of no return, when somebody else comes in to use the urinal. Which isn't quite as bad, because pissing won't take that long, unless it's some old guy with a bad prostate or a young man who whizzes quick enough but decides that this being a private enough place, decides to pop a few pimples while he has the mirror to himself. Chuck handled this by not stopping altogether but by slowing down the strokes so as not to make any noise audible outside the stall and forcing himself to breathe as naturally as he could, which had the counteracting effect of heightening his internal arousal in much the same way as slow and sensual lovemaking can drive you more out of your mind than primitive pounding (one of the great mysteries of human life), making it harder and harder to keep the noise down.

But then, Oh my god!, it started. Not the big if-you-were-thrusting-you'd-have-to-just-about-scream kind of orgasm, but that little creeping kind where you think you might be able to hold it back, but no way in hell, and Old Mr. Johnson started contracting, just enough so ejaculate was seeping out, kind of like the little guy was vomiting into his throat, and Chuck realized that he was still facing out like he was taking a dump and the specimen jar was still on the back of the toilet.

"Shit!" he said and then stifled it back because zit boy was still out there. He clenched up his perineum as hard as he could (as if the same muscles that control bladder release are the same ones that control orgasm, which isn't even possible, and had the result of making things worse). He spun around with his thing still in his hand.

By the way: Concerning the word *thing* here. Why can't there be a Goldilocks word between *penis* and *cock* that you could just use in passages like this? Nobody ever worries about finding a middle-of-the-road synonym for *elbow* or *ankle*. No wonder the whole human race is so neurotic, what with having to choose between clinical and vulgar all the time.

Anyway: Chuck grabbed the jar and got it under his dick, the little bit of semen dribbling forth sort of oozing down the inside of the glass, more like his wang was weeping rather than gushing in the fullness of its vitality. (Men will understand, but women may not, that that kind of tepid release can go one of two ways. It can either keep on weeping until the full load is emptied out [but with a minimum of ecstasy], or it can kind of clam up and figure it'll just hold off until the next time, which may sound good in theory, but until that next time, the body to which the member is attached will feel desperately horny. The best thing to do to avoid said horniness is to go at it real fast right away and with barbaric enthusiasm so that with luck, said member will relinquish its reluctance and send forth the full abundance called for in Genesis 1:28.) So Chuck went at it with a vengeance (thinking discovery was at this point worth the risk—but he kept his teeth clenched to cut back on the growling), with so much vigor that a lot of what was supposed to make it into the jar didn't (also partly because he was having trouble keeping his eyes open), but enough (he hoped).

The next thing you know, Chuck is standing at the nurse's desk and the nurse is nodding toward the counter because she will be damned if she is going to take a chance on touching his hand by taking the jar from him. As it was, she wouldn't even pick up the jar right away. "Did you wipe this off before you brought it out?" she asked (again a lot louder than she had to).

Chuck nodded.

"Did you wash your hands?" (There was an implied "You disgusting *fuck*!" somewhere in the question.) To which Chuck didn't say anything, not one single word and he didn't nod neither, but was getting that look on his face that reminded the nurse that there's only so far you can push a person and they are going to push back and since she figured that anyone crazy enough to put up with as much humiliation as a vasectomy eventuated (not to mention the brutal discomfort) might just be on the edge of don't-give-a-damn, so she didn't ask again. She just told him he could call tomorrow for the results. (But she did grab a tissue and put it between her persnickety virginal fingers and that filthy jar when she took it from the counter.)

On the drive home, Chuck just kept thinking about how good it was going to be without a rubber, warm and slippery and soft, and Mattie pliant and yielding like when they were still in high school. Just thinking about her like that started getting him stiff again, and he just let it. He didn't touch himself or anything, just let himself feel the sensuous union he was having with the universe as he and it melded into blissful suchness (he didn't think that of course, him being a machinist and all—but he did let himself relax and enjoy the moment). And it wasn't going to be all that long before he could be with Mattie sans rubber because they'd been using the last ones up quicker than he'd thought they would. Over the last couple of weeks, Mattie had been puzzlingly amorous and had initiated their doing it more than once and not said no when he did. Strange. But Chuck wasn't about to look a gift horse in the mouth. He'd take it. The next afternoon he called the doctor and *Praise God Almighty, free at last!* Sperm count: 0!

Chapter 23
Mattie Has an Idea

[Wherein Mattie shifts her plan into high gear
(that little fox).]

On the Saturday after Chuck tested clean (*Praise the Lord!*), he and Mattie went through their usual Saturday night date thing, except she was already naked when he got into bed and smiling, and as easy as she was to look at just naked, she was *real* easy to look at when she was naked and smiling. Chuck went through the motions with the condom (because he couldn't tell her he was clean because of all the solos) and while he was rolling it down over his manhood, she murmured how nice it was going to be when they didn't have to use them anymore. Holy cow! What was getting into this woman?

And then the next night, just after 3:00 in the morning (he knew because he looked at the clock with its radium-painted hands and numerals), he felt her climbing up on top of him, naked again. She kissed his neck and slid slowly down his body, her inner thighs embracing his outer ones, kissing and breathing on his chest and all the way to his naval, her breasts feathering him the length of his torso until they ever so lightly grazed him where it really counted and reached in to fondle his peepee and man, did the little guy ever respond (and Chuck's heart too—which sped up like he was back at football practice and had just done five sets of wind sprints). Chuck was about to ease her to the side so he could get the next rubber but right in that moment it seemed like a really inconsiderate and insensitive thing to do, and what the hell, they didn't need it anyway—it would have only been to keep up appearances—and she'd think they'd just been lucky when nothing came of it. So he didn't. Mattie stood up straight on her knees and spit in her hand and rubbed the wet on him and straddled him at the exact right spot and slid down on him. And, Oh, it was sweet! So very, very sweet.

The next morning Mattie made a change, which on the surface might not seem like that much of an adjustment, but given how rigid the morning schedule always was, was actually kind of a big deal: She didn't put on a house dress until after Chuck left for work. She made his breakfast still in her nighty, not even with a robe over it. And not one of her faded, flannel nighties either. She had on the shiny beige rayon nighty she saved for Valentine's and their anniversary. Of course, when Chuck came down for his breakfast, he couldn't help but notice and he couldn't help but think about how so, so sweet last night had been, but given how much of a morning person he was, he didn't say anything. However, he did rush through that first cup of coffee and as Mattie refilled his cup said, "You look real good in that, you know." Which, for Chuck, may as well have been him having a whole semi load of American Beauty roses and orchids from Kocher's delivered to the house and a string quartet outside playing Italian opera music and a singer right under their bedroom window serenading Mattie like she was the Princess of Norway.

Mattie was all set with her answer: "I wanted last night to last a little bit longer." Which, like Chuck's flowers and music, may have well been, "As soon as the kids are out of the house, I am going to slap myself down naked on this table and fuck your brains out and I am going to keep on doing it until they get home or you pass out, whichever comes first."

Almost anyway.

They looked at each other for not quite a minute and then went back to looking at their coffee. Chuck leaned back in his chair and stretched his arms, the signal that he was going to say, as he did every morning, "I better get moving if I want to be on time." Mattie had been watching for it, and when he took in that deep breath which was the real signal he was going to say that thing about getting moving, she jumped in before he had the chance and said, "I been thinking." Not only did Chuck not take that deep breath, he didn't take in any breath at all, because, as every married man knows, when his wife says that she's been thinking, the odds of him saying something anywhere close to right the next time he opens his mouth are about as close to zero as they can be and still be called odds.

"Uh huh," was all Chuck said.

"I'd forgotten how nice it is without the rubber. Maybe we should hurry up and see how quick we can use up the rest of the box so we can have it like that all the time."

Oh my, thought Chuck, oblivious to the alarm bells that were clamorously tolling, tolling, tolling all around him. Oblivious even to the diminutive silver bell daintily tinkling right beside his coffee cup.

Chapter 24
A Bump in the Road

[Wherein Hank and Delores's transactional
relationship finally throws up its hands and
gives in to the inevitable.]

When there was just one more un-smitten heart on Hank's
card, Delores said why didn't he make an appointment to get
tested tomorrow and they make a special night of it, maybe
throw in an extra one for good measure? Hank said it sounded
good to him, so he made the appointment and they had their
night.

They both got kind of silly and worked into the
foreplay as much of what they had learned in the months
they'd been together as they could and took their time, this
being the grand finale before Delores moved back out to her
dad's trailer, and who knew when they would have another
chance? Delores even tried to put the condom on with her
mouth when they were both breathing real, real hard and so
ready to go that they couldn't wait anymore, which maybe
looks easy in erotic movies but if you think about it, there has
to be some kind of trick to it, because: Seriously?

Hank went down to the hospital after work the next
day and of course he gets the same army nurse and she does
the same thing she did with Chuck, trying to get him all
embarrassed, so with any luck at all the young man wouldn't
be able to do it and she could have another crack at him the
next day. But Hank held his ground and almost said one of
the couple of retorts he had rehearsed for her, different retorts
for different snippy things she might say. Like if she said to

take his time, he'd say, "No problem, I'll just imagine being in bed with you, which means I'll have to work it extra just to get hard." And if she said, like she did the first time, to make sure he got enough in the jar, he'd say, "What? You hungry?" But he didn't. It would have been just plain mean and even if she was mean herself, he didn't have to be. As it turned out, he didn't even remember what she said. He just went in and teased out the sample, not having to deal with any awkwardness there might have been if somebody else came in like Chuck had to deal with, because nobody did.

He tried to make it just a medical and mechanical thing, but he couldn't because he kept thinking about how much he was going to miss Delores, and that made her the only thing he could think about, but not naked in bed or anything—just the two of them out on the porch on Sunday mornings with the paper and going out to Rudy's on Fridays for supper and driving to the park in the evenings to feed the deer. But to be honest about it, maybe he didn't think about her being naked, but he did imagine her swaying up the stairs in that way she had where all her parts just seemed to know how to show each other off, which no matter how many times she'd climbed those stairs, still made him turn his head to watch.

The next day Delores was already in the house when Hank came home from work. "This is the big day," she said and Hank said he guessed it was. She thought he would make the call right away because that had been the whole point all along but he dawdled. Being it was a Friday, he took his work clothes down to the cellar and put them by the washing machine. He went to the bathroom and asked what she wanted to do for supper. Maybe they could go out to eat. And lots of other little things like that until Delores finally said, "You want me to call them?" (Which she couldn't do, because doing that is not anywhere in the point of this narrative, but it would have been a really interesting passage to write, what with all the potential for asides it would have—especially if that army nurse answered the phone.)

Hank said he knew he was just putting it off and went over to the phone and picked it up and waited for the operator. He gave her the number and pretty soon Delores heard him say could he speak to his doctor's office and then it was a couple more minutes and Hank gave his name and then there were a couple more minutes before Hank said, "Okay. Thanks."

As soon as Hank hung up the phone, Delores could tell he'd failed. He didn't even have to tell her. "Oh, Hank," she said. Hank didn't know what to say so Delores said, "What's next?"

"They said I have to go ten more times and then go back for another test." For a minute, he looked like his dog just died. But only for a minute. He brightened up right away and said, "What the heck, let's get dressed up and go over to Sharon and find a fancy place to eat."

"Sure, but there's something I got to do first."

Hank thought whatever it was she wanted to do had to do with her moving out, maybe packing her lady things that she didn't want him to see or calling her dad. He thought he'd give her a little privacy, so he said, "Sure, we got lots of time. I'll just go up and change clothes."

"I'll be right up."

When she came into the bedroom, he hugged her and gave her a nice little kiss and said she did know how much he appreciated her being here and she said she did. She almost said she would have done it for free just to be cute, but it wouldn't have been funny at all—it would have just ruined things—you have to see your tender moments when they come and you have to savor them—because there will come a day when there won't be any left and you will be godawful sorry for any that you messed up.

Hank said he was going to go wait for her in the kitchen and take her time. There on the kitchen table, right at his place, was the card he'd given her the first day—with ten more hearts drawn on it and a long string of brand new x's and o's all along the bottom.

Chapter 25
What They Talked About Without
Talking About What They Talked About

[Wherein Chuck and Mattie demonstrate an
intriguing form of narrative that could
reasonably be termed *performative deception* by
continuing to try to get each other to believe
something that isn't true through elaborate
dramatic fictions, acting out lies without
actually *telling* any (except for one single
pronoun, which is pretty amazing technique on
my part when you think about it).]

Mattie waited until Chuck was just about finished with his second cup of morning coffee before she said (with an enigmatic little smile), "Guess what."

Chuck looked at her across the top of his cup and was about to say something snarky because on this particular morning it was taking him a little bit longer than usual to stagger his slow-waking self to civil. But then he remembered how amorous Mattie had been these last couple of weeks and said (which he tried to do real nice, and you got to give him credit, he got pretty close), "What?"

Again with the smile, but this time trying to make it a little naughty, Mattie said, "We're down to the last condom," which got Chuck's attention, both because it meant they could start doing it skin to skin and also because he could finally drop the charade about not having had nineteen ejaculations when he really did.

Mattie went on. "How about I call the hospital and make an appointment for you to get your test tomorrow after work and we use it up tonight?"

Uh oh, thought Chuck, and then he thought real fast about how to handle this, which was taxing, him being a machinist and all and used to being methodical (which does not mean dumb or slow—it just means methodical) about absolutely *everything* like we learned back in Chapter 7. It took him a second to think of something and that second actually worked out because he got a little red in the face being scared to death that Mattie might figure out about his solos, but which Mattie just thought was hesitancy over getting tested, which she couldn't even begin to imagine how embarrassing that had to be. He said, "I think I'd rather make the appointment myself. I'll call them during my dinner break."

"Okay," Mattie said. "But make sure you do. I'm as anxious as you are to get there." He gave her a look that she took to mean, "No damn way you are that anxious," but actually indicated relief on Chuck's part.

All the way to work, Chuck worried over in his head how he was going to pull this off. There were so many places where he could make a mistake and get found out. Like what if she told one of her friends (which she would never do, but what if she did?) and that woman's husband worked in the machine shop and took that day to tell her something funny somebody said during dinner break and you should have seen old Chuck McAllister laughing his butt off. Or what if somebody they knew was also getting a test tomorrow and Mattie said they must have run into Chuck and when they said they didn't see him, she would get suspicious. Even with all the possible things that could go wrong, Chuck had had enough practice lately in plotting out devious solutions that by the time he got to work, he'd come up with a pretty elegant plan.

He'd drive the few blocks to work so he could have the car to go down and get the test. During dinner break, he'd go out to the guard shack where there was a pay phone. He'd put a nickel in and pretend to dial the hospital, but would really be calling the number for the correct time and he would talk to it.

This is not as weird as it might sound, because back then, there were people who would call the time and later on the weather when the phone company started that service because they were lonely, not because they didn't know what time it was or were trying to figure out what to wear tomorrow. Later on, when long distance information was free, lonesome people would call information in some place like Hawaii and ask for the number of the Howard Johnson's and the operator would ask which one and they would say something like, "The one closest to the airport," and she would give them the number and they would tell her how much they appreciated her help and that very brief conversation with a stranger would, if they were lonely enough, be a little bit of a comfort and respite from the loneliness. I don't think Chuck would have done that, but you don't have to be lonely to pretend to be talking to somebody. Embarrassment over his masturbation secret would have done it for Chuck. All he had to do was imagine Mattie's disgusted (and disappointed) look if she found out.

After work Chuck would drive down street and look to see where the Broad Street cop was and find a nearby meter with no time on it and park there but not put any money in and that way he would get a ticket and that would be proof positive that he'd been down street. He would "forget" to pay it and take the ticket in the house and tell Mattie he didn't see it until he was halfway home and he would pay it the next day on his way to work. (Back then, the parking fine was only fifty cents. The ticket was actually a little yellow envelope with the date and time and meter number and cop's signature. You'd put a half dollar in, seal it, and drop it in a box at the end of the street. The police didn't even keep a separate copy—it was crime and punishment on the honor system.)

He'd get out of his car and walk to the hospital and go to the lab and hope that the army nurse wasn't there (this was the one hole in his plan—because if she was and given her winning personality, likely to decide she had it in for him—oh my God!). He'd go in and use the men's room and he'd stay in there a good long while and when he came out, he would kind of slink back out into the hall like he really was sheepish and nonplussed and if anybody asked, he could say the test was private and he didn't want to talk about it and who cared if they started a rumor?—it would just make the whole thing more believable to Mattie if it managed to get back to her.

So he made the fake call, put in the rest of his day's work, and went home where Mattie was waiting in her slinky beige nightie and had his favorite supper braising in the oven. She gave him a real passionate kiss when he came in the kitchen and told him the girls were at her mother's for the night so they could have the house to themselves for later on and her mother would make sure they got off to school in the morning and could he smell the pie she baked that afternoon? She said why didn't he go upstairs and take a nap and she would call him when supper was ready. Chuck said okay and it was nice of her to make the pie, but on his way upstairs, all he could think was, This is weird. He lay down and did fall right to sleep, but he couldn't enjoy it because he had that dream where you're in school and have to take an important test that is all that's standing between you and graduation but you forgot the room number (except for Chuck it was a dream where he had to machine a part which was critical to an engine that would save the world from imminent catastrophe and he had lost the work order with the machine sequence on it and was going to have to guess).

He awoke to Mattie kneading his shoulders, which did feel awful good, and her saying supper was ready. She had her leg under her butt where she was sitting on the edge of the bed and when she got up, the nightgown hung up on her hip for a second so Chuck got a good look at her legs and what was between them and it doesn't matter how many times you've seen it, when it flashes sudden like that, it always gives you that special tingle and he forgot about weird and thought about *later*.

Mattie had put a tablecloth on the table and lit candles and Chuck had to admit that supper with all those little touches was nice. Mattie had things to say about the weather and gossip she heard and cute things the girls said at breakfast. When they finished eating, she said she was going to just let the dishes go until morning and why didn't they go in and watch some television. "A little, but not too much, if you get my drift," which Chuck did get and part of him was wondering if there was a way to skip the television altogether, but why take the chance? Just let things take their course. Which they did (and not to give it short shrift, but that course ended in a hell of a tumble, even with the last condom) and then it was the next morning when Mattie once again waited for Chuck to get into that second cup of coffee before telling him she had an idea. (Which made Chuck hold his breath again, because when your wife says she has an idea, God knows what you are in for. It's even worse than when she says she's been thinking. The best thing is to not say a word, except maybe, What is it?, but even that is risky because you might not get the tone of voice just right and being off even slightly can lead to catastrophic consequences. Chuck just smiled, but only a little bit so Mattie wouldn't think he was patronizing her.)

"If your test comes back that you're sterile, how about we ask Mom to watch the kids again this weekend and we go up to Conneaut Lake and rent a cabin? There'll be plenty vacant what with it being out of season and all. And cheap too."

Chuck held back a wince, not because of the idea, but because of the word sterile, which had a kind of pejorative ring to it.

"C'mon," Mattie said (thinking Chuck was being stingy and leaning over so her breasts showed). "Just imagine how much fun we'll have." And Chuck said Yes.

So Chuck went through his little song and dance at the hospital the next day (fortunately the army nurse was not there—all that worry for nothing and isn't that almost always the case when something's just hanging out there and you are a nervous wreck over it?—and Chuck getting more relaxed at every step when it didn't end in the apocalypse). He made another faux phone call for the results the day after that, and when he told Mattie his sperm count was zero and they were good to go, she actually said, "Yippee!"

And so they had their weekend at Conneaut Lake, most of which they spent in the cabin, pretty much only going out to eat and that one time late Saturday night when they went down to the water when no one was around and did it on a picnic table (but not naked just in case, Chuck with his pants down just enough and Mattie with her skirt hiked up just enough too), which was about as wild as they had got since high school. Altogether they did it eight times from Friday night to Sunday afternoon, the last time standing up against the kitchen table. All eight times were so very, very sweet because they were really touching, not guessing at touching through a film of latex. Both nights Chuck pretended to fall asleep right away, but was really only waiting for Mattie to go to sleep herself because he wanted to watch her for a little while before he drifted off, not wondering why, after seven years of marriage, he would still want to do that.

Mattie wanted to stop for supper on the way home (to make the weekend last a little bit longer she'd said) and what could Chuck say? Even dizzy as he was from the weekend trysts, he was clearheaded enough to realize that this was maybe something he could keep going after they got home—at least for a little bit longer—and that was sure worth the price and extra time of a restaurant. They came up on a rustic, roadside diner, announced on a peeling old sign as Mom's Place. They had open-faced sandwiches—Mattie got turkey and a ginger ale and Chuck meatloaf and a root beer. Mattie sighed and said that being at the cabin was really nice, wasn't it and Chuck said back that nice didn't even begin to describe it and they should do it again sometime. Mattie said she would like that.

And *then*:

Mattie got a real serious look on her face and smiled at the same time (a special trick all women know) and took Chuck's hand in both of hers and said, "I have some news and I hope you like it."

Oh shit, Chuck thought as he felt his balls sucking up almost to his chest, because every married man (and a lot who are almost married and have already begun to make dumb mistakes) knows two things for absolute sure when he hears his wife (or almost wife) tell him that she has news that she hopes he will like: 1) He is so not going to like it, and 2) He has to do whatever it takes to make her think he does. (It's even worse than when she says she has an idea or been thinking. Talk about orders of magnitude!)

So Chuck put on the most nondescript face he could muster and said as softly and as tenderly as possible given that, in that moment, breathing itself was a serious problem, "You know I'll like it. [....] Tell me." (He knew he paused just a little too long before "Tell me," but maybe she wouldn't notice.)

Mattie gave his hand a gentle little squeeze and said, "We're going to have another baby." (This is the verbal part of Mattie's lie, and contains its one flaw. If she'd said, "*I'm* going to have a baby," then the integrity of her performance would have remained intact. But genuine duplicity is really, really hard, so we can forgive her this one little slip.)

Oh *shit*.

There followed an indeterminate space of time during which Chuck went in and out of consciousness but with his eyes open, somehow remembering to hold on to his inscrutable expression but tempering it with a slight smile now and again, and Mattie just going on and on about how excited she was and how nice it would be to have a tiny baby to take care of again and it must have been that time they did it in the middle of the night and she really did mean to get up for a condom, but she didn't know what came over her. Then she said she did know what came over her: She was just so worked up with the romance of it all that she didn't want to wait even one more second.

The whole time she was talking, Chuck was doing calculations in his head. Mattie must have had somebody over while he was at work and who not only did it in his own house and bed, but *used his own rubbers, for Christ's sake*. At least once anyway. That was why the count seemed off when he put together his plan for counting out the nineteen. It really was off, and that dark look Mattie got for a second when he told her about how he was going to keep track wasn't his imagination—there was a damn good reason for it. Also, when he remembered the nineteen, he thought, Damn, I should have counted that unprotected night and I would have got to the pretend-count, zero-to-go one round quicker. Also, a weird part of him was relieved that the extra miles he'd seen on the car's odometer hadn't been his imagination either.

Mattie finally said, "If it's a boy, we'll name him Charles, Jr., of course, but if it's another girl, would you be okay with naming her Blessing?"

Chuck came to. "Blessing?"

"It would be kind of a spiritual name, like Joy or Grace or Harmony, and to remind us of how lucky we'll be to have her."

Chuck looked down to Mattie holding his hands and saw the scar she got when he raced out on the football field to take care of her and remembered the bandage and them in the car when he kissed her hand so gentle and what it led to. And then he wasn't mad or hurt—he was scared, scared that he was going to lose her to somebody else, which would have been worse than having to tell her about his jacking off to get to the nineteen quicker. And that all by itself would have been harder than telling her he knew he wasn't the baby's father. Oh boy.

"Blessing's perfect," he said.

Chapter 26
Chuck and Hank Share News

[Wherein Chuck and Hank bring each other up
to date, but leave a lot out of the stories. Don't
worry that you might miss something
important because they are so hesitant to share
intimate details. I've filled all that in for them,
either here or in a previous chapter.]

"Who'd a thought?" said Chuck as the label fell from the neck
of his Carling Black Label.

"Who'd a thought, is right," said Hank.

"Would you do it again?"

"[…] Yeah, I would."

The two friends nursed their beers and communed in
silence, coincidentally emptying their bottles at the exact same
time and setting them down with the half-hearted finality that
comes from many, many rehearsals. Hank motioned to the
bartender that they'd have another round and said
offhandedly, "Me and Dee's getting married."

"Holy Christ!" said Chuck.

"Me and Dee's getting married," was all Hank said, thereby
avoiding telling his friend about the sappy exchange he and
Delores had that led to the decision and also avoiding some
good natured ball busting from Chuck, which even if it is good
natured, you don't necessarily want to deal with right in this
particular second.

Here's what happened.

After Hank's next ten ejaculations (among which were some rather creative ways of achieving same), he tested clean (which makes sperm sound like a disease, but clean also implies a desired outcome, so you know what I mean). At supper the next day Delores was toying with the card with the twenty-nine hearts and arrows and Hank was watching her doing it. He said he guessed she would be moving back with her dad and she said she guessed so. Hank was thinking how weird it was that he wasn't suggesting that they do it one last time before she left, but instead was thinking about how much he was going to miss Sunday mornings and supper at Rudy's and going to the drive-in to actually watch the movies. And laughing when Delores came up with one of her ribald comebacks right out of nowhere. And the delicate way she held her coffee cup. And the way she hummed in the bathroom. Once he got started thinking about all those things, he just kept going. In his head he went on and on and on about how nice just being with her was, and when he did think of their being together in bed, it was with her asleep with her cheek on his chest and her warm breath on his skin and how thinking about that didn't even give him a hard-on. And that was worth a lot more than the measly four hundred dollars it took for him to figure that out.

Delores felt him looking at her and she felt something else which was the familiar tingle, but instead of down there, felt it all over, in her chest and shoulders and face and especially in her arms, which she wanted to wrap around him and cling to him like a little girl in love with her daddy. She felt him thinking all those thoughts about her, without actually knowing what they were exactly, but knowing in a general way that they were real nice.

After a good long time she said, "You know, we could make this permanent."

Hank said, "We could, but if you think we got neighbor trouble now, can you imagine what it would be like if we was going on year after year?"

"Not if we was married."

Hank almost got that thing where his balls were being sucked up into his stomach, but his natural aversion to matrimony got waylaid by his millwright nature to look for a solution and in less time than it took for his balls to get a decent start, decided that being married to Delores would be about the best thing that ever happened to him. But he had to keep up appearances, so....

"You got it backwards, don't you. I'm supposed to be the one to ask you."

"So ask."

"[...] How about I just say Yes?"

Then they got up and kissed and hugged and laughed a little bit and then did it right there on the table, except it wasn't all raw id but was mostly nice and sweet and lovingly tender (though there was just enough id that by the time they got to the moment of penetration, they were both quivering and breathing like monsters in a horror show and Delores actually hissed out, "Fuck me!" because Hank seemed to be taking just a tad too long to get to that moment—and without a rubber, it was Wow! Also, Delores's breathless "Fuck me" was all Hank needed to assuage any vestige of doubt he harbored about whether he'd made a good decision).

The first thing Delores did after they sketched out some tentative plans was go out and tell her dad who said, "You went and got yourself knocked up, didn't you? I told you to be careful."

"Jeez, Dad, no. It's for love."

"You sure?"

"Of course I'm sure. Wouldn't do any good to try and hide it if I was knocked up."

"Well then."

Delores said the wedding was going to be at Hank's house and she wanted him to give her away and did he have a suit he could wear?

"Do I have a suit? You just wait and see!"

Then he got up out of his easy chair and hugged his daughter, just hugged her and hugged her and hugged her like he was going to hold onto her forever, which I can't even begin to tell you how out of character that was for him, and after all that, he gave her a sweet little kiss on her forehead, which was even more out of character.

Okay, back to our friends at the Rusty Bolt.

Hank said he was wondering if maybe Chuck would be his best man and Chuck said, "I'd be honored." Which is something you should know by now is never anything Chuck would think to say on his own, but he'd heard it in movies (especially war movies) when one character asked another character to be his best man, which meant "I'd be honored" had to be the thing you should say in a situation like that.

The beers came and Chuck said, "This one's on me" (which is another thing they said in the movies after somebody asked you to be their best man). They clinked bottles and took a swig.

Then Chuck said (his face getting just a little dark and his feeling a little guilty about what he was going to say because of this being a celebration and all on account of Hank's terrific news), "I got some news too—Mattie's pregnant."

"Holy Christ!" said Hank.

Another moment of silence as the two friends contemplated the momentous pregnancy (so to speak) of what had just been said.

"You mess up?" Hank asked.

"No. I got tested clean."

????

"But Mattie didn't know it."

????

Chuck glanced over to the bartender to be sure he wasn't looking their way and then under the bar made the universal jacking off gesture.

????

So Chuck explained (with more than a trace of embarrassment) about the two counts, one with just the rubbers, which was the count Mattie thought was the real count, and the *real* real count that included the nuts and bolts out in the garage and the night Mattie came on to him and they did it without a rubber and what he suspected happened. (Don't forget that Chuck and Hank could have this kind of intimate conversation on account of they'd played football together. Also, since Chuck was going to be Hank's best man, they were now connected on some deeper plane, rather like blood brothers. Also also, even though it was embarrassing for Chuck, he knew he could trust Hank not to say nothing to nobody about him jacking off—which was real, real important.)

Hank tried to comfort his friend: "Oh shit." Which didn't really help, so he tried again: "Maybe it is yours. Rubbers aren't a hundred percent." Which didn't help either.

One more time: "We should get as drunk as we can."

And so they did. Which helped a lot.

Chapter 27
The Wedding

[Wherein we learn about ham loaf and deer
rifles as events continue their suspenseful crawl
toward the climax, but with growing
momentum. Plus everybody is dressed up,
which in Western, PA, in 1954 was almost as
good as a county fair sideshow.]

Hank and Delores set their wedding date for a Saturday in late March. They neither one wanted anything fancy. They'd have it at Hank's house, which would be a little strained given all the guests they expected, even if they were only inviting family, close friends, and a few co-workers. The co-workers part is always tricky because somebody's feelings are for sure going to be bruised given that you can't invite everybody from work—in Hank's case, he would have to have extended invitations to over a thousand men, because once you invite somebody from your own department, then there will be workers that that man knows who will feel slighted if you don't ask them and then if you invite them, you have to invite the workers *they* know, even if they are barely acquaintances of yours, etc., etc., etc. Plus Delores would face the same kind of tricky etiquette situations on her side because of her having been at the diner since high school and all the people she knew out in Number Five. Plus some people would just show up— you could count on that—neighbors passing by and probably the lowlifes who pranked Hank's mailbox, just out of a perverted kind of curiosity (hoping maybe some of the women would strip naked and run through the woods brandishing torches high above their heads in homage to Baal and thereby validate all of their self-righteousness—and also when they found out there wasn't a preacher, would get their noses all up in the air because a wedding is supposed to be something sacred on account of its being holy matrimony and all).

After talking it over, the lovers decided they'd just invite all the people they *wanted* to invite and ignore the ones they *should* invite, and anybody who got their nose out of joint, got their nose out of joint. But it was still going to be a lot of people and there wouldn't be enough chairs for everyone to sit on. So they borrowed a couple of truckloads of folding chairs from a local Grange and stacked them up in the barn until the day before the ceremony. They had to borrow the truck to carry them in too. You'd think that Hank would own a truck (on account of how he has here within been characterized), but he didn't, and I realize that this may be late in the game to point this out, but have I even once suggested that Hank owned a truck?

About a week before the big day, Hank and Delores stood in the open barn door with their arms around each other's waists and studied the stack and said there was no way it was going to work—no way all those chairs would fit in the living room. Hank said maybe if half the people sat on somebody's lap. They went through all the possibilities of who could sit with whom (like Delores's dad sitting on Hank's cousin's lap or Big Fred sitting on Aunt Martha), which got them laughing so hard, they forgot they had a big problem, which turned out not to be a problem at all because a couple of days before the wedding, the weather turned warm, with the prediction being for unseasonably mild temperatures and clear skies all through the weekend and they decided to have it outside. Which made things a little frantic because they had to rush around and borrow some picnic tables so people could eat outside too, and it wasn't until then that they realized that they hadn't thought through anything at all, not just seating for the ceremony. Where would they have sat people if they had tried to have all those guests eat inside, let alone have a place to put out all the food?

By the way: This is one reason why telling stories is so hard. Sooner or later, something is going to happen that just doesn't fit, like that scene in *Native Son* where there are more people in Bigger's cell than it could possibly hold. In this case the problem is my wanting to have the wedding at Hank's house (because as Hank said, "Screw church!" [and Delores agreed]), but there couldn't possibly be enough room on account of my having rendered Hank as the kind of guy who had lots of friends and no doubt a pretty big extended family (even though we haven't explored his relatives even a little bit—because why?), so something isn't going to jive just right no matter how hard I try. I just want you to know that I know that having the weather break is a straight-out *deus ex machina* intervention and thereby truly lame. But this far in, I don't really see any other way. People who know the area might suggest that I have the wedding take place in the park, where they could hold it in one of the pavilions which can handle pretty big crowds, but it has to be March (for reasons that will become clear soon) and nobody would ever have reserved one of the park's pavilions for an outdoor wedding in March, so the original plan had to be for inside Hank's house, and it wasn't until I got to right here that I realized that in the *real* real world, it wouldn't work, but this isn't real at all, so: *Voilà!:* warm weather!

Anyway: Food would be potluck. Music would be Hank's big mahogany console record player. Hank asked the same justice of the peace who fined him for defending

Delores to do the honors (which Hank thought was kind of a cool thing to do and made him think about inviting that shit stomper he gave the black eye to just for fun [but only for a second]).

They bought simple gold wedding bands down street at Royal Jewelers, Delores not at all interested in an engagement ring, even though Hank tried to persuade her that she deserved one and he would be proud for her to wear his and she could even pick it out herself right there on the spot. She said, "What I *deserve* doesn't matter. What I *want* is new dishes"—Hank's dish set not even a set, since maybe three plates matched and most of the second-hand "silverware" was pitted where Hank had ground off the rust with an emery wheel. Hank said, "Okay" but went back to Royal and put down a refundable deposit on a ring just in case. (Hank seemed to have a natural talent for the kind of husbandly wisdom it takes most men years and years of learning the hard way to acquire—even millwrights—which would go a long way in making his and Delores's a fairytale marriage.)

Hank had an old refrigerator in the barn that he manhandled onto the back porch. He ran an extension cord through the window to power it. They filled it up with pop and beer. The only outside grill Hank had was a little handmade thing he'd welded together from scrap, which wouldn't have been near big enough for all those people, but was perfect for a picnic for two, so they borrowed cast iron griddles and arranged for Ron, the diner's substitute cook, to make hamburgers on the stove inside. (Obviously I'm just making names up as I go along here, with no regard for any elided meanings. You can change them if you want. Like you could change Ron to Buddy and it would still fit, maybe fit better. By the way: I know a fiction writer who names every single male protagonist Booger the first time through and then changes it to a real name sometime during the rewrites. He says he lets the character tell him what his name should be. By the way he explains it, you can tell he is trying to sound real, real smart like he's going for a panel at the next AWP about how fictional names in narrative are socially constructed and therefore beyond the author's conscious control and *always* detrimental to any enlightened reading of the text. But c'mon, for crying out loud. Booger? Seriously?

Anyway: Delores sent away for a record of "Here Comes the Bride" and they tested it out on Hank's console (and it's a good thing they did, because it was scratched and they had to send for another copy).

Hank's brothers and cousins and Delores's dad came over early on the big day to help out with last minute details, like running out for condiments (which, can you believe it, neither Hank nor Delores thought to stock up on [an especially egregious oversight for Hank, him being a millwright and all and almost always thinking the whole problem through, but preparing to be married will really play mess around with your brain in ways you can't even imagine, so we should give him the benefit of the doubt]) and setting up the tables and sweeping the back porch and wrestling the record player outside.

The ceremony was supposed to start right around 11:00 a.m. People started showing up about an hour ahead of that, every one of them loaded down with covered dishes, everything that makes a Western PA get together a thing you really want to put on your bucket list: Fried parboiled chicken, braised round steak, potato salad, macaroni salad, baked beans, more baked beans, even more baked beans, cold sliced venison, three-bean salad, glazed ham loaf. (Ham loaf all by itself is worth the trip. Google it.)

And pies—every single lady who came carried a pie with more care than you would give a box of dynamite (knowing that they would be judged on two things: how quick their pie disappeared and how many men buzzed their way asking if they wouldn't mind baking one just for them [and if you can't bake a pie good enough to keep your man at home, well that's your problem, not mine] and they better guard their pie with their life). Cream pies, fruit pies, mince pies. Pies with icing. Pies with woven crusts. And every woman knowing she was the only one who really knew what she was doing when it came to pie. (I've seen conversations about whether or not to salt piecrust devolve into hair pulling, down-on-the-floor-and-roll cat fights in about thirty seconds. And I am not making this up!)

Delores was getting really anxious and had a "couple" bottles of beer to settle her nerves before going upstairs to get dressed. She used the main bedroom and Hank and her dad used the second bedroom—where they waited for the JP to come up and talk to them and they could work out the details for how this was going to go (nobody having thought a rehearsal was necessary).

Delores's sister Alice handled all the other details: The order of the "procession," the flower girl and ring bearer, setting up the order of the records, etc., etc., etc. Alice was also Delores's "maid" of honor, that term applied to her being more than a little ironic in that she shared Delores's precocious proclivities for reproductive freedom and there were more than a couple of young men in attendance, married or not, who hoped to cash in on those very proclivities before the day was over. Their names, Delores and Alice, connote much about their family life out there in Number 5, a certain kind of rustic and individualistic affect, the names evoking images of truck stops at midnight and clothes hanging outside and double clutching. And then that all breaks down when we find out their dad's name was Eugene, making one wonder if his whole familial production and process was an overcompensation for being picked on when he was a kid because of his having such a lame name.

Around quarter after eleven, Alice snuck Delores and her dad and the ring bearer and flower girl into the barn. (Don't worry about how she did that with all those people milling around drinking beer and saying things like they never would have thought any girl would have got old Hank and somebody coming out with the tired adage about how a man chases a girl until she catches him and people saying, "Boy, ain't that the truth?" Just assume Alice was real resourceful and got the job done without one single soul seeing her do it [again, the magic of literary fiction at work], except Mattie, because she had to coordinate the music.) When the wedding party were all in place Alice yelled for everybody to take their seats, and while people were jostling over the best chairs (without regard to bride and groom sides), went into the barn herself and took a big deep breath.

At 11:30, only a half hour late, Alice gave Mattie the signal, which signal Mattie relayed to Hank and the JP in the kitchen. Out they came, Hank in his shiny suit that changed colors and the yellow tie and socks and the shoes with the Cuban heels and cleats and a deep purple aster in his lapel. Jaws dropped.

Mattie, who was as big as a barn herself by then, waddled to the porch and heaved herself up the steps and switched on the record player (see why this chapter had to be set in March?). The first record wouldn't drop down the spindle and she had to do that thing where you catch the tone arm and slip your thumbnail between the two bottom records to get things started and set the arm down manually, but she couldn't get it to work, so Hank went over and gave the console a little tap in just the right spot and shined a real nice and warm smile down on Mattie so she wouldn't be embarrassed, showing yet again the amalgam of millwright and country charm that made him such a catch in the first place.

Hank waited for the record to start, one of several piano concertos he and Delores had picked out in the Five and Ten's record department, the particulars not being important, just that they wanted something classy for their wedding. The flower girl and ring bearer meandered out of the barn, not quite sure what they were supposed to do, looking around at the grounds and all the people and the girl dropping the flower basket. The kids' mother (they were Hank's niece and nephew, the most adorable set of twins you ever saw) went back and took them by the hands and guided them all the way up to the porch and told them to just stand there until she told them to sit down. And they did that thing where kids kind of wiggle around while they keep their feet in the same spot. Everybody just went, "Awww...."

Then Chuck and Alice came out, Chuck a little awkward with how to hold his arm, chivalry not a thing he had ever studied, but they both managed a decorous solemnity while still radiating hope for the future. And they almost kept in step (almost probably being better than not at all, but who's to say?). When they got to the porch, there was some confusion with the kids because their mother had told them to hold on to the rings and the flower basket and not give them to anybody (the kids being generous little souls). As hard as it is to convince kids to do something, once they get it in their heads, it can be really tough to dislodge, and they didn't want to give up their parcels to Chuck and Alice. Their mother had to go up and tell them it was all right, which wasn't as intrusive as you might think, because she'd planned all along to go up and lead them back to their seats once they'd turned their burdens over, them being innocent little lambs and all.

The last concerto record fell right after they got the kids back to their seats, which was just about perfect because it made for a nice interlude before the wedding march where everybody could settle in and wait respectfully while the concerto played all the way through. Some of the attendees had been to church weddings (not a lot, because of there being so many elopements or a couple just going to a preacher's house with their wedding license and asking him [always *him* back then] and the preacher would beam and beam like their coming to him was just the most blessed thing that ever happened in the whole wide universe and the entire time he was deftly zipping through the ceremony and wondering if the Pirates had scored that runner on second and why do kids always want to get married when the game's on the radio?

Fortunately, those who had been to church weddings knew to stand up and turn around when the wedding march started and everybody who didn't got the idea, even if they were righteously confused, and they all got turned around in a kind of ragged synchronicity reminiscent of the way a big Italian family make their way from the street into the banquet hall where they will be celebrating their matriarch's eighty-fifth birthday (seeing such an event should also be on your bucket list—that box is checked on my list thanks to my wife's very extended Sicilian family).

Out came Delores and her dad, Delores in her red dress and a red pill box hat (no veil), upon seeing which several ladies who were borderline religious gasped and one guy actually said, "Oh shit," to which his wife jabbed him in the ribs with her elbow. But as outrageous as Delores's wedding dress may have been, Eugene stole the show. He wore a double-breasted, pinstriped brown suit that hadn't seen sunshine since the '20s and a white shirt with French cuffs and a high starched collar that held his head in place like a vise. A paisley tie (mostly brown and yellow) clamped down whatever part of his neck the collar didn't, the tie held to his shirt with a gold-plated tie clasp in the shape of a skeleton key (a wedding gift from his ex-wife to let him know he held the key to her heart, now and forever [which proved not to be at all prophetic as she had left him three years later for a mechanic who made better money]). But the capstone to the outfit was the shoes: Patent leather, tan and brown wingtips polished like mirrors and tied with white laces. The man was a vision!

Delores and Eugene stopped at the bottom of the steps and waited for the march to finish, everybody in the yard stone-still silent, realizing that they would never in their lives see anything like this again. When the music died away, the JP, with an unexpected penchant for the dramatic, held up one arm for a moment as if he were the Pope about to bless the crowd in St. Peter's Square, the guests altogether mesmerized.

"Who gives this woman to be married to this man?"

And Eugene all but lost it. His voice cracked as he said, "I do," not getting the *do* half all the way out. As sweet as it was, it was also scary. Real scary, because when somebody goes to a place that out of character, you can't anywhere near predict what will happen next—it might even mean they were going completely off their rocker and about to go berserk and start killing people with their bare hands. He recovered by giving Delores a quick kiss on her forehead and squeezing her arm just ever so slightly before hustling to his seat and just about busting through his suit trying not to cry. Afterwards some people (after they got over being scared) said it would have been the best part of the whole day if Mattie hadn't had to go and steal the spotlight.

Delores handed her sprig of red and white carnations to Alice, and right off the JP did the "We are gathered together" thing, which he got out of the JP manual but elaborated a little with religious stuff, being careful not to say *God*, given how adamant Hank and Delores had been about that, but did throw in some *thee's* and *thou's* and even the word *sunder* and finally got to the, "Do you Henry take this woman Delores, blah, blah, blah."

The whole time that Hank was repeating after the JP, Delores held her right hand to her breast with the first two fingers held in a shallow vee, and stuck out the tip of her tongue, and ran it across her lips like she was a sneaky little garter snake, and it was all Hank could do to hold back laughing. Most of the women guests thought Delores's little hand gesture was her holding her hand to her breast as an expression of the limitless love she held in her heart that was almost more than she could keep in there and it was any second going to burst right out of her in a cascade of pastel flowers, rainbows, and angel wings. A few of the men thought what they would give to be that hand (a real out of place thought to be having at the man's wedding, but as long as you don't say it out loud, what's the harm?).

Hank had to turn his face away from the guests so they wouldn't see that he was trying hard not to laugh, which everybody took to mean he was choking up like Eugene, the women *aww'ing* silently inside so as not to embarrass him and unable to not compare Hank to their own husbands and those husbands thinking they would never have took Hank to be so pathetic and if he thought he was in pain now, just wait for a few years until he was real good and married. It turned into a story Hank wouldn't live down for decades.

When it was Delores's turn and she got to her "I do," she added, "All except the obey part," and some people gasped, some laughed, and Eugene beamed. God, was the man proud of his little girl! The JP rushed straight to the "I pronounce you man and wife" part after which Delores and Hank did their "Praise Jesus" and "Amen" antiphonal thing, which had what few religious people who were there hopeful for the newlyweds' souls in spite of their living in sin for all these months and everybody else thinking, "What the hell?"

With the ceremony out of the way, the party got started, people scurrying for the food and making sure they got their share of the beer and trying to get decent seats (not all the picnic tables were in tiptop shape). Alice put on a stack of happy records, starting out with Dean Martin's "Think About Me," which made the women think Delores and Hank were making this day just about the most romantic stretch of sunshine they'd ever been part of and the men thinking, Oh for Christ's sake!

At one point Hank said he had to use the bathroom and excused himself. When he came back out, he switched the record to Guy Mitchell's "Heartaches by the Number" and stood on the porch grinning at Delores, who went up and gave him a playful little slap on the chest. "That's for that thing you did," Hank said (meaning with her tongue during the vows). He took ahold of her and gave her a deep, wet kiss and held her tight while he whispered in her ear to just wait until they got to Niagara Falls and he'd show her how good he was with *his* tongue.

By the way: I have taken significant license with the songs, given that the wedding happened in March 1954, and the songs weren't out until the late '50s and even in the '60s— inviting the question as to whether in any narrative the detritus of its details should fit the times or fit the sentiment. And yes, getting both right should be the objective, but sometimes you just got to choose, because there is only so much that a person can be expected to know. Plus, nobody's perfect.

Anyway, back to Hank and Delores having fun with the record player and sharing a wet kiss: Delores said she couldn't wait for Hank to show her what he could do with his tongue and how about right now? Hank said what if your dad sees and Delores looked around and said where was he anyway, she didn't see him anywhere and it wasn't like him to wander off someplace when there were so many good looking women in tight clothes to flirt with. Hank caught a glimpse of Eugene as he ducked around the shed and said, "There he is—I'll go get him." Around back of the shed, there stood Eugene, with tears rolling down his cheeks and him blasting his nose in a red bandana. Resting his hand on Eugene's shoulder, Hank said real gentle, "Just between you and me, she makes me cry too sometimes." (Hank left out that the reason he sometimes cried because of Delores was that she had fellated him so amazingly that he thought maybe he had died and was in heaven and wept reverential tears of joy and gratitude, but that is not the kind of thing you share with your brand new father-in-law, especially if that father-in-law is a man like Eugene.)

Eugene said, "Well, just between you and me, you say one goddamn word and I will cut your balls off and ram them down your throat."

Hank said, "No chance, Dad," and Eugene said, "Shit," on account of he just that second realized he had a son-in-law who was going to be calling him Dad, a milestone of enormous consequence for a man like Eugene who still considered himself to be in the full vigor of his youth.

They went back to the party just as somebody put on Benny Goodman's "Sing, Sing, Sing," and the gang really started popping. This crowd had learned to dance during WWII, and could they ever jitterbug. It was crazy, couples flying around in the driveway and up on the porch and out back—everybody switching partners and laughing and going back and grabbing another plate and then more dancing like everybody had stumbled into another dimension and come out in the middle of a James Cagney musical. Things were trying real hard to come to a head.

Even though Hank and Delores had stipulated that there were to be no gifts, Hank's friends had pitched in and bought him a new .30-06 for the occasion. Now Hank was the one to almost be overcome with emotion. Of course, they all had to try it out and so they set up pop and beer bottles in a line by the edge of the woods and everybody had a crack at trying to break the bottles but, being tipsy, nobody did. The shots scared some of the kids and their mothers said the men should stop shooting, but they didn't and one of the women got real assertive, telling them they could stop this nonsense right the hell now or there was going to be goddamn hell to pay and one of the men (who didn't have an especially warm relationship to the woman's husband [cordial enough on the surface, but cool at the same time]), told him that if he couldn't control his wife, somebody else sure as hell would. And then the fight almost got started and it would have been epic and ended like they all do with whoever the two were that started it laughing together afterwards and telling each other how you really got me, while rubbing their black eye or split lip or whatever, and drinking beer together way into the night before passing out.

Yes, it would have been epic—that is if Mattie hadn't picked that exact second to have her water break, the event that resulted in her giving birth early the next morning to a two-month-premature, 9-lb, 10-oz baby girl.

Chapter 28
Blessing

[Wherein Mattie and Chuck at last figure out
what is important. But they still keep their
secrets, proving that though they may realize
that they have sometimes been hurtful to each
other and are truly sorry about it and really do
want to make things right, neither of them is
what you would call dumb.]

It took a few minutes for the news about Mattie's water
breaking to sweep its way through the melee of celebrants.
The look on her face got the attention of the two women
sitting across the picnic table from her, and then when they
stuck out their necks to gawk at her, that got some other
people's attention who exclaimed, "What's wrong?," and that
provoked a quandary in still more people over whether to
watch the fight or figure out what was going on with all those
women over there at the table. Sometimes you got to pick
something to miss out on and just hope you made the right
pick, with the deciding factor usually being which was more
likely to make the better story on down the line. But the stress
of having to choose evaporated when the woman who was
responsible for the fight getting started in the first place saw
the clutch of females fluttering around Mattie and decided she
better get over there before she missed out herself (she being
the kind of woman who just had to be in charge). Without an
audience, the two men who were about to throw punches
took a quick look at each other that said, "You just wait,

motherfucker!" and dropped their fists and started over to where all the commotion was along with everybody else.

Mattie tried to stand up and the women next to her told her to sit down and be careful, she didn't want to strain herself just then and some other women went inside and cleared everybody out of the living room and somebody asked Hank where he kept his clean sheets. They made up a bed on the couch for Mattie and all but carried her inside so she could lie down and the men wondered if they should be boiling water. The women shooed away any man who tried to go in the house. They got Mattie's maternity pants off while Delores fetched one of her flannel nightgowns (her coming down the stairs with the nightgown raised a couple of eyebrows, because not everyone believed she'd really been living with Hank all these months).

The men clapped Chuck on the back and told him, "Way to go!" Chuck was himself thinking about "Way to go," but not in the way his friends and relatives were but more like, Which way was this thing right in front of him about to go? And was he a dad or a chump, and what was he going to do if when he saw the baby, it looked like one of the neighbors instead of him and should he say something, but that would mean unveiling the secret of his masturbating his way to nineteen, and oh, is this ever a mess.

All the arrangements got themselves brought together, less about people making rational decisions and more like a case study in chaos theory with all the random scurrying and buzzing about, and what worked itself out from all that babble was that Chuck would take Mattie to the hospital and their girls would stay at the house where Eugene would keep an eye on them until Chuck had a chance to come back and take them to Mattie's mother's. (Delores and Hank had asked Eugene to stay at Hank's house while they were off on their honeymoon to Niagara Falls to "watch out for robbers," but the real reason was they thought it would be a nice gesture to give him a place where he could do his business inside for a week.)

One of the men took a couple more shots with the .30-06 until the guy whose wife yelled at them said, "Dammit! You trying to get me shut off?" He checked that the gun was unloaded and leaned it up on the back porch railing and told Hank to make sure he put it up before he and Delores left, which they couldn't do until Mattie was out of the house, Hank being a man and all, and so not allowed in the same room as a woman in labor and wouldn't be allowed to go inside to change into his traveling clothes. But as soon as the women got Mattie on her feet and on her way to the car, Hank and Delores went upstairs and got changed.

There was a moment when they were both naked at the same time. Hank pulled Delores to him and embraced her in just the gentlest way, holding her breasts to his chest and running his hands down her back, and said it didn't feel any different and boy, was he ever relieved—they say things change after you get married. Delores asked him if there was something he wanted to do with that hard-on. What was he going to do, say no? So he kissed her long and hard. Delores said they better make it quick before somebody figured out what they were doing and Hank said he didn't want it to be quick—he wanted for them to take their time and as hard as it was for them to stop, they broke away from each other and got dressed.

Noticing that Hank's erection wasn't going away and Hank kind of embarrassed about it, Delores walked over like she was going to give him a kiss but instead of that, came down with the heel of her shoe on his bare instep, hard, but not hard enough to do any real damage. Hank had to bite back the big ouch that was working its way up his throat and said, "What the hell?" Delores pointed to his pants and said, "It's gone isn't it?" Hank just shook his head and said they better get moving and grabbed their suitcases.

Setting aside for a second the fact that those "couple" beers Delores drank had a little something to do with her stamping on Hank's foot, there was no doubt about it: This was going to be a marriage of equals, a forward looking arrangement that over time evoked some pity for Hank (along with envy about who he got to screw compared to whoever was pitying him in the moment got to screw [including some introspection on how much potential humiliation from the community of real men you could put up with if you had a woman like that {given how hard it was to find that always tenuous balance between keeping your wife in line and keeping your mouth shut with a wife who was only real cute and not put-your-lights-out gorgeous}]) and a mix of "that bitch" and "good for her" feelings about Delores from the women of Mercer County.

They got themselves into the car amid a big fuss and ado of waves and smiles and back slaps and the men in the party wishing the newlyweds would get the hell going so they could get back to the beer. Finally they drove off, tin cans clattering behind them and bouncing like zombie alcoholics staggering on the macadam until, one by one, the twine strings holding the cans to the bumper broke and they were down to the last one which didn't want to let go and just kept on clanking on the road. After Hank pulled over and untied it and got back in the car, Delores said she wondered if there had been nineteen cans back there when they started out. Hank said, "Is that all you got on your mind?"

She said, "Pretty much," and pointed to a lane going back into the woods.

"I give up," Hank said and drove far enough up the lane to where he figured nobody from the road could see them and so what if they did?

It wasn't slow, but it wasn't quick either. It was just right.

Back at the house, things got back to being fun, nobody even thinking about picking a fight because Eugene set himself up on the back porch in a big steel rocker with the .30-06 cradled across his lap, and even though nobody had seen him load it, they weren't about to take a chance. The celebration went on until way after midnight, boisterous and rowdy and a few couples making their way out into the field or up in the barn's loft, not all of the pairs married to each other, but nobody found out, so no more violence, although one of the trysts resulted in a pregnancy (of course, it did—somebody should write a book about it [maybe themed around the intersection of desire and loss and how that crossroads is never just about sex {well, not *never*, but mostly it isn't}]).

All the way to the hospital, Mattie sat in the passenger seat looking straight ahead with her jaw clenched and her eyes vacuous. Chuck thought it was because she was being stoic and trying hard not to show how much she was hurting, but that wasn't it (she hadn't even had her first contraction). She was praying silently. Please, Jesus, let it look like me. Let it look like me. Oh, please, please, please. Chuck was praying too, sort of—to himself. His mantra? Keep your goddamn mouth shut, keep your goddamn mouth shut, keep your goddamn mouth shut.

Mattie's first contraction hit just as they arrived at the hospital. Chuck double parked the car and waited for it to pass. He sat in a state of impuissant panic as he wondered if he should lay his arm across her shoulders or console her with soothing crooning sounds or should he just leave her alone. Thank God for Chuck the contraction passed fairly quickly and Mattie said she could go in now. He helped her out of her seat and through the door, at which point the nurse on duty gave them a bored kind of a look and then realized they had a woman in labor on their hands and she was in grave danger, being as she was guided by a man. She picked up the phone and pressed a button so that her voice came over the intercom, "Maternity to the front desk," mostly calm, but with enough of an edge to it that you just knew that what maternity heard was her screaming, "Oh my God! Get out here everybody!" And out maternity came, a brigade of women with a gurney.

They phalanxed around Mattie and pushed Chuck to the side and got Mattie on the gurney and told her it was going to be all right dear. They told Chuck to get out from underfoot and then they were gone. Lucky for Chuck he had been through this twice before, so he knew where the fathers' waiting room was and went there after he parked the car, where he spent the rest of the afternoon and early evening leafing through two-year-old *Life* magazines and smoking cigarettes. For a long time, he was all by himself until a little after dark a young kid, probably not even old enough to vote, came in all fidgety and his eyes wild and couldn't even keep still long enough to sit down. Chuck asked him was this his first time and the kid stammered out that it was and how long was it going to take. "As long as it takes," Chuck said and told the kid that his first had taken twenty-six hours and the youngest about half that long, and talking about his girls reminded him he was supposed to have gone back and picked them up at Hank's and taken them to Mattie's mother's. Oh shit!

Chuck found a pay phone, but when he went to dial, realized he didn't have any change and nobody in the hospital had change either and he had to run outside and find some place open (turned out to be the newsstand) and came back and couldn't remember Hank's number and had to call information first and when the operator asked him if he would like her to ring the number for him, he could have kissed her.

Somebody who was pretty drunk answered and it took them a couple of minutes to figure out what Chuck was asking for and then a few more minutes for Eugene to come to the phone. Chuck said he was sorry and he'd be right out. Eugene said for Chuck not to worry about it—him and the girls was having a fine time and why don't they just stay at Hank's for the night, it being Saturday and all, and they didn't have to be in school the next day. They could work it all out tomorrow—just go back to the waiting room. Chuck told him he couldn't thank him enough and that he'd let him know when he'd be out.

What Eugene didn't say was that the girls had found Delores's closet and dresser drawers and makeup case and used their discoveries to play dress up. And they got Eugene to play along with them. When he came to the phone, he had a filmy blouse thrown across his shoulders, a housedress tied around his waist and lipstick mostly on his mouth but a lot of it was on his chin. One or two partiers thought about ribbing him but don't forget, Eugene had that reputation of his, and you would have to be a whole lot drunker than they were to make that mistake. The fact of the matter was that Eugene was in heaven, feeling for the first time what it must be like to be a grandfather and how he couldn't wait for Delores to give him a grandchild. Poor guy.

Chuck went back to the hospital and tried to doze a little in the waiting room, which was real hard on account of the young kid absolutely could not sit still for more than a few minutes at a time. Every couple of hours a nurse came out and told them how their wives were doing (always fine, but babies come when they come and they just had to be patient). Finally, just a little after 4:00 in the morning, the nurse told Chuck that he had a beautiful baby girl and mother and child were doing fine.

Chuck got up to go inside to see Mattie, but the nurse said he had to wait for a while. The doctor had put her under and she was still really groggy and Chuck should go get some rest and come back around 9:00. Mrs. McAllister should be fine by then. Chuck asked if he could see the baby, assuming she was in the nursery. The nurse told him that the baby's temperature was just a little bit low and they'd put her in an incubator off the main nursery, which was all to the good given that Mrs. McAllister wouldn't be able to give her any attention until she was more awake, but Chuck would have to wait until then to see his little girl. She saw Chuck's worried look and reassured him that nothing was wrong, that it happened all the time and she was as healthy as healthy could be and what a set of lungs she had on her!—she'd sure let the world know she was here.

Reluctantly Chuck left and went home. He'd known for a long time that there wasn't any arguing with nurses, especially after what he'd been through right in this very same hospital last summer (oh well). But no way he was going to be able to sleep, him being so worried that Mattie was all right. It doesn't matter what doctors and nurses tell you, you don't really know until you see your loved one for yourself and she says something that makes you know she's fine, especially if what she says is cranky or sarcastic, which tells you she truly is herself, and you are so relieved and happy that she's snippy that you don't even try to be snippy back. All that verbal chaos bouncing around in Chuck's mind made him feel like he had stepped out of his body and was looking at himself like someone else would see him and it occurred to him that he really was worried and less about whose baby it was and more about his wife—to the point where he was about to become a nervous wreck if he didn't see her pretty soon.

He took a bath and put on clean clothes (not church clothes, but good clothes like he was going down street on Friday night) and used some Brylcreem on his hair, which he hardly ever did, and shaved extra close and splashed on a little witch hazel. And the whole time, he was thinking and thinking about what maybe could be waiting for him at the hospital and what he should say depending on who the baby looked like. He tried and tried, but he just couldn't get anything in his head to rehearse with. Finally he drove back down street and parked on Broad Street right around the corner from the hospital and just walked up and down the street, from Main to the railroad tracks and back again, over and over and over, and just thought.

When he passed the Five and Ten for about the seventh or eighth time, he noticed a display of Easter candy in the window, with a cardboard Easter bunny and baskets stuffed with pastel-colored cellophane grass and yellow peeps and chocolate rabbits and piles and piles of jellybeans. He remembered holidays with the girls when they were just toddlers and how excited they got, especially the night before, and how it made him and Mattie feel real close and they could have that all over again and he should start planning for it. And then he got the strangest thought he ever had in his whole life. He wondered how much of the situation Mattie had got herself in was because of him. And then he had an even stranger, much more complicated thought.

It occurred to him that every day was like the raw stock he fed into his lathe, that the day wasn't what it was when it started. It was what he made it to be between then and nighttime. It was his job to drill and polish and turn the darkness that the day came out of and make it into something daylight bright that he and his family could use. He realized that most of the time he'd made a lousy job of it and the day had to be tossed on the scrap heap, that there had been very few days he'd made as true to the specs as he could, like when he and Mattie went to Conneaut Lake and after how nice it was, her telling him about the baby. And Chuck being afraid he might lose her.

What if he worked as hard on making him and Mattie as perfect as he did the parts he machined for those big engines? What would happen then? And maybe she had gone with someone else and maybe she hadn't, but being honest about it, who could blame her? When it came right down to it, all she needed was for somebody to want her and he knew he did and used to show it like the time in the car after she burned her hand. If he'd been half that attentive in the years since, and if he hadn't pulled those cheap little tricks on her like pulling the sheets tight (which he saw now was just plain mean and should have been the last thing he would ever think of doing to the one person in the entire world he loved with all his heart), she wouldn't have had to look for somebody else who *showed* her that he wanted her. Oh man, he didn't like thinking like that. But he knew for sure that he wouldn't like being mad and twisted up inside if it turned out the baby wasn't his and he turned that into something he'd be real sorry for, and that would be almost as bad as Mattie finding out he'd been jacking off so much. But not near as bad as if she left him.

By then it was almost six and just getting light. The newsstand would be opening. He walked down and went in and bought a Sunday paper to take to Mattie and a box of cigarillos to pass out at work tomorrow. He thought about going out to Kocher's to get Mattie some flowers, but remembered it was Sunday and they'd be closed—which turned out not to be a problem because thinking about things in a new light had got him all resourceful and he figured out a way that had to do with going down to the diner and swiping an empty quart milk bottle from the wire crates out back and then snipping daffodils from the Tower Church flower beds to put in the bottle and quite creatively tucking in some fern leaves he found in Dad's Restaurant's flower boxes.

The waiting room was empty. Chuck guessed the kid was a father now. Poor guy—had no idea what he was in for—how hard it was going to be and how totally worth it all at the same time. Pretty soon it was nine o'clock and he tracked down a nurse and asked if he could see Mattie and she said she would check and be right back. But it was a different nurse who came out—it was that army nurse.

The army nurse had come on at 7:00 and when she saw the name on Mattie's chart, put two and two together. And the four she came up with took her back to the war and all those boys she had tried to comfort and how some of those broken young men got Dear John letters from sweethearts and letters from wives who were going to have babies and they were so sorry but they thought it best if they got a divorce. She wished she had broken the rules back then and burned those letters or at least held them back until the boy was a little better. Or died. One boy in particular drifted up out of the backwaters of her memory, a wisp of a freckled kid from Georgia who cried like a baby when he read the letter and to whom she gave a handjob after lights out and told him that there was a beautiful and gracious southern belle back home waiting for him. The girl just didn't know it yet. She remembered how she had had to go outside when he died and hide behind a half-track so no one would see her weep.

Chuck was all kinds of flustered when she came out and sat next to him in the waiting room. By God, if she up and gave him a hard time like she had before, he was going to lay into her for sure and not stop at just calling her witch either. But she gently laid her hand on his arm and with an angelic smile, told him how beautiful a wife he had and how lucky he was to have her. And that he had an even more beautiful baby girl. She said, "Make sure you tell them what treasures they are. If there's anything I can help with, just speak up." Chuck could tell that she wasn't being sarcastic this time. That she really was being sincere. She gave him Mattie's room number and left. Chuck could have sworn she trailed a haze of golden light as she walked away.

Striding down the hall amid the ether and bleach smells and the new mothers nursing their babies and a doctor making notes in a chart, Chuck bucked himself up. No matter what, he was resolved to smile and be happy and tell Mattie she done good. But "no matter what" is one thing when you are walking down the hall and another thing altogether when you walk in your wife's room and she looks like she just got found guilty of treason and was going to the electric chair tomorrow and she looked that way because she was nursing a little girl with the reddest hair you ever saw and nobody on either Chuck's or her side of the family was anything other than brunette, not a sibling or uncle or aunt or grandparent or first cousin or nth cousin (no matter how much removed), as far into the generations up and out as he could remember.

In spite of his resolve, Chuck couldn't help himself and just up and blurted out, "I never wanted to believe it"—and

Mattie stopped breathing and got a look on her like a man would get if he just felt his balls getting sucked up into his chest.

Chuck realized his mistake in saying he didn't want to believe it as soon as it came out, but fortunately for him, his season of introspection had sharpened his wits (as illustrated by his using a stolen milk bottle and stolen flowers to show his wife how much he loved her) and he right away came out with, "I thought Grandpa made it all up."

Mattie, seeing just the slightest shadow of an umbral lifeline of hope, reached out for it. "Made what up?"

"Grandpa said his dad had red hair and there was almost always a McAllister with red hair, but sometimes it skipped a generation or two. He said it was the angels playing tricks on us. I never believed him until now—I thought it was just a story for little kids."

Mattie breathed again as her metaphorical balls drifted back from her chest to her groin where they belonged. Chuck asked if he could hold the baby and Mattie handed her up to him. He chucked the child beneath her chin and said, "Welcome to the world, Blessing." Then he looked at Mattie, smiling like she was just the most precious thing in the whole wide beautiful world and loving her was the only thing in his life that mattered to him, and it took him a couple minutes to figure out that the strange feeling he was having was because he wasn't pretending—he really meant it.

Epilogue

Hunter

Hunter finished out the term at Theil while applying for positions at southern universities. The University of Arkansas offered him a named chair, where he began several novels of longing, loss, and regret set in a fictional Appalachian county whose county seat felt a lot like Mercer, PA. He had a series of affairs with young faculty members from various departments and two or three of his colleagues' wives. Each one left him when she figured out that she wasn't the inspiration for the woman in whatever novel he happened to be working on at the time.

One Saturday night he found himself in a roadside tavern just north of Fayetteville, drawn in by the sign outside: *Live Entertainment: Gayle Krause and the Leftovers*. Gayle sang in a dusky alto that, depending on the song, drew forth memories of anything from jasmine honey to fifty-year-old, barrel-aged bourbon. She wore a pencil skirt that maybe could have been tighter but not by much and a full-sleeved, electric-blue satin blouse with four-inch heels to match. She kept time with a silver-jingled tambourine. The Leftovers were a gaggle of misfits on the high side of middle-aged, but their music was as haunting and wistful as early morning fog twining over the Ozarks.

When it came time for last call, the bartender signaled to Gayle as she wound herself down from "It Wasn't God Who Made Honky Tonk Angels." She crooned into her mic,

"Last call, folks, which means we got time for just one more. Anybody got a request?"

Hunter half stood from his table in the shadows and said, "Faded Love," not shouting exactly but in a voice that barrowed its way right through the drunken appeals for, "Move It on Over" and "If You Got the Money."

Gayle did that cute little thing women country singers used to do, twirling her hips left and right like she was a shy little girl in a frilly dress, but she sure wasn't a shy little girl and her dress sure wasn't frilly.

"You sure about that, cowboy?"

Hunter lifted his glass, nodded, tipped his invisible hat, and sat back down.

Smiling toward the audience, Gayle said, "Looks to me like somebody needs theirself a good cry." Nodding to the band, she said, "Okay then, 'Faded Love.'"

The band was down a fiddle player for the intro, but the steel guitarist was a more than adequate surrogate. The man could make that guitar come about as close to shedding real tears as wood and wire can get.

Gayle's voice turned soft and trembling as she looked straight at Hunter through the entire number. What with the way she let the lyrics drift out of her as if she were letting go a deep and soulful pain and the steel guitar plaintive as Sunday morning remorse and the clouds of cigarette smoke circling her raven-black hair, the song hovered over the room as much benediction as music.

In the morning Hunter awoke to her getting dressed. "Hey," he said, "breakfast?"

"Cowboy," Gayle said, "There's one too many women in this house. I think it's best if I just leave you to the one who got here first." She didn't even kiss him goodbye.

That afternoon Hunter called his wealthy father for the first time in years and asked if it was too late to come home and work for him. His father's voice fairly boomed through the line with a love as bounteous as it was pure. "Damn, son, ain't such a thing as too late. You get your backside over here right now. We'll spit-roast us a yearling and stay drunk for a month."

So Hunter went home, threw out all the novels he'd written, and made do with being rich.

He never found out that he was a father.

Mattie

Mattie and Chuck had ten more good years together. Chuck was almost too tender with Blessing, his other two girls more than a touch jealous of the attention he showed her, which manifested in little things like his taking her to Isaly's for ice cream on Saturday afternoons, just the two of them, and is probably part of the reason both her sisters got pregnant and had to get married before they'd graduated from high school, a way to get Chuck's attention. Mattie blamed herself, thinking it must be something they got from her, the way Blessing got her red hair from Hunter. But it all worked out for the girls—the oldest's husband was a pattern maker and the other's a mechanic, jobs that were steady and paid well, so that they led solid and comfortable blue collar lives.

Every year Chuck took two weeks of vacation in a row, the whole family going on a trip the first week to someplace close like Washington, DC, to see the monuments or up into Canada to camp out. Then he and Mattie would leave the girls at Mattie's mother's and spend the second week at Conneaut Lake, making love in the cabin and walking around the amusement park. Chuck would always win something for Mattie on the midway, and she would always say he should give it to one of the girls and he would do what he could to win a couple more prizes and if he didn't, he'd just buy a couple.

Chuck tried to be mindful that how he comported himself every day affected Mattie, going so far as to set the alarm a few minutes early so that he could have a cigarette before going downstairs, a way to shed at least some of the grouchiness so he wouldn't be gruff with her and could actually talk to her straight off, even as she was serving out his breakfast, and always kissing her first thing when he came down. And though he was wrong in his belief that the reason the condom count was off when this whole story started was that Mattie's lover was using them right there in Chuck's bed, lying down on that bed every night with the ghost of whoever it was kept him always aware of how close he came to losing her—and maybe could again. He was almost grateful to the man.

Given that the other girls obviously weren't going to make it to college, Mattie put all her hopes in Blessing, especially after what happened when Blessing was five. From the day Blessing was born, Mattie read to her, book after book after book. One day the phone rang during reading time and Mattie left Blessing alone with the book they were reading. When Mattie came back, there was Blessing looking at the book and speaking the story right out loud. Mattie figured the child had memorized it. She expressed the exaggerated praise we show little kids when they've done something we are either very proud of or very surprised by. She exclaimed how smart

Blessing was to have learned the whole story. Blessing said, "*No*, Mama, I'm *reading* it."

Mattie got another book that they'd read together many times, and sure enough, Blessing "read" it right through too. Still unconvinced and thinking Blessing had memorized all the stories, Mattie took the little girl down to the Five and Ten that afternoon and bought a few new books. Blessing was able to read them as well, though she did stumble over some of the words.

Blessing read her first novel when she was in the second grade, *Black Beauty*. She thought it was about a real horse and somehow the horse was either able to write the story (maybe by holding the pencil in its mouth) or could speak (to maybe just one special person and nobody else could hear) and dictated the story. By the end of second grade she'd read all of both Grimms' and Anderson's fairy tales. In third grade she read *The Prince and the Pauper*, a moment of lost innocence for her. Except for the fairy tales, she thought all of the stories she read were true. When she read Twain's footnote about the Prince's whipping-boy and realized that the prince and his pauper friend were fictions, she was initially crushed, but came over time to see how true fiction really is and started making up fairy tales of her own to tell her imaginary friends, sometimes in a secret language that only she and they could understand.

Chuck died just a few days after the child's tenth birthday. The chest pains came sharp and hard while he was standing at his lathe, the pain so bad he had to lean against the machine. But he drilled down through the pain to a place where he could still be strong and waited for the piece in the chuck to be finished. Twirling the chuck loose, he held the part up to his face, saw no flaws in the metal, and dropped the part into the finished bin. He powered down the machine, took off his apron, and turned and walked away, making but about five steps toward the locker room before collapsing. Bubbles boiled out of his mouth as he tried to whisper something down there on his back on the hard concrete floor, but none of the men who'd rushed over could make it out. Whatever it was he said, he said with his dying breath.

Mattie and Blessing took it really, really hard, Mattie altogether lost without Chuck. With the insurance money (and the bit of a settlement the Bessemer gave them), she and Blessing had enough to get by for a couple of years without Mattie's having to get a job. She listed the house for sale and got her full asking price that November. On the day of settlement, she packed up the car with what clothes and sundries she and Blessing would need for a while and a folder full of all her important papers. She left a note for the new owners that they could keep or dispose of the furniture as they saw fit, closed out her bank accounts, loaded Blessing in the car, and just drove. South at first, down Route 19 all the way through Pittsburgh and into West Virginia, where she found a wooded back road and took it and just wandered for days, south and east and west and north and south again, crossing and re-crossing state lines, just rambling until she came to a sign along a river road that said Brigard County and took the road until it branched, one path going onward toward a cut in the hills where it disappeared and the other over a bridge into a town carved into the side of a ridge, its terraced streets rising like a dirty stairway to the foothills of heaven. She drove across the bridge, parked the car, and pulling Blessing to her, kissed the child on the forehead. "Here," she said.

Delores

Hank and Delores went on pretty much as they had in the months before their wedding. Delores kept her job, because what was she going to do all day if she didn't, what with Hank hardly making any mess at all and pretty much cleaning up after himself when he did and her with as much energy as she had. Later on, she took some night classes in dictation and typing and got a job at the college, first as a filing clerk, but eventually working her way up to be the dean's secretary.

When General Electric opened up a plant at the edge of town, Hank saw the writing on the wall for the Bessemer and put in an application and was hired the next day, for a little less money, but more in the long run because he would draw two pensions when he retired. Besides, money wasn't a problem at all, because Hank already had a pretty decent savings account, and when his grandmother died, she left her house to him, which had been paid off for two generations. He sold it for way more than what he owed on his articles of agreement, leaving him and Delores free and clear on the house and with an even bigger nest egg than what they started out with. So he and Delores really had it easy in the money department, with no mortgage and no kids. (The not having kids part continued for years to confirm that rumor about how Delores had got a back-alley abortion and had to have a hysterectomy when she was young—rumors don't die back there—they're like weeds that hide in the wintertime only to come back stronger spring after spring. Hank and Delores just put up with it.)

Nearly every Friday they went to Rudy's for spaghetti and took in a movie (though they never did that thing in the

Guthrie balcony again—but they did do it at the drive-in every once in a while, just for old times' sake.) They bought an Airstream trailer and went on a long vacation every summer, taking turns deciding where they should go. Hank favored mountains and places like Glacier National Park, while Delores loved barren spots like Death Valley and the Painted Desert. Those long trips gave them chances to work on their goal of making love in all forty-eight states, the Airstream being a convenient way of just slipping off the road and into each other, kind of a portable hot-pillow joint without the sordidness.

They got the idea for the forty-eight states during their honeymoon, its giving them a third state in addition to Pennsylvania and Ohio (where they'd snuck off from the Canfield Fair midway during their nineteen ejaculations period and done it under the grandstand, where someone "accidently" spilled a root beer on them). They were so intent on the goal that they even took short weekend trips without the trailer just to get in a couple extra states. Once they took a weekend to get Maryland, Delaware, and New Jersey. After they'd found an isolated spot in Delaware, Hank said he couldn't figure out for the life of him why anyone would want to live there—and then he saw New Jersey and understood.

Getting all the states is harder than it sounds. Big states like Montana are easy because you have time to sexually regenerate in between, but the small states are a challenge. For example, when they went through New England and passed through Connecticut, Rhode Island, and Massachusetts in just a couple hours, they had to make a choice. They decided to skip Rhode Island and have a long seafood lunch in Boston to give Hank time to get recharged. They'd get Rhode Island on the way back. But they didn't, since they forgot the plan was to do Maine, New Hampshire, and Vermont during the return leg of the trip (New Hampshire and Vermont themselves being pretty tricky). On their trip to Florida, they took a little detour to clip Kentucky and Tennessee, and since there wouldn't be enough recharge time to get both states, pulled off on a side road right at the state line. While Delores stood outside and gave guidance, Hank worked the trailer back and forth until the bed lay in both states. That way they got two for the price of one (which they didn't see as cheating, because their game, their rules). All things said though, they did pretty well, making it to almost forty states. (Alaska's and Hawaii's admissions to statehood threw them a curve, but they figured that out by saying that only the states already in the Union when they got married counted.)

At first Delores was worried about her dad, how he would get along by himself, but the old fart went and knocked up Steel Car's office manager, a woman only a couple years older than Delores. They got married and he moved into her house outside of Greenville. Eugene signed his trailer over to a friend who was working hard to drink himself to death— Eugene thought it would be easier if he could do it indoors, even if it didn't have a place to crap. The gesture so moved his friend that he did something about his drinking, not going all the way to abstinence, because, c'mon for crying out loud, but cut way back and even started going to church where he almost found Jesus but not quite, because, c'mon, for crying out loud.

Eugene's new wife was so critical to Steel Car's operation that they let her work when she was pregnant, almost to the end if you can believe it, and gave in to her insistence that they make Eugene a supervisor, which Eugene had sworn he would never do—he always said he had too many friends at work—but turned out to be really good at, the kind of tough but consistently fair boss that his men could respect and stand up for. He didn't get a granddaughter, but he got the most beautiful baby girl he'd ever seen (except for his other daughters, of course) and spoiled the child rotten.

Hank retired when he was sixty-two and died a couple years later. He just stopped breathing in the middle of the night. It was less his breath stopping that awoke Delores and more the loss of the rhythm of his heart, she always, right up until the end, sleeping with her face on his chest. She lay there beside him for a good long while, not quite smiling but almost, thinking that he deserved that kind of death, quiet and not bothering anybody—pretty much the way he'd lived. Finally she got up and called Cunningham's and they came out and got him and his wedding suit, which was a little tight after all those years, but Cunningham just slit it up the back and no one could tell.

Delores wore her red dress to the funeral, which was notable for its lack of a clergyman and for a bunch of Merle Haggard and Hank Williams songs coming over the sound system. Instead of a preacher she just had some of Hank's family and friends tell stories about him, most of them pretty funny, but some jerking a couple tears here and there. There was no graveside service. Delores just went out to Crestview with the undertakers and watched while the workmen put him to bed, the whole time holding her fingers to her chest in a vee and believing in her heart that Hank saw it and was laughing his eternal backside off.

Back home she took down a composition book from a shelf in the bedroom closet and sat on the bed and leafed through it and ran her fingers down the pages filled with hearts with arrows through them. Some of the hearts were outlined twice and some of them had stars around them. Two numbers stood out on each page, the number of hearts on the page and the total number of hearts up to that point in the book. Looking out into the air beyond the walls, she whispered, "You know, big guy, if you'd a hung on just a little longer, we'd a made it to five thousand." As she put the book up, it occurred to her that it had been years since she'd given herself a good talking to and that she had Hank to thank for that. "Bless your heart," she said.

Delores was still pretty hot in her mid-sixties and chased by more than a few men, but she never went with another man. Not once. She did however have a friends-with-benefits arrangement with one of the women who taught in the English Department, a forty-something woman who specialized in the Metaphysical Poets. Delores would never even think of cheating on Hank with a man, but she figured another woman was just girls' night out.

And every March, on her and Hank's wedding anniversary, she baked a split top banana bread, filled the cleft with apple butter, took it out on the front porch, and ate the whole luscious thing all by herself.

ACKNOWLEDGMENTS

I reached out to the dozens of people who in ways large and small contributed to the successful completion of *Nineteen to Go* to thank them for their help and to let them know that I was going to graciously acknowledge their assistance right out loud in this final section of the book and was that all right? To a person, they all declined to be so recognized, with responses ranging from "I prefer that you not" to "Don't even think about it" to "Hell no!" Clearly such universal reticence to be singled out for praise illustrates how this text inspires humility in its readers—which, on a personal level, I find profoundly gratifying. So to all of my humble, anonymous admirers, I hereby proclaim my heartfelt thanks. BTW: This ubiquitous reluctance to be singled out is also why *Nineteen to Go* doesn't have a dedication page.

ABOUT THE AUTHOR

James Carpenter is the author of the novel *No Place to Pray*. He lives in the New Jersey Pine Barrens with his stunningly beautiful wife, Rosetta, where he is currently at work on a novel that will be hailed as a breathtaking masterpiece of American Gothic fiction.